MW00774940

MUDDLED MATRIMONIAL MURDER

Cupcake Catering Mystery Series Book 6

KIM DAVIS

Cinnamon & Sugar Press

Muddled Matrimonial Murder

By Kim Davis

Chapter 1

"I s something wrong?" I reached over and placed my hand on my best friend's arm as he scowled at his phone.

"What's the matter? Is the groom a no-show?" Tillie chortled as she raised her margarita glass as if saluting Brad. With her free hand, she smoothed down her platinum-silver hair and tucked a silky strand behind her ear. Her large diamond stud earrings glittered in the candlelight.

I probably needed to move the pitcher of margaritas away from the octogenarian's side of the table, given the slight slur I'd heard in her words.

My boyfriend, Brian, must've thought the same thing because he slid the pitcher away from his grandmother, placed it in front of me, and winked. "Maybe you'd better take control of the margaritas, Emory. Gram's getting punchy."

"Actually, that is the problem." Brad clenched his teeth then tossed his phone, screen side down, onto the table. "Gabe's not going to make it."

"Oh, Brad. I'm sorry." Tillie set her glass down. Her painted-red lips turned downward, but nary a wrinkle could be seen on her smooth face, thanks to her having the best cosmetic surgeon in Orange County on speed dial. "I only meant it in jest and had no idea it was even a possibility."

"It shouldn't have been a possibility," Brad muttered. "Gabe promised he'd be here."

"Is it work?" I filled Brad's margarita glass to the brim then topped my own glass.

"So he says." He took a swig of the icy drink. "He promised he wouldn't take on any new cases and told me he was close to wrapping up open ones or passing them on to another detective. There shouldn't have been anything so pressing that he couldn't make it tonight."

Gabe O'Neill, Brad's intended, was a homicide detective in Newport Beach. I'd first met him on a balmy Southern California night, when he'd investigated a murder that occurred at Tillie's Halloween party. He'd suspected me of killing the Bavarian barmaid, and it'd taken some time for us —well, me—to get over his accusations and become friends. But if he broke my best friend's heart, I would have to give him a piece of my mind.

"Well, I say we need to carry on with our celebration and pretend your groom is virtually here." Tillie clinked her spoon against her glass. "I'll start with the first toast. Brad, you've become like a grandson to me, and I wish you all the happiness in the world. Don't focus on the minor setbacks that happen in relationships, like murders, and get in the way of plans. Instead, focus on the joy your beloved brings to you on a daily basis."

"You're right, Tillie." Brad raised his glass to her and then to the rest of the table. "Gabe is an honorable man, and finding justice for victims is one of the many reasons I admire him. And I'm fortunate to have all of you here to celebrate with me and support me when life doesn't go according to plan."

Murmurs of "Hear! Hear!" fluttered around the table as we raised our glasses. I looked fondly at our group of friends and family, who had gathered together to celebrate the upcoming nuptials only two weeks away. Tillie had organized the event, complete with a party bus to cart us door-to-door, with the first stop at the new Mexican restaurant that overlooked the Newport Harbor. After dinner, we'd be heading to a rollicking musical stage production and, from there, a nightclub for dancing and nightcaps.

My mother, Addie, was the next to offer up a toast. "I'm so happy for you, Brad. May you have love, happiness, and a lifetime of joy with Gabe."

Brad and I exchanged furtive glances and tried not to smirk. We'd been best friends in high school, but when Brad left for college, my mother had done everything she could to make sure our friendship ended. She thought we'd been romantically attracted to each other, and she wanted me to marry her choice... a man who turned out to be nothing but a snake and was now, thankfully, my ex-husband.

Brad, being the great friend he was, didn't hold it against my mother... much. And truth be told, she wasn't the same person she'd been ten years ago. Confessing that she'd given up a baby for adoption and then finding and connecting with my half sister, Vannie, last year, had given my mother a new outlook on life. She'd become kinder and much less critical of those who were less perfect than her... like me.

The rest of the group took their turns toasting Brad, with a bit of roasting thrown in by his mom, Reina, and his sister, Marigold. Reina didn't act like a woman who'd just turned fifty. She was a bit of a bohemian, wore her long honey-blonde hair in a single braid, and dressed in fashions that were popular in the sixties. She spent as much time as possible on the water, surfing the waves, and as a result, her overly tanned skin was already showing wrinkles from sun damage. Brad tried to make time to surf with his mom at least a couple of times a month.

Marigold, several years younger than Brad, was a single

parent, a stay-at-home mom to a toddler and an infant. Every time I'd crossed paths with her, she looked perpetually exhausted. She had short-cropped honey-blonde hair, and as she'd put it, she was a wash-and-wear gal. Even though she hadn't lost the baby weight, Marigold still dressed like a teen in midriff-showing T-shirts and tight jeans that had strategic tears. Even though Brad wouldn't admit it, I knew he financially supported his sister, allowing her to be home for her children. Since neither Brad nor Marigold ever talked about the father of her children, I'd not pried.

By the time all eleven of us had had our say, the margarita pitchers were empty, and the servers appeared with our plates of food.

Vannie scooted into the empty seat that had been reserved for Gabe, and we both did our best to try to keep Brad entertained while we ate. After another round of margaritas, he seemed to relax a little, but I couldn't help but notice that the crease between his sun-bleached eyebrows had deepened. His gray eyes misted over once or twice, and he rapidly blinked as if to clear them.

Vannie got caught up in a conversation with her grandmother, Tillie, and Brian, who was her half brother as well as my boyfriend. Let me set the record straight that Brian and I were in no way related. My mother had had a relationship with Brian's father while they were in college, which resulted in the birth of Vannie, who'd been given up for adoption. Our parents had broken up and gone their separate ways while still in college and had gone on to marry other people.

I nudged Brad, trying to force him to meet my gaze. "What else is worrying you? I can tell there's more bothering you than Gabe getting caught up at work and not making it here tonight."

He sighed and toyed with the beans and rice on the enchilada platter that sat before him. He'd barely taken more than a few bites of the spicy dish. "Gabe's best man, Colin, flew in from New York a few days ago and will be here through the wedding."

"They were college roommates, right?"

"Yes. Anyway, they've been spending a lot of time together, which I understand, except it's always when I've got other commitments or can't make it. When I suggest the three of us do something, they always have an excuse that it won't work." Brad raked a hand through his wavy hair, which was the same shade as his mother's and sister's. "I just get the feeling that Colin is trying to drive a wedge between Gabe and me."

"Why is Colin here so early? Your wedding isn't for another two weeks." Unlike Brad's, my appetite hadn't diminished, so I forked a piece of tamale smothered in guacamole and shoved it into my mouth.

"He says he hasn't had a vacation in over five years, so he decided to take the time off and see some of the sights in California." Brad huffed. "As if Gabe isn't busy enough at work as it is, Colin's been pestering him to take a few days off and head up to Napa for some wine tasting."

I raised my eyebrows.

"Yep. You guessed it. I wasn't included in the invite." Brad's shoulders slumped.

"But surely Gabe wouldn't go without you." I twisted a lock of my usually frizzy red hair around my finger. Vannie had helped tame it with product and a flat iron before our evening out, but I knew all her efforts would be for naught by the end of the night. My hair was relentlessly stubborn when it came to keeping it under control.

"No, but I think he feels guilty for having to say no, so he's going out of his way to spend all his free time with Colin." Brad slapped my hand away from my hair. "Stop messing with your hair. It looks great, and you're going to ruin it."

"Sorry. It's just I feel so bad that Colin's trying to come between you two. Have you told Gabe how you feel?"

"Of course. But he assures me I have nothing to worry about. That he and Colin are like brothers and nothing more. Blah, blah, blah." Brad's scowl deepened. "I'm so angry at Colin I could just kill him."

I shuddered. Too many dead bodies had come my way, and I hoped never to see another one in my entire life.

Brad elbowed me. "You know I don't mean that literally, Em."

"I know, but I can't help but worry that something could happen."

Tillie dinged her glass again. "Finish up your drinks, party people. Our chariot awaits to escort us to more entertainment, and then we'll dance the night away at the Canyon Club."

Chapter 2

I woke the next morning to a pounding headache and a pounding on my door. Piper and Missy, my two rescue dogs, added a chorus of barking that did nothing to help. I vaguely remembered that Brian had said he needed to leave early to catch some waves with his surfer buddies before heading to work. Obviously, he hadn't imbibed nearly as much as I had. Piper and Missy's barking turned into happy whines, so I knew I'd better answer the door instead of ignoring it like I wanted to do.

My bedside clock indicated it was only seven, much too early after crashing into bed only four hours ago. After stumbling out of the covers, I threw on a robe and made my way to the door of my luxurious pool house, courtesy of Tillie and her generosity. She lived across the alleyway in a mansion of a house replete with bay views and a boat dock. Throwing open the door, I came face-to-face with a scowling Brad.

"What are you doing here so early?" I opened the door wider so he could step inside without tripping over the prancing dogs, who were eager to get their usual adoration from him.

He held up an extra-large coffee and a white bakery bag. "I knew you'd need these to get you going."

"I'm not going anywhere except back to bed." I took the coffee from him anyway and took a long swig then collapsed onto the sofa. "Can you bring me some aspirin?"

"Eat the bagel. You'll give yourself ulcers if you don't have something on your stomach first." He handed the bakery bag to me, wrinkled his nose at my hair, then sat beside me.

"Fine. But that still doesn't answer my question of what you are doing here. Shouldn't you and Gabe be making up or something after last night?" I massaged my temples.

Brad rubbed his palms over his cheeks, which hadn't been shaved that morning. "He never came home last night."

"What?" I turned to look at my best friend. "Did he send you a text or anything?"

Brad nodded then threw himself against the back of the sofa. "At six this morning, I got a text. All he said was he was tied up with a case, and he'd call later. So far, I haven't heard from him, and he hasn't responded to any of my fifty texts and calls, which, by the way, go straight to voice mail."

"It's only been an hour. Maybe he's in a meeting and can't respond." I took another swig of coffee.

"He could at least send me an emoji letting me know he's received my texts." Brad took the bag from me and retrieved the bagel then handed it to me. He took out an apple fritter and began eating it.

"Hey, where's my apple fritter?" I tried handing the bagel back to him.

"Given your level of intoxication last night, I thought you'd need something bland yet substantial." He smirked. "I don't think I've ever seen you have so much fun before."

"You can blame it all on Tillie, whatever it was I did." I vaguely recalled a mechanical bull and Brian trying to peel me up from the floor after I'd been thrown off. The throbbing of a bruise on my left hip reminded me that I'd fallen hard. "Anyway, you missed a lot of the fun when you ditched us at midnight, Mr. Cinderfella."

He grimaced. "I know, but I just couldn't stop worrying about Gabe's lack of response to my texts and calls. I needed to sulk by myself."

"I'm sorry." Placing my hand over his, I gave him a quick pat.

"I suppose you don't remember your promise to help me take wedding gifts over to the house and go over all the things you need to get done before the big day." Brad closed his eyes, and I thought I heard him mutter, "If it even happens."

"Oh yeah. I did promise something like that." I bit into the raisin bagel and chewed. Brad had thoughtfully added some cinnamon cream cheese between the slices. "But why do we have to go so early?"

"I couldn't sleep, and I didn't feel like being alone." He frowned, then his cheeks pinked. "Sorry. I didn't think about how hard you partied last night and how late you must've gotten to bed. Brian went surfing, right? I didn't interrupt anything… I hope."

I smacked his arm then absentmindedly wiped off some of the cream cheese that I'd smeared onto him. He fished around in the bag and gave me a napkin.

I wiped my hands and then my mouth. "Yes, Brian went surfing. And for what it's worth, I'm really sorry about Gabe not showing up."

"I know. It'll work out one way or another."

I really didn't like the sound of that, but I let it drop. "Give me fifteen minutes, and I'll be ready to go. Can you feed the dogs while I shower?"

"Sure, but take your time. Your hair looks like it needs some extra care." He shrugged. "Besides, I have nothing else to do today, so there's no rush to get going."

"If that's the case, why don't you scramble us some eggs?"

I popped the last bite of bagel into my mouth. "Or French toast, if you prefer."

"You do remember I'm not your hot chef boyfriend, right?" Brad smirked. "I can make passable scrambled eggs and French toast, but that's about the extent of my cooking. Do you have a preference?"

It was my turn for my cheeks to heat. I'd gotten spoiled with Brian cooking delectable breakfast dishes whenever he stayed over, and he encouraged me to ask for whatever tickled my fancy. "Of course I didn't get you mixed up with Brian. Scrambled eggs will be fine."

"Uh-huh." He flicked his fingers at me, palms facing downward. "Go take your shower, and I'll see what this nonchef can make."

I took the hottest shower I could tolerate then spent too much time trying to minimize the bags beneath my eyes and untangle my frizzy red hair, despite using extra conditioner in the shower. By the time I made it to the kitchen, dressed in comfy stretch leggings and an oversize sweatshirt, Brad's scrambled eggs were a cold, unappetizing glop on my plate.

"Sorry. I should've waited to cook them." He toyed with his own glop of eggs. "I'm not thinking clearly."

"You're forgiven, since you already brought me coffee and a bagel." I picked up the two plates and dumped the eggs into the dog food bowls. Missy and Piper gulped them down as if they hadn't eaten in a year then turned around and looked expectantly at me, begging for more. "I'll make us some fresh eggs if you'll pour us more coffee and toast some bread."

"Do I need to make the coffee?" Brad went to my cabinets and pulled down two mugs.

"I'm sure Brian made it and placed it in the carafe to keep it hot." I pointed at the jug sitting next to the coffeepot then began cracking eggs into a bowl. "Do you want cheese in the eggs?"

"However you make it, I'll eat it." He poured coffee into the mugs then added a large splash of milk into mine.

After whisking the eggs, with a couple of teaspoons of water added and a dash of salt and pepper, I poured them into the hot skillet. Once the eggs were barely set, I plated them and sprinkled some shredded cheddar cheese over the top.

Brad took a plate, added a slice of toast to it, and sat at the table. "This looks so much better than mine."

"Now that you're going to be a married man, perhaps I should teach you to cook." I giggled then took a bite of eggs.

He scoffed. "Gabe's a fine cook, and I get by when he's not around."

"It wouldn't hurt to surprise him by cooking for him once in a while."

Brad's face fell, and he pushed the eggs around on his plate. "What am I going to do, Em? What if he wants to call off the wedding and this is his way of avoiding telling me?"

I tried to console my friend, but all I could offer were empty platitudes. I had no idea what was going on in Gabe's head any more than Brad did.

Chapter 3

Despite Brad's worries, we headed to Gabe's grandparents' Huntington Beach home, where the wedding and reception would take place. They'd bought the mini mansion a decade ago but only used the house a few times a year. The rest of their time was divided between the homes they owned in Boca Raton, Cape Cod, Vail, and Hawaii. Gabe never let on how wealthy his family was, and I had to respect his dedication to serving the community in law enforcement.

When Gabe's parents had found out the couple was planning on a quick courthouse ceremony with a small gathering of friends afterward, they'd insisted on a more formal affair at the Huntington Beach home. We'd managed to whittle Gabe's family's guest list down to seventy, and with Brad's family and friends, we expected one hundred people. It was still far more than either of them wanted.

Even though Gabe's grandparents and parents wouldn't arrive in town until the day before Thanksgiving, Gabe and Brad had the keys to access the house to prepare for the nuptials scheduled for the Saturday after Turkey Day. Since I was acting as the impromptu wedding planner, after theirs absconded with all the money they'd paid up front, Gabe had made sure I had a key as well.

As we drove, we discussed all the items to be done over the next two weeks before the ceremony. I checked my notebook for the things that needed Brad's input, although for the most part, he was leaving it entirely up to me and my family, who I'd conscripted to help.

"The florist is having trouble getting enough cranberry-colored rose petals for the flower girls. Can we fill in with white and blush petals?"

My two seven-year-old nieces, Sophie and Kaylee, were the flower girls. They were enthralled with the satin-and-tulle champagne-colored princess dresses they'd get to wear along with the crown of flowers for their towheaded tresses. My dogs, Piper and Missy, would each be carrying a soft basket of rose petals—attached to the tops of dog vests—for the girls to throw as they made their way down the white satin runner.

My almost-two-year-old nephew, Tommy, would be the ring bearer. Instead of attaching the actual matrimonial rings to the pillow, fake rings would be displayed to minimize any disaster, such as Tommy or the dogs swallowing the rings. He'd walk between the two girls, but it was anyone's guess if he'd actually make it all the way down the aisle. In my opinion, which I'd expressed often, the inclusion of the kids and dogs had all the makings for it either going oh-so-wrong or their stealing the show. Brad didn't care in the least, and Gabe was leaving all the planning up to his intended.

"Sure, as long as there are enough petals to make it all the way down the runner." Brad turned on his signal and switched lanes to speed around a tourist driving a car with a Florida license plate.

I couldn't blame the tourist. The ocean view from the Pacific Coast Highway, or PCH, as locals called it, was glorious. The sun sparkled on the swells and the crashing waves. Surfers, garbed in slick wetsuits, sat atop colorful surfboards, waiting to catch the next wave. I wondered if one of them was Brian. I'd forgotten to ask him which surf spot he'd planned on visiting. The crystal-clear day displayed Catalina Island in full view. Only thirty miles off our coastline, Catalina was a tourist destination, with several ferries departing daily to keep up with the demand.

"The alterations are done on your tuxes, so I'll pick them up tomorrow." I added a calendar reminder so I wouldn't forget. "Have you and Gabe gotten your marriage license yet?" I knew they hadn't, but I needed to keep prodding Brad so it wouldn't fall through the cracks.

He groaned. "Send Gabe a text, and ask him to schedule a time. He's the one holding up the process."

I thumbed a quick reminder to Gabe, despite knowing I wouldn't receive a response. "Done. Brian has the menu under control, and his sous chef, Sal, will be the head chef for the reception. I don't think there's anything else I need to worry about on that front."

Brian was the owner of and chef for Oceana, an upscale restaurant in Laguna Beach. After Sal had been accused—and then cleared—of murdering my twin's catering client, he'd quit and gone to work for Brian. He'd rapidly proven his worth and had recently taken over Oceana's catering services after my sister decided she could no longer take on the workload.

"They've got something for the vegan guests to eat, right?" Brad asked.

"Definitely. Brian made wild-rice-stuffed acorn squash for dinner the other night. It was tasty and filling. Plus, it's perfect for autumn." The dish had been made with Parmesan cheese, but Brian promised he'd sourced a tasty vegan cheese to substitute. "He's got several appetizers that will be vegan as well."

"Good." He turned into a gated community and gave his name to the guard. While we waited for the gate to open, he turned toward me. "How much more wedding stuff do we have to discuss? I'm going to turn into a Groomzilla if I have to deal with much more."

We'd only gone through a fraction of the things we needed to discuss, but I decided to have pity on him. "I won't bother you with all the minute details and the thousand phone calls I have to make to follow up with the vendors, if that will make you feel less stressed."

Brad pulled to a stop in front of the imposing house. The Spanish-style home, with a red terracotta tiled roof, had wrought-iron balcony railings, and arched windows graced the front of the house. The variegated bluestone walkway to the front door complemented the ivory-painted exterior.

"Until things stabilize with Gabe, that's probably for the best." He gave me a weak smile. "And I'll keep on him about making time to get the license."

"If something really needs your decision, though, I'm going to have to bother you." My mind was going a hundred miles a minute as I thought about everything that needed to be coordinated with only two weeks to go.

There was the photographer, the videographer and his drone, the stringed quartet, the DJ, the florist, and the cake bakery to confirm. I'd need to go over the list with the rental company, who would be providing everything from table and chairs to linens, China, crystal, and flatware. I'd also scheduled shuttle buses to cart guests back and forth from the school we'd contracted with to leave parked cars and I needed to tell them what time to show up. Then there were wedding programs, dinner menus, and place cards to pick up from the printer. And, not the last thing by far, was making sure the temp employment agency had enough maids scheduled to clean up after guests inside the house and keep the six bathrooms refreshed and stocked with amenities.

We each gathered a few wrapped gifts, most with elaborate bows and ribbons, and walked to the front door. Brad balanced his stack of gifts in one hand and fit his key into the forged-iron door lock. Before he could twist the key, the door inched forward.

"That's odd. I thought I locked up two days ago when I left." He toed the door inward, and I followed him inside. "The alarm isn't beeping either."

"Do you think we should wait in the car and call the police in case someone broke in?" I backed up, toward the open door.

"I don't hear anyone. Let's check it out first." Brad headed toward the kitchen. "I was distracted and probably forgot to set the alarm and lock up when I left. Gabe called me just as I was leaving, and well, we were arguing. Again."

"Lead the way, if you think it's safe." I shifted the packages in my arms. "Where do you want to put the gifts?"

"I've been storing them in the butler's pantry. When the rental company drops off the tables, you can set one up to display them there." He shook his head and huffed. "We clearly stated no gifts on the invitations, but do Gabe's family and acquaintances listen? Nope."

It was clear to me that this wedding was putting both men on edge. "It sounds like you should have eloped and then told the family about your marriage after you got back from Costa Rica. It's not too late to go ahead and do that."

Brad rolled his eyes. "That's what Gabe and I were arguing about two days ago. I'm all for eloping because this wedding is turning into a circus, and his family just keeps putting more and more pressure on him. Did you know they invited another twenty guests last week without asking?"

"*What?*" My screech echoed in the vaulted-ceilinged living room. I wanted to pull my hair out. "And you're just now telling me?"

"Relax. Gabe at least has a good understanding of the logistics of things, and he put his foot down. The guests have been uninvited, but it caused a lot of angst between

Gabe and his parents, which kind of got carried over to me."

We reached the butler's pantry and added the gifts to the piles already stacked on the black marble counters. I was relieved to see the gifts still there because that meant the house hadn't been burglarized.

"Before we bring the rest of the gifts in, I want to show you what my cousin sent me from Italy." He waggled his eyebrows. "I should have brought the ingredients so we could test it out and imbibe while we work. You know... hair of the dog and all that?"

"No, no, no. I'm not drinking any more alcohol until your wedding." I elbowed him. "So, what is this mystery gift, and where is it?"

"It's a black Italian marble muddler and cocktail shaker. She had our monogram engraved onto the shaker." He pulled me toward the door leading out of the pantry. "I can just envision the bartender making our signature cranberry mojito cocktail at the reception using them. You've figured out the recipe for the cranberry mojito cupcakes, haven't you?"

"Yes, and the bakery has already tested the recipe with their ingredients, and I approved it."

Brad and Gabe had wanted a signature cocktail with corresponding cupcakes using the same flavors. With Thanksgiving only two days before the wedding, the guys decided—with a little nudge from me—that cranberry flavors would be appropriate. Plus, the cranberries would lend a festive color to the reception. With a nod to the matrimonial theme, white fondant and white embellishments, such as flowers and edible pearls, would cover the cranberry buttercream frosting.

I followed Brad through the formal dining room, which was double the size of my living room and kitchen combined, and into the media room, as Gabe called it. It was a wide-open area with a glass wall that could be fully retracted to open to the outdoor living space and the expansive backyard beyond. From a previous visit to the house, I knew there was a wet bar tucked around the corner of the wall that held a humongous flatscreen TV surrounded by built-in bookshelves. Our footsteps clacked on the white marble flooring, and we stepped around the plush rugs that covered the areas in front of white sofas grouped into inviting seating arrangements.

As we turned the corner to reach the wet bar, Brad came to a sudden halt. With my attention diverted by some of the book titles, I slammed into his back.

"Oh my gawd! This can't be happening." Brad started backing away from the wet bar and stepped on my foot.

"Ouch!" I tried pushing him away, but he wouldn't budge. I peeked over his shoulder then gripped his arm hard enough to elicit a yelp. I might have screamed, or maybe it was Brad.

A woman was sprawled out on the white marble floor. Blood pooled beneath her dark-brown hair, which fanned out from her head. Her dark-brown eyes stared unseeing up at the ceiling. A bloody marble muddler lay next to her outstretched hand.

Chapter 4

"How the heck did she get here? And how did she even find me?" Brad scrubbed his face with his palms.

I'd pulled us out of the house, after checking for a pulse—there was none, and she was stone cold—and we now sat in his car while we waited for the police to arrive.

"You know who she is?" I hadn't recognized the woman, and I thought I knew most of Brad's friends and employees.

"Do you remember me telling you I had a stalker a few years ago?" Brad shuddered. "It's why I don't share my true identity on social media."

"Yes… Don't tell me that is your *stalker!*"

"I'm afraid that's the case." He stared at the house. "How did she find me?"

The shrill whine of a siren filled the air, and a black-and-white police car pulled up behind us.

We stepped from the vehicle, and I came to a halt when my ex-husband, Officer Philip Martinez, got out of the patrol car.

"Great," I muttered to Brad. "You take the lead on this."

Philip had developed more paunch since the last time I'd

seen him, but he still had the same cocky swagger. He brushed a lock of wavy black hair away from his forehead while his brown eyes flicked up and down my body. I was glad I'd worn an oversize sweatshirt that hung halfway down my thighs.

"Well, well, well. It looks like the murder magnet strikes again." Philip's lips curled up in a sneer. "And now you've dragged someone else into your mess."

"Is a detective on the way?" I didn't wait for Brad to take the lead. I'd had it with Philip's arrogance and the way he'd belittled me for way too long.

"I need to determine whether one is required." Philip jutted his chin toward the house. "Let's go take a look."

"What part of a dead woman lying in a pool of blood with the murder weapon right next to her makes you think a detective isn't required?" I'd heard Philip had recently tried to get a promotion to the homicide unit but hadn't passed the test required to start training. I wondered if his desire to become a detective had anything to do with my reputation for solving murders. He'd always had a competitive streak where I was concerned, thus the belittling.

Before Philip could answer, an unmarked black sedan pulled into the driveway. A tall man dressed in black slacks and a white button-down shirt that contrasted nicely with his caramel-colored skin stepped from the vehicle. I heaved a sigh of relief and gave Detective Nathan Hawkins a quick wave. It might have just been my imagination, but I thought he rolled his eyes up toward the sky. He'd investigated the last murder victim I'd had the misfortune of stumbling across.

Philip stood taller and sucked in his gut. "Detective Hawkins, I haven't had a chance to secure the house yet. Would you like me to do so?"

Detective Hawkins looked from me to Philip and back to me. "Do you think anyone other than the victim is in the house?"

"I don't think so." I gulped. "Given the color and viscosity of the blood along with how cold and rigid she is, I think she's been dead for quite a while."

Detective Hawkins pursed his lips and gave Philip the side-eye. "Wait here, and Officer Martinez will accompany me to be sure."

Brad and I returned to the car and waited another five minutes. Philip exited the house and stomped to his car. He got in, slammed his door shut, then roared off. Detective Hawkins strode over to our car and motioned for us to join him.

I jerked a thumb over my shoulder, toward the street where Philip had sped off. "What'd ya say to him?"

"I put him on notice that if I heard any more talk about murder magnets, he'd be demoted to meter reader."

I couldn't help but laugh. "Thank you for that."

"Crime scene techs should be here soon, along with the coroner." He held out his hand to Brad. "I'm Detective Hawkins, and I've already had the pleasure of meeting Emory a couple of months ago. And you are?"

Brad shook his hand. "Brad Ruller. This is my fiancé's grandparents' home and our wedding venue. We were just going over the wedding details when we found her."

The detective pointed at the house. "Shall we go to the living room, and I'll take your statements while we wait? Or would you feel more comfortable remaining outside?"

Knowing that the living room was far enough away from the victim, I suggested we go inside. A few neighbors had exited their houses and were warily watching us. The last thing I wanted was for someone to take photos or videos of us and post it on social media for the world to see. The detective retrieved an iPad from his vehicle, and then Brad and I followed him inside.

We tried to make ourselves as comfortable as we could on the overly firm tufted white sofa and wingback chairs.

"I'd normally separate you for the statements, but since I

know Emory is presumably innocent, I'll talk to you both in the interest of saving time before the coroner arrives." Detective Hawkins picked up his iPad and tapped. "How do you spell your last name, Brad?"

"R-u-l-l-er. I should mention that my fiancé is Detective Gabe O'Neill with the Newport Beach PD."

"Congratulations on your upcoming nuptials. I take it he can vouch for you last night?"

Brad's face drained of all color. "Unfortunately, no. I was with Emory and a bunch of friends until about midnight. Gabe has a case that kept him away from home all night long. I picked up coffee and pastries at six forty-five and got to Emory's house around seven this morning."

Detective Hawkins raised his eyebrows. "Well then, let's hope the death happened while you were with your friends."

"I was with the same friends, and then Brian stayed with me until around six this morning. I think." At least, that was my best guess. I barely remembered him kissing my cheek before he left, and not once had I opened my eyes to check on the time.

The detective sighed. "Alrighty, then. Do either of you know the victim?"

Brad glanced at me, and I gave a subtle nod.

"Well, the truth of the matter is…" Brad cleared his throat. "Well, she used to stalk me. I had a restraining order against her, and once I moved down to Orange County a couple of years ago, I haven't seen or heard from her since."

Detective Hawkins lowered the iPad, and the creases around his hazel-colored eyes deepened. "Do you know her name and where she's from?"

"I knew her as Zara Yeager, but I was told when I filed the restraining order that she had a couple of aliases. I have no idea what name she was using now." Brad rubbed his hands together as if to warm them. "The last time I saw her, she was in San Jose. But that was over two years ago."

The crime scene van pulled up in front of the house. All three of us strained our necks to catch a glimpse of the crew as they hopped out. They were dressed in white coveralls and carried black totes.

Detective Hawkins stood. "Wait here. I'll have more questions for you."

Brad and I crowded around the window to watch as Detective Hawkins strode out to meet the crew. He extended his hand to an older woman who wore her iron-gray hair cropped short. She was diminutive and, if I had to guess, even shorter than my five-two stature. But where I was pudgy, thanks to sampling more than my share of cupcakes and buttercream, she had a petite frame. The group entered the house but bypassed the living room. I assumed they were heading straight for the wet bar area and the victim.

Brad flopped back onto the sofa then wiggled in an attempt to find a more comfortable spot.

"Are you going to text Gabe and tell him about this? He should probably hear it from you rather than from someone else." I brushed several strands of dog hair from my leggings. It reminded me I needed to get Missy and Piper an appointment with the groomers a few days before the wedding so they'd look their best. I added another reminder to my notes.

"I don't know what to tell him." Brad stood and began pacing. "Ya think 'Hey, babe, there's a dead stalker in your grandparents' house' is going to smooth things over between us?"

"Nooo…." I stood and paced alongside Brad. "How about telling him you're in trouble and really need him to call you? Then you—or I if you can't—can explain the situation when he calls back."

"But I'm not in trouble. Right?" Brad glanced out into the hallway. When he didn't hear anyone coming, he continued, "There's no way they can think I had anything to do with her death. Right?"

"It's going to be okay, Brad. Detective Hawkins is one of the best at his job. He'll find out who did this."

"Why, thank you for your vote of confidence, Emory." The detective came back into the living room and sat down. He swiped a hand over his shaved head. "I trust that means you'll let me do the investigating instead of poking around and putting yourself in danger?"

"I never mean to get involved, but I can't help it if people would rather gossip with me over cupcakes and coffee than talk to the police."

"You have a good point, but I can't condone putting your life in danger. Again." Detective Hawkins opened the iPad. "Ms. MacGraw, the coroner, made an estimated guess that the time of death was between midnight and two, based on the temperature of the body. That could be a bit problematic for you, Mr. Ruller."

Brad visibly tensed, and his shoulders migrated up until they almost reached the bottom of his ears.

The detective pointed his index finger at us. "Can either of you tell me how the victim came to be in this house and who might have wanted her dead?"

Chapter 5

B rad and I answered, "No," at the same time.
"Do either of you know anyone who might be able to provide that information?"

"I have no idea." Brad shook his head. "Like I said, I haven't seen or heard from her in over two years."

"I'm assuming you told Detective O'Neill about Ms. Yeager?"

"Of course. When we met, he wanted to know why I stay anonymous on social media." Brad crossed his arms in front of his torso.

"Could he have been keeping track of her to make sure she didn't have the opportunity to get to you again?" Detective Hawkins put the iPad down on the glass coffee table.

"He never mentioned anything about it. As far as Zara getting into the house, I may have forgotten to set the alarm and lock the door." Brad looked sheepish. "Gabe and I were having a, um, discussion as I was leaving, and I might have been distracted. I honestly can't remember if I left the house unlocked."

"The family doesn't have a spare key hidden outside, do they?"

"No. Only Gabe's grandparents, parents, me, Gabe, Emory, and the housekeeper have keys. I'm pretty sure they're all accounted for."

"Should Brad call Gabe and see if he's been tracking Zara?" I asked.

"I'd rather talk to Detective O'Neill myself before you speak with him." He picked the iPad back up. "Can you give me his cell number and yours? If he doesn't answer, I'll have the dispatcher radio him."

Brad rattled off both ten-digit numbers. The corners of his mouth drooped downward.

"Thanks. I'll let you both leave now. You can be expecting a call from me soon, Mr. Ruller." Detective Hawkins tapped numbers on the screen of his cell phone then stood.

"Wait!" I jumped to my feet. "When can we have access to the house and the grounds? I have a gazillion things I have to do here to prepare for the wedding."

"I'll call you when we've finished with the crime scene. It might be as early as tomorrow, depending on what we find." He gave Brad a long look before striding toward the back of the house without another word to us.

"Come on. Let's go back to my house." I grabbed Brad's hand and pulled him to standing. "We need to discuss this with Tillie and Vannie."

Brad moaned. "There's not going to be a wedding, is there? He definitely thinks I killed Zara."

"Don't overreact. Of course the wedding is going to happen."

"But the house is a crime scene, and nothing ever goes according to plan. It could be a week or more before we can come back, or I could be rotting in jail for murder."

"Stop worrying. We know you're innocent, and the house won't be a crime scene for more than a day or two. I'll have a service come in to disinfect everything." I pushed him toward the door. "No one will ever know that a murder happened here."

"Gabe will know, and he'll have to tell his parents and grandparents." Brad opened the front door and stepped onto the walkway. "They're going to blame me."

"Just stop right there."

Brad came to a complete standstill, and I slammed into his back.

"Why'd you stop in the middle of the walkway?" I pushed him forward.

"You said, 'Stop right there.'"

"Oof. I meant stop with the negativity and blaming yourself. Did you kill her? No, you did not. Did you invite her here? No, you did not."

Brad turned to face me. "But…"

Before he could say another word, I held up my hand. "Nor did you ever lead her on or ask her to become infatuated with you or ask her to stalk you. Gabe isn't going to blame you either."

"It's just a lot to take in right now." He unlocked the Tesla doors using the app on his phone.

"I completely understand." I showed Brad how much my hand was shaking. "I think I need some coffee and something sweet to eat. This has been a shock and probably even more so for you."

"I know just the place with a view of the waves."

We hopped into his car, and Brad headed back to the PCH then turned toward downtown Huntington Beach across from the iconic pier.

After parking in the multistory parking garage, we walked to a café that boasted of its outdoor patio with scenic views of the beach and the pier. I grabbed an empty table and settled into the wicker chair while Brad ordered coffee and pastries for us.

Once we'd eaten our fill, Brad looked around then lowered

his voice to barely above a whisper. "I'm feeling really guilty. Part of me is relieved that she's dead. I no longer have to look over my shoulder all the time, wondering if Zara will find me and make my life a living nightmare again."

Brad had never shared the details of the stalker with me before, aside from stating he had had one. But if she'd made his life a living nightmare, then could Gabe have done something to protect the love of his life? I shook my head. Gabe had been working last night so would have an alibi. Besides, I didn't see him murdering Zara, especially in his grandparents' home. He was smarter than that, and if he ever decided murder was needed, as a very last resort, he'd know how to make it virtually unsolvable.

"I'm so sorry you had to go through that." I reached over and clasped my friend's hand.

Brad gave my hand a light squeeze before releasing it and picking up his coffee. "Don't you go thinking Gabe might have killed her either."

"I can't believe you'd think I'd even consider that." My cheeks heated, and I hoped Brad wouldn't notice.

"I can practically hear those cogs in your brain spinning, and I know how you think." He glanced at me over the rim of his mug. "I'm serious, Em. You can't even think for a second Gabe had anything to do with this."

"I won't, and I pinky promise." I held up my left pinky and hooked it around Brad's finger. Why was Brad so adamant about it? Could he be entertaining the same suspicions? Gabe had been acting odd lately. Was it because he was trying to figure out a way to stop the stalker and the situation got out of control?

"Do you have any other ideas on who might have wanted her dead?" I asked.

"I don't have a clue."

"That's no help. How can we investigate if we have zero suspects?" I thought for a moment. "We need to do a deep dive on the internet to find out where she's been the last two years and what she's been up to. Do you think Gabe would use his resources at the police department?"

"You're asking if my Gabe would jeopardize his job to do that?" Brad snorted. "Not in a million years, especially since there's already a competent detective investigating."

"You're in the software developing business. Can't you access more than what us normal barely computer-literate people can? We need to find out if she's been stalking someone else too."

"I'll see what my guys at work can dig up, but I highly doubt we can go as deep as law enforcement can as far as criminal records or restraining orders." Brad pursed his lips. "Although I have a young kid—his name is Ethan Soros—I hired last year. He's reportedly an expert hacker. Let's see what we can find through the usual channels, and I'll approach him as a last resort."

"That sounds like a plan." I drained the rest of my coffee. "I'm ready to go if you are. It's time to let Tillie and Vannie know what's going on."

We walked to the parking structure and headed south on the PCH. About ten minutes from my house, Brad's phone rang. Gabe's name flashed on the center dash screen. Brad bit his lower lip then answered the call.

"Hey," Brad said. I hoped that Gabe picked up on the icy tone so he'd know how his actions had hurt.

"Where are you?" Gabe sounded congested.

"I'm taking Emory home, and then we were going to go over wedding plans with Tillie and Vannie."

Gabe exhaled loudly. "Can you come home? I really need to talk to you. It's… It's urgent."

"I guess." Brad rolled his eyes. "Give me about thirty minutes. I'll be there after dropping Emory off."

"Actually, bring her here. We have a lot to talk about, and she might be useful."

"Gee, thanks, Gabe. I always aim to be useful." I didn't bother trying to hide my sarcasm. "Even if you refuse to answer texts or phone calls from your fiancé."

"I apologize for that, and I hope you'll both forgive me when you hear why I was incommunicado." Gabe cleared his throat. "I'll see you in about ten minutes or so?"

"We're on our way." Brad disconnected the call without saying goodbye.

Chapter 6

B rad and I both gasped when Gabe opened the front door to their home. He had a large knot on the side of his right temple, which his golden hair couldn't hide, and the skin around his eye was turning shades of blue and purple.

"Babe, what happened?" Brad rushed to the door and held Gabe's face between his hands. "Have you been to the doctor yet?"

"I'll be okay." He motioned for us to come inside. "There's no need for a doctor."

"You might be concussed." Brad held onto Gabe's hand and led us toward their open-space great room. A fire burned cheerily in the stacked stone fireplace. "Can I get you some ibuprofen or some tea?"

"There's no need to fuss over me." Gabe sank down onto the cognac-colored leather sofa, and Brad followed suit. "We have more important things to discuss."

I chose to sit in the matching armchair. After kicking off my shoes, I tucked my feet beneath me and wrapped my arms around my midriff. I had a bad feeling that whatever had happened to Gabe was even worse than what I could imagine, and I wasn't sure I wanted to be a part of it.

"Let me at least get you an ice pack for the swelling." Brad started to stand, but Gabe pulled him back down. "Who did this to you?"

"I don't know. But I'll explain what I do know if you stop fretting." Gabe smiled to take the sting out of his words.

Brad mimicked zipping his lips closed then rolled his hand in a circle as if to give Gabe the floor.

"I heard you two discovered the body of Zara Yaeger." Gabe covered his mouth with the palm of his hand for a moment. It looked like he felt nauseated. I had to agree with Brad that he needed to seek medical attention.

"Yes. We did." I answered for both Brad and myself. "Did you know she was in town before this?"

Gabe closed his eyes and slowly nodded. "Four days ago, Colin and I found her snooping around the backyard of our house. Of course, I immediately recognized her, since I'd completed a background check on her as soon as Brad told me about his stalker when we met."

At the mention of Colin, I noticed Brad's lips straighten to a hard, thin line.

"She tried to play it off that she'd heard the house was for sale and she was interested in buying it. I finally convinced her I knew all about her stalking and if she didn't leave Brad alone, I'd make sure she spent a long time in jail. At that point, she left, and I thought she'd leave town and go back home. I mistakenly didn't think to get any of her contact information or follow up by searching her records."

Gabe paused and swallowed hard. "Yesterday morning, she called my cell phone. I have no idea how she tracked down my personal number, but she did. Zara said if I paid her ten thousand dollars, she'd leave town and never bother you again. I tried tracing her phone, but she used a burner."

Brad's mouth dropped open. "You didn't..."

"Unfortunately, I did. I didn't want her ruining our wedding, nor did I want you to be constantly looking over your shoulder for her." Gabe clasped Brad's hand. "She said to bring the cash to my grandparents' house at seven last night. I'm so sorry. I should have told you."

"Was she dead when you got there?" I asked.

"I never saw her. When I opened the front door, the alarm was already turned off. I stepped into the house, and someone hit me on the side of the head, and that's the last I remember of being at the house and the last I saw of the money."

Brad gasped and touched Gabe's cheek. "You're lucky they didn't kill you along with Zara."

"I know, although it appears their goal was to set me up for her murder."

"What do you mean?" I felt chilled, but whether it was from the weather or from my growing unease about Gabe's story, I didn't know. I pulled a cashmere throw from the back of the armchair and draped it over my legs.

"Whoever knocked me out dumped me and my car out in Riverside, in the middle of nowhere. When I came to, I couldn't find my keys, and my cell phone was dead." Gabe shivered. "It was almost three in the morning, pitch black. I thought about walking to try to find a road and help, but I was so dizzy and nauseated I decided to wait for morning light."

"Gabe, you have to see a doctor. It sounds like you have a concussion," I said.

"Not yet. We have other things to worry about." He twisted to meet Brad's gaze. "A bit before six, when it got light enough, I started walking west, hoping I'd find a road and help. But then I found my keys about fifteen feet from the car. I plugged my cell phone in to charge the battery and drove to the office to clean up and start hunting for Zara. The second my phone came back on, I sent you a text so you wouldn't worry."

"Instead of coming home." Brad's face fell. "Didn't you

know I was worried about you no matter what your text said this morning?"

"I didn't think about that. And in my defense, I really wasn't thinking straight. My only concern was trying to track Zara down and keep her away from you."

"Did you go back to your grandparents' house to see if she was still there?" I asked.

Gabe hung his head. "I started to drive down their street later this morning but saw the police, coroner's van, and paramedics. I turned around and came home, hoping Brad was here and unharmed."

"And you found out it was Zara who had been murdered when Detective Hawkins called you?"

Gabe nodded, although slowly, as if it hurt to move his head. "Here's the bad news. He found the security footage which shows me coming to the house at seven last night, but it doesn't show me leaving. Apparently, there was a neighborhood power outage shortly after I was attacked, and it lasted for several hours. That means there is no way to prove someone attacked me and left me out in Riverside, unconscious."

"If someone drove you out to Riverside, then they must've had an accomplice pick them up and drive them back here. I'm not sure when Zara was killed, but the coroner thinks it was sometime between midnight and two." I hugged my knees to my chest. At times like this, I wished I had Piper and Missy to provide comfort. My earlier concern had been warranted. This was so much worse than I'd anticipated.

"It gets even worse. She was bludgeoned to death, and the murder weapon is our muddler. It most likely has my fingerprints on it, since I'm the one who put it on the wet bar. And most damning, I was the only person seen entering the house the night she was killed."

I furrowed my brow as I tried to make sense of everything.

"Then how did Zara or the person who attacked you get into the house without being seen on the security footage?"

"Probably through the back. My grandparents never bothered to have cameras placed back there." Gabe again covered his mouth with his hand for a moment. "Until I'm cleared, I'm on administrative leave."

Brad gasped. "Oh, Gabe. That's not good."

"That's why I wanted Emory here." Gabe looked at me with trepidation. "I know I've been harsh with you in the past, telling you to stop interfering with investigations. This is hard for me to admit, but I think I need your help. I can't access any records or files to track Zara's movements, nor can I try to find out who she's been interacting with since she arrived in town."

"Don't your injuries exonerate you? Surely they can't think you'd hurt yourself just to create an alibi." I pulled the throw closer around me.

"I'm afraid that's exactly what they'll think. It wouldn't be the first time a perp has injured themselves, hoping it would provide an alibi."

Brad and I exchanged glances, and I nodded. "We'll do what we can. Tell us everything you can about Zara, from when you first researched her to when you saw her and spoke with her."

Chapter 7

I t turned out that Gabe didn't know a whole lot about Zara. When he'd met Brad, she was residing in San Jose. Since then, she'd moved to Half Moon Bay, where she worked as a sales clerk for a bookstore and seemed to keep to herself. There hadn't been any new complaints about stalking.

"Do you know where she was staying here in Orange County?" I wondered if the police already had that information. Squeezing my eyes shut, I tried to picture her body. I hadn't noticed a purse, but maybe she'd put her car keys and ID in a pocket.

"No. I didn't think to interrogate her. I only wanted her away from here." Gabe's voice sounded flat, as if all life had gone out of him.

"Brad, did you notice any cars parked close to the grandparents' house? Especially cars that didn't seem to belong in the neighborhood?" Most of the homes had, at a minimum, three-car garages, so there weren't a lot of vehicles parked on the street. The vehicles that were parked in driveways or curbside were of the luxury persuasion: BMWs, Mercedes, Teslas, Range Rovers, and Lexuses.

"Not that I recall." He furrowed his brow. "With the guard at the gate, how did she get in anyway?"

Gabe lifted his chin, which had practically been resting on his chest. "There's a footpath entrance to the neighborhood on the west side. The gate backs up to the urban forest and Huntington Central Park. It would be a piece of cake sneaking in, especially after sundown."

"Presumably, that's how the killer got in too. He probably followed her here." I tapped my index finger on my chin. "What I don't understand is the timing. Why knock you out at seven and then come back and kill Zara later?"

Gabe appeared deep in thought then let out a long breath. "My hypothesis is that the killer is the one who contacted me and told me to bring the ten grand. Once he—or it could be a strong woman—had me out of the way, they arranged for Zara to meet me here later to collect the money."

"Why not deal with both of you at the same time? Especially since there's got to be an accomplice." Brad stood and headed to the kitchen. "Keep talking. I'll be able to hear you while I get an ice pack for your head."

"I don't need it." Gabe crossed his arms in front of his body.

"I don't care. It'll make me feel better, whether or not it helps you." Brad headed to the kitchen, located at the far end of the great room. A long island with a white-and-gray-swirled quartz top divided the dining table from the kitchen area. High end stainless-steel appliances dominated the kitchen, while the countertops were pristinely clear of any clutter. He opened the overly large French-door-style freezer door and extracted an ice pack. Gabe kept his eyes glued on his fiancé's movements.

"Well?" I asked. "What's your opinion on Brad's question?"

Gabe tore his gaze away from Brad and turned his focus to me. He mulled over the question for a moment. "This is only a guess, mind you, but I think the perp wanted to make sure the timing precluded me from having any type of alibi."

"But why you? I'd think Brad would be the person to set up, given Zara was his stalker." I hesitated a moment. "You do know that Brad left our party early because he was upset about your, um, lack of response and doesn't have an alibi either."

Gabe's face fell. "That's truly unfortunate. But think about it. If they'd intended to set Brad up instead of me, I'd have all the county's resources, with access to information to help solve her murder. With me on administrative leave and evidence pointing at me, I have my doubts the perp will be found."

"You don't have faith in Detective Hawkins?" I asked.

"He's got a solid reputation, but he's going into the investigation knowing I had the motivation, the means, and the opportunity to kill Zara. He's probably going to think that Brad is my accomplice." He placed his elbows on his knees then buried his face in his palms. "If I were investigating the crime and had the evidence Hawkins has, I'd be thinking we both committed the crime too."

"We don't need any of that negative talk." Brad sat back down and handed Gabe an icepack wrapped in a white tea towel. "I thought I'd leave my tech as a last resort, but we need to have him track down where she was staying right away. From there, we can see if anyone knows if she was in contact with other people besides Gabe."

Gabe stood abruptly. "I think I'll excuse myself from your planning. I don't need to know, and I don't want to know about anything illegal going on."

"It's probably for the best. I'll take Em home, and then I'll pick you up and take you to urgent care. You need your injuries checked out."

"I'm fine." Gabe's shoulders slumped.

"You can say that all you want, but I'm taking you to the doctor." Brad placed his hands on his hips.

"Guys, I'll just wait out in the car." I picked up my purse, slung it over my shoulder, and scurried out of the house.

Brad wasn't long in joining me. He blew a raspberry. "That man can be so stubborn sometimes."

"Does that mean you gave up on dragging him to the doctor?"

Brad grinned. "Gabe may think I did, but my sister's best friend is a doctor. Marigold will have no problem convincing her friend to make a house call later today."

I laughed but had to agree that it was in Gabe's best interest to receive medical attention.

Once we arrived at my pool house and parked in the double garage, next to my cherry-red SUV, I texted Tillie and Vannie to see if they were home. They were, so Brad and I headed to Tillie's bayfront mini mansion. The second I opened the massive wrought-iron-and-frosted-glass front doors, I heard claws scrabbling on the travertine flooring, heading from the kitchen, down toward the extra-wide hall-way, and into the two-story foyer where we stood.

Piper and Missy barreled into us, their furry tails circling like mini helicopter blades. They acted like they hadn't seen us for days when, in fact, it had been mere hours. Tillie followed behind but at a much slower pace.

"I'm glad you kids are here. Vannie and I were just going over the Thanksgiving Day menu, and we need your input." Tillie bent over to ruffle Missy's curly apricot-colored fur. "We've decided to host an open-house-style brunch for friends and family to drop by earlier in the day, and then we can serve dinner at five."

Inwardly, I groaned at the amount of work I had to complete for the wedding and now the investigation, but I still managed to produce a weak smile. "A brunch?"

Tillie turned and motioned for us to follow her. "There are a lot of people coming into town for the wedding, and they already have plans for Thanksgiving dinner, like Gabe's parents and grandparents. Vannie and I thought brunch would be a nice way to extend hospitality before the wedding and allow Brad and Gabe's family and friends to get to know one another without the formality of a huge dinner. What do you think, Brad? Your mom and sister thought it was an excellent idea."

Brad's suntanned face—from hours spent surfing waves—paled. He gulped several times. "Maybe? Um, I'd probably better run it by Gabe since, well, I'm not sure there's going to be a wedding."

"What? No wedding? Why?" My half sister, Vannie, stood at the kitchen's entrance with her hands on her hips, which were rounded like my own. Her copper-red hair tended toward frizzy, the same as mine, while my twin sister, Carrie, was blessed with sleek hair that was more auburn than our clown red. Vannie also had the same generous sprinkling of freckles over her face as I did.

"Let's go sit in the kitchen, and we'll talk about what's happened over tea." I tugged on Brad's arm and led him into the spacious kitchen, which was a chef's dream.

I'd spent many, many hours baking cupcakes in the space, and it had become the hub for conversations and confidences shared between friends and family. When I'd first met Tillie, a small bistro table with two uncomfortable chairs had occupied an alcove in the kitchen. Since then, she'd swapped it out for a long farm-style table with bench seating so that a large group could gather together in the inviting space, which overlooked the bay.

Vannie filled a stainless-steel teakettle with water and set it on the burner. I gathered teacups and saucers while Tillie pulled a bottle of brandy out of the cupboard.

"It sounds like we need a little tipple with our tea." She splashed generous amounts into each cup.

Once we each had a bracing cup of hot beverage in front of us along with a mounded plate of white chocolate cran-

40

berry cookies sitting in the middle of the table, Vannie pointed at Brad. "You're not calling off the wedding just because he had to work and couldn't make it last night, are you?"

"It's not that." Brad rubbed his face with both palms. "It's just that…"

I decided to put Brad out of his misery of trying to explain. "Gabe's being investigated for the murder of Brad's stalker, and Brad doesn't have an alibi either. Obviously, if they're arrested, the wedding can't take place."

I wasn't sure I'd ever seen Tillie rendered speechless. Her mouth dropped open, and her eyes widened.

"You're joking." Vannie elbowed me. "Just so you know, it's not funny."

Brad coughed then cleared his throat. The words tumbled out in a croak. "It's no joke. Em and I found the victim this morning, and Gabe's now on administrative leave while they investigate."

Tillie rubbed her hands together. "I guess this means we've got a case to solve!"

Chapter 8

"Since we have less than two weeks to clear Brad's and Gabe's names, tell us what you know." Vannie took a bite of cookie.

I quickly explained how we'd found Zara and what had happened to Gabe. "We all know they're both innocent, so we have to find out who wanted Zara dead."

Brad slapped his palms onto his cheeks and closed his eyes. "This is hopeless. Zara wasn't from around here, and no one knew her except for me."

"It seems like whoever did the deed covered their tracks pretty well." Tillie pursed her lips. "How are we going to go about finding more suspects?"

"First thing tomorrow, I'm going to have one of my, uh, computer experts hunt down where Zara's been staying and see if he can dig up anything on her." Brad took a sip of the brandy-laced tea then screwed up his face before swallowing. He placed the teacup back on the saucer and pushed it away from him.

"Ooh, a hacker!" Tillie pointed at Brad. "I think I'd like to come watch him in action. Or is your hacker a she?"

"His name is Ethan, but I don't think he'd appreciate anyone hanging over his shoulder."

"Or breathing down his neck," I added.

Brad stood, picked up his still-full teacup and saucer, and placed them in the sink. "I need to head back to Gabe and make sure he gets some medical attention."

"Keep us posted on how he's feeling." I threaded my arm through his. "I'll walk you to the door."

After Brad kissed Tillie's cheek and said his good-byes, we walked to the front door. Piper and Missy stayed with Tillie in the kitchen, most likely hoping she'd slip them some treats. I'd long since given up on scolding the octogenarian for spoiling the dogs.

"I'll call you tomorrow morning, once I talk to Ethan."

"Maybe I should meet you there. That way, we can start investigating just as soon as he gets a hit on where she's been staying." I giggled when I saw Brad's eyebrows rise. "I promise not to hover over his shoulder, and I'll bring some muffins in for your staff."

"In that case, meet me there at nine. You can park in my spot, since the lot will be pretty full by the time you get there." Brad opened the door.

"Won't you need the parking space?"

Located in a small strip of offices, Brad's business was close to the Orange County airport in Irvine and had been allotted only seven parking spaces to cover the number of employees. I'd often had to park a few blocks away and walk, since the few visitor spaces were always taken.

"I'll get there early enough to park in one of the visitors' spaces." Brad swept a hand through his hair, and his wavy locks sprang right back into place when he dropped his arm to his side.

"Hope you don't get a parking citation from the monitor." I smirked, knowing Brad and the self-proclaimed site manager had butted heads several times over frivolous infractions she'd brought against him and the other companies occupying office spaces.

"That nosy parker can stick her meaningless warnings in the trash. She has no authority to break our lease or collect monetary penalties on behalf of the owner. Maybe I should take some of your muffins over to sweeten her up." He shook his head. "Naw. She'd probably think I might be trying to poison her."

"I'll bring a few extra, in case you change your mind."

Once Brad left, I scurried back to the kitchen. Vannie stood at the sink, refilling our teacups with hot water, while Tillie rubbed behind Piper's ears. Missy had flopped onto the travertine floor, her hind legs sticking up in the air. She snored gently.

"It's such a shame something like this is taking away from Brad and Gabe's joyous day." Tillie looked wistful. "I wish I knew what I could do to help them."

"Surely Gabe's friends at the station will help him. Or at least pass along information he can use to clear his name. Right?" Vannie added extra cookies to the plate still sitting in the middle of the table.

"I'm not really sure. Gabe seemed kind of freaked out when Brad mentioned getting his employee to look into tracking down Zara's movements and where she's been staying around here." I accepted the cup of tea from my sister then set it on the table to cool a bit more before sipping. "He actually left the room and said he didn't want to know what we were doing."

"He's a by-the-book kind of guy." Tillie stretched across the table and retrieved the bottle of brandy. "Do you want another little tipple?"

"No, thanks. I'm good as is." I blew on the tea to hasten the cooling.

Tillie set the bottle down after adding a splash to her cup. Her mouth was set in a grim line. "I'll only bring this up once

—and please promise me that it goes no further than us three."

Once she'd gained our promises, she continued. "How certain are you of Gabe's innocence?"

Vannie gasped. "How can you even consider Gabe?"

I bit my lower lip then sighed. "I had the exact same thought. He's devoted to Brad, and if he thought Brad's life was in danger, Gabe would do anything to protect him."

"Was the stalker that dangerous?" Vannie asked.

"Brad said she'd made his life a living nightmare, so I'd say yes." I should have asked Brad for details when I'd had the chance. If I brought it up now, he'd reasonably assume I suspected Gabe. "And for the record, Brad doesn't have it in him to kill anyone."

"I agree, but wouldn't Gabe go through legal channels to stop the stalker? It seems a bit excessive to jump straight to killing her." Vannie sat beside me.

"Maybe he tried that, and the legal system failed." I shrugged. "Or he saw how the legal system had failed since she managed to track Brad down anyway."

"What about the money Gabe supposedly got to pay off Zara?" Tillie asked. "Do you think that really happened or that he made up the story as a ruse?"

"I don't know." I thought a moment. "His injuries were definitely real, and I can't begin to imagine doing that to yourself. I'm pretty sure he's got a concussion."

"Yeah, it seems out of character for Gabe to do something like that," Vannie said.

"What makes me hesitate to really consider Gabe as a true suspect is that he's intelligent. Why kill Zara at his grandparents' house and then leave her for Brad to find her? He could have found an easier way to get rid of her without bringing attention to himself or to Brad."

"But he assumed Brad would be with us most of the night, giving him an ironclad alibi," Tillie said.

"But he had to have known either Brad or I would be the one to find the body. I don't think he'd do that to either of us."

"What if he planned on getting to the house first to 'discover' the body and you beat him to it?" Tillie bounced her index and middle fingers up and down on the word *discover*.

I stood and retrieved a scratch pad and pen from Tillie's junk drawer, which wasn't junky at all. "I need to write down all the pros and cons in suspecting Gabe."

Vannie leaned into me and watched as I wrote down our conjectures. When I'd finished filling in the two columns, she said, "I think the circumstantial evidence might make Gabe look like the number-one suspect, but I truly believe he's innocent. Whoever did it really covered their tracks."

"That's our entire problem. There are no other suspects." I tossed the pen back into the drawer and wadded up the page I'd written on and threw it into the trash.

"Give it time. Perhaps Brad's guy will track down some information that will point us in the right direction." Tillie sipped her brandy-laced tea. "Since we can't talk about other suspects at this point, let's schedule our next Sunday family dinner. I'm assuming we'll postpone until the first Sunday in December?"

"I think that's the best plan. There's too much to do to get ready for Thanksgiving next Sunday, and then everyone's going to be exhausted after the wedding." I tapped my calendar open and made a note. Late last summer, we'd started a weekly family dinner at Tillie's house. It was potluck style, and it wasn't uncommon for a few friends to join us. I'd enjoyed becoming closer to my sisters as well as seeing my nieces and nephew on a consistent basis. And since pets were a part of the family, my nieces brought the kittens, Tigger and Patches, whom we'd rescued a couple months before. Even Piper and Missy looked forward to romping then snuggling with the kittens each week.

Initially, Tillie and I had planned on adopting the kittens, since my sister Carrie was allergic to cats and had to keep her kitchen up to code for her catering business. But my nieces, Kaylee and Sophie, had finally worn their mother down. Carrie endured weekly allergy shots, which helped a lot, and cat-proof barriers had been installed to keep the darling kittens from entering the kitchen when she was working.

"I realize you're right, but I do miss our gatherings." Tillie opened up her own phone and scheduled the dinner. "I'll send an email to everyone so they can plan accordingly."

Vannie tapped her fingers on the table. "We also need to go over the details for our Thanksgiving gatherings, especially if we're going to add brunch to the festivities."

We spent the next hour working on the details, and Vannie volunteered to let Brian, Carrie, and our mother know about the plans. Once we'd reached a consensus on what we'd each fix and the menu, Vannie and I made a quick ravioli vegetable soup along with a green salad for dinner, then I headed to my pool house with the dogs in tow.

Chapter 9

The blaring alarm clock startled me awake the next morning. I'd slept fitfully and would have preferred to sleep in instead of getting up before sunrise to bake muffins for Brad and the cupcakes that needed to be delivered for a dinner party that night.

Brian had called around eleven the previous night to let me know he was still working at his restaurant and would crash at his house instead of coming to mine. Because of a growing waitlist for reservations at Oceana this week, I suspected I wouldn't see him until Thanksgiving afternoon. I'd miss him, but it would give me more time to clear Gabe and Brad of murder.

Brian and I had begun house hunting in September but so far had struck out on finding something that would suit us both. We'd thought we'd found the perfect house—and it was only two blocks from Tillie's home—but the couple decided to call off their divorce and reconciled just as we put in an offer. They withdrew their property from the market, and we'd been searching ever since. With the holidays upon us, our Realtor told us to relax and not expect anything until after the first of the year. I could tell Brian's patience was wearing thin, and he'd stopped coming to stay with me after work as often as he had just a few short months ago. I couldn't blame him, though, since his restaurant's holiday business kept him busy until the wee hours of the morning.

Piper and Missy laid their snouts on top of my bed, and Missy whined.

"Okay, I get the message." I threw the covers back, rolled out of bed, and rubbed their heads.

The dogs pranced around me as I dressed in yoga pants and a pumpkin-colored long-sleeved tee. I used to keep the doggie door to the backyard open during the night, but a nocturnal critter—an opossum, if you must know—accessed the doggie door and created quite a commotion, to say the least. The poor, frightened creature ended up comatose, and I had to call animal control after locking the dogs in my bedroom. Before they could arrive, the opossum came to, and I managed to herd it outside through the wide-open French doors. It wasn't an experience I wanted to repeat.

After letting the dogs into the backyard, I filled their bowls with kibble then got the butter and eggs out of the refrigerator. I'd let them come to room temperature while the oven preheated and I collected and measured out all the other ingredients.

The season seemed to call for cranberries, so I'd decided to make muffins using canned cranberry sauce. That way, I could use the muffin recipe year-round instead of waiting for cranberry season to come around. I began by creaming butter with both granulated sugar and a bit of brown sugar for an added depth of flavor. Using some sour cream to increase both richness and moistness, I next added in an egg, some vanilla extract, and lemon zest. Once it was combined, I slowly mixed in flour, baking powder, baking soda, and salt.

When the batter was thoroughly mixed, I dolloped in canned cranberry sauce with whole berries and swirled it around with a butter knife. I wanted a marbled effect so it wouldn't disappear into the batter. After dividing the batter between twelve muffin tin cups, I doused the tops of the batter with a heavy sprinkle of white sparkling sugar then placed them in the oven to bake.

The dogs, tired of chasing early birds and squirrels, came back inside and gobbled up their kibble. They turned their liquid toffee-brown eyes up at me, begging for treats. Missy even sat on her hind legs and placed her front paws in front of her chest. It always made me think of Oliver Twist saying, "Please, sir. I want some more." I couldn't help but laugh, so I gave them each a homemade dog biscuit made with dehydrated liver, oatmeal, and eggs.

While the muffins baked, I started on the cranberry-orange cupcakes. I'd made the sugared cranberry garnish the day before as well as the fresh cranberry sauce for the frosting. The procedure was pretty much the same as the muffins, except instead of sour cream, I used buttermilk and alternated adding it to the creamed sugar mixture with the flour mixture. Once the batter was combined, I stirred in some chopped fresh cranberries then filled the cupcake tins just as the timer dinged to remove the muffins from the oven.

While the muffins cooled, I brewed a small pot of coffee then poured some, along with a generous splash of milk, into a large mug. I took a big bite of the almost-cooled muffin and concentrated on the flavors and texture. I thought it could use an extra punch of lemon so jotted a note on my recipe to try adding a small amount of lemon extract to the batter next time. Since Tillie was still insistent about hosting a Thanksgiving drop-in brunch, I'd make a couple of batches of these for those who wanted something light.

WITH A CUPCAKE TOTE IN HAND, I pushed the glass door open and stepped into Brad's office. I placed the tote that contained the muffins on the slate-gray countertop that divided the reception area from the receptionist's built-in desk... that was, if Brad had a receptionist. His software company didn't have uninvited drop-in visitors, so the desk remained bare.

Brad poked his head through the doorway that led down a hallway to more offices. "Right on time, Em. I'm starved."

"Of course you are." I smiled as I opened the tote to showcase the baked goods nestled in little indentations that kept them in place. "I brought eleven muffins, since I had to taste test one of them."

"My employees are going to be disappointed you didn't bring any for them." Brad snatched a muffin from the carrier and was about to pick up a second muffin.

"No way, dude. Emory brought those for all of us." Sylvia, a recent college graduate, slapped Brad's empty hand away from the muffins. She carefully examined the treats then chose one. "What's the flavor today?"

"Cranberry and lemon. It's a new recipe, so let me know what you think."

Sylvia brushed her long, straight black hair away from her face then took a bite. She chewed thoughtfully, whereas Brad had inhaled the first muffin and was in the process of taking a second one.

"It's a bit light on the lemon flavor, but overall, it's good. It's not overly sweet, and I like the crunch of the sugar on top." Sylvia flashed me a thumbs-up. "Thanks for the snack, but I need to grab a cup of tea and head back to the dungeon. The taskmaster has me on deadline."

Brad pretended to crack a whip then extended his hand for a fist bump. Sylvia obliged, flashed a smile that showcased perfectly straight white teeth, and headed back down the hallway. I enjoyed the camaraderie Brad had with his employees. They might work hard, especially when there were deadlines, but they were well compensated and treated with respect, and they all seemed to have the same type of bantering humor.

"Come on back, and we can put the muffins in the break room before we talk to Ethan." Brad led the way down the hall then turned right into a bright, open room. There were three round tables. From past experience spending time sitting in the break room, I knew the black leather chairs that surrounded each table were comfortable. A stainless-steel refrigerator sat beside a long granite countertop, upon which sat a microwave. There was a full-sized oven, an induction cooktop, and a full-sized stainless-steel dishwasher. Brad had spared no expense for his employees, and it wasn't uncommon for him to order in lunch or dinner for everyone when they were on a tight deadline.

After placing the muffins in the middle of one of the tables, I followed Brad back down the hallway to Ethan's office. He sat hunched over his keyboard with two extra-large monitors dominating his desk.

Brad lightly knocked on the doorframe. "Is now a good time to review what you found, Ethan?"

Ethan straightened and pushed his black-framed glasses up the bridge of his nose with his index finger. The thick lenses made his black eyes seem owlish. A hank of dark-brown hair fell across his acne-scarred forehead. Even though I knew the man was twenty-five, I couldn't help but think he looked like a high-schooler.

"Oh, yeah. Now's fine." He rolled his chair to the far side of the desk and gestured for us to come stand next to him.

The monitor sitting on the right side of the desk showed a large map of Orange County. Multiple red and yellow digital pushpins dotted the map. Ethan handed us each a sheaf of papers.

He pointed at the monitor. "Each of the pushpins represents where she used either a credit card or her debit card."

"How did you…" I bit back my question when Brad scowled at me. I suddenly remembered that Ethan was a hacker, and his skill wasn't something we should ever discuss. Especially if anyone else was in the vicinity.

Ethan ignored me and went on as if I'd never interrupted him. "The subject left Half Moon Bay on September fifteenth and arrived in Anaheim on the sixteenth."

I gasped. Zara had been in the area for almost two months. Had she been stalking Brad the entire time, or had she been trying to track him down and only recently had success?

"You can tell from the printouts I gave you that she moved to a new motel every few days and eventually ended up at a small apartment complex in Irvine a month ago. The lodgings are represented by the red pins." Ethan pointed at a spot on the screen. "The yellow pins represent other places she used her credit or debit card, like gas, food, and shops."

I glanced down at the pages in my hands and found not only the names and the locations Zara had visited but also the dollar amounts and, in some cases, the items she'd purchased. Ethan was scarily good at hacking.

"I printed out the map with the pins. The page should be at the very back of the packet I gave you. I also included a high-res photo of the subject." He tapped his fingers on the keyboard, and the monitor went dark. "Is that everything you needed?"

"It's everything and even more than I'd hoped." Brad clapped the young man's shoulder. "Thanks, Ethan."

"No prob." Ethan pushed his glasses back up again. "Let me know if you need anything else. Anything at all."

Brad nudged me toward the door. "Thanks, bro. This should do it for now."

I hustled out into the hallway and made my way to Brad's office. It wasn't any larger or more sumptuous than any of his employees'. They were equally nice with top-of-the-line equipment and ergonomically comfortable chairs.

Brad closed his office door once we were inside and tossed

the pages onto his desk. "I feel like Detective Hawkins should have this information, but there's no way to give it to him without admitting I hired a hacker."

"What if we say we stumbled onto where she lived, and then maybe he can take it from there?" I flipped through some of the pages. Zara had spent quite a bit of money over the two months she was in our area. Although until she rented the apartment, she'd stuck to staying at budget motels.

"Oh sure. He'll believe that we just guessed that she was renting an apartment in Irvine instead of staying at one of the thousands of hotels, motels, or Airbnbs in Orange County." Brad swept a hand through his hair then went to sit on the small sofa against the wall.

Brad wasn't kidding about the thousands of lodging options. With Disneyland a main feature in Orange County, in addition to other theme parks, beaches, and recreational areas, there was a myriad of places to choose from. There would be no way anyone would find Zara's motel or apartment just by guessing.

"I don't know what the answer is. Perhaps we should take her photo and go check out the apartment complex. Maybe someone there will recognize her and be able to tell us if she's had any visitors." I paged through the information until I found the apartment complex. "Can you leave work now? I don't have to be back home until one to frost cupcakes before delivering them."

"Give me ten minutes to reply to a couple of emails, and then I can probably spare about an hour."

"Sounds good." I sat on the sofa while Brad moved to his desk and sat down.

A chime sounded. Brad frowned before jumping up. "That's the front door. I must've forgotten to lock it when you came in. Be back in a jiffy."

Brad's footsteps echoed down the tiled hallway.

"Mr. Ruller, I have some more questions to ask you. Is

there somewhere private we can meet, or would you prefer to come down to the station?" Detective Hawkins's voice was loud and clear.

I glanced down at the papers I held and the sheets that were scattered on Brad's desk. I scrambled to collect them all into one pile and shoved them into my purse. We'd both be in huge trouble if the detective found evidence of the hacking.

"We can meet in the break room. Emory dropped off muffins, and there's fresh coffee, if you'd like some." Brad's voice was louder than usual.

I assumed it was to give me a hint where he was taking the detective so I could avoid running into him.

"No, thanks. I'm fine." Detective Hawkins cleared his throat. "Is Emory still here? I thought I saw her vehicle in the parking lot."

Great. There'd be no way to sneak out of there now. I hoped Brad didn't think he'd need to lie, because the detective would see through him in a heartbeat.

"Uh, I think she's still in my office. Do you want to speak with her?"

"Not unless she's got some new information to tell me. And by that, I mean she'd better not have anything new, since I don't want either of you sticking your nose in the investigation."

"Nope. We were just going over wedding stuff. You know how it is."

Detective Hawkins grunted, and then I heard the door to the break room close. I took the opportunity to make sure none of the incriminating papers had been left behind, and then I hightailed it out of the office. Not knowing how long Brad's interrogation would go on, I decided to go check out the apartment complex on my own.

Chapter 10

I t was close to ten by the time I accelerated onto the freeway to head south on the 405. Traffic was fairly light, and it didn't take long to get to the Culver Drive exit. I turned east and drove on the multilane road, hitting every red traffic light along the way. My phone chimed, so I snuck a peek while sitting, waiting for the light to turn green. It was a reminder to pick up the tuxes. The shop was located on the very road I was on, so I decided to stop before I headed to the apartment complex.

The shops in the plaza were just beginning to open, so I easily found parking in front of Signore Bespoke Studio. Bells on the door tinkled when I pushed it open and stepped inside. The pewter-gray carpet was plush, while soft over-head lighting made the room seem inviting. A dark mahogany counter dominated the back of the room, while matching shelving and mirror frames liberally covered the walls.

"Good morning. How may I help you?" An older man, perhaps in his late fifties, with distinguished salt-and-pepper hair trimmed short, stepped from behind the counter to greet me. He appeared to be of Mediterranean heritage, and if the name of his shop was any indication, then I guessed he was Italian.

"Hi. I'm here to pick up the tuxes for the Ruller and O'Neill wedding." I dug in my purse for the receipt and hoped none of the pages from Ethan escaped. I should have kept them safely in the trunk of my vehicle.

"Ah yes. Give me just a moment." He picked up the handset of a black phone and punched a button. "Nina, please bring up the O'Neill and Ruller tuxes."

He replaced the handset and smiled at me. "It'll only be a moment. May I check your receipt and your ID?"

I handed them both to the man, who checked them against the screen of his computer and then handed them back to me.

He pursed his lips then glanced toward the back-room door then looked at me. "I don't mean to be indelicate, but I understand there's been an… unfortunate incident. I hope it's resolved before the nuptials."

I guessed it shouldn't come as a surprise that word had spread about the murder. I was sure it had made the newspapers that morning, and any mention of Brad or Gabe would be sure to trigger the curiosity of anyone who had worked with them on the wedding.

"I'm sure it will be. The detective heading up the case seems very capable." I didn't want to share any gossip with the man, if that was what he was fishing for. Yet I couldn't be exactly rude and ignore him.

"I understand the young lady had recently moved from Half Moon Bay." He inclined his head toward me and lowered his voice. "Did either Mr. O'Neill or Mr. Ruller know her?"

"I'm really not at liberty to talk about the case. I'm sorry. I wish I knew more." I turned my attention to the back-room entrance and hoped Nina would be bringing the garments out soon.

"Forgive me. I didn't mean to pry." He twisted his hands together. "It's just that my assistant Nina used to live in Half Moon Bay, and she seems to have known the, ah, lady in question. She's a bit distraught, as you can imagine, but she might be able to help the two gentlemen."

"Oh!" That was interesting news. "Did your assistant recently move to Orange County?"

"She's been here about a year. Nina's a capable seamstress and has been a huge asset to my business." He glanced around as Nina entered the showroom carrying two black garment bags and hung them on the clothes rack that stood next to the counter. "I'll let Nina show you the garments to make sure they meet with your approval. I'll be in the back if you have any further questions for me."

The proprietor—I never did catch his name—winked at me before he disappeared into the back room.

"Hi, Nina. I'm Emory."

"Nice to meet you, Ms. Emory. Would you like to inspect the tuxes? I can place them on a mannequin, if you'd like." Nina began unzipping the garment bags with her long, slender fingers. She appeared to be in her mid-forties. Silver strands of hair were threaded throughout her almost-blue-black French braid. Her olive-toned skin seemed a bit sallow, and dark circles looked like smudged bruises beneath her eyes.

"There's no need to go to that much trouble. If you can remove them from the garment bags and hang them here, it should be sufficient." I had no idea what I was supposed to be looking for anyway. As long as there were no apparent rips or missing pants, I was sure it would be fine.

Nina quickly did as I asked. I ran my hands over the lapels of the jackets and admired the fine handiwork.

"I understand you moved from Half Moon Bay last year," I said in a hushed voice. "And you might know a mutual acquaintance."

Tears quickly filled Nina's eyes. "Did Dominic tell you I knew Zara?"

I nodded but held my tongue, hoping Nina would continue.

"She worked at the bookshop I frequented, and we became friendly. Zara is… I guess I need to get used to saying was… younger than me and seemed a bit lost, so I befriended her." Nina swiped a finger beneath her eye. "We kept in touch when I moved down here to be closer to my mother, and it was at my invitation that she came down to visit."

"When did she come down?"

"The first time was about two months ago. She spent a week staying over by Disneyland. She said she'd never been to the theme parks before and wanted to explore the area. We went out to dinner a couple of times."

"When did she come back?" From the records hacked by Ethan, it appeared Zara had stayed in the area the entire time. I had to wonder why she kept it a secret from Nina.

"She came down every couple of weeks. She said she wanted to relocate, and last month, she told me she'd finally rented an apartment and was looking for a job." Nina brushed nonexistent lint from the sleeve of the tux. "Zara was a bit vague about why she wanted to move down here, and I never found out if she'd found a job."

"Did she ever question you about any of the clients who came to this shop?" I wondered if Nina had inadvertently mentioned Brad's name and that was how Zara found him.

Nina's cheeks turned pink, and she dipped her head. "I'm quite embarrassed to say I did talk about my clients with her."

"And you mentioned Brad? Mr. Ruller?"

If possible, her cheeks blazed an even deeper shade of pink. "Yes, and I'm so ashamed to admit it. It was highly unprofessional of me, and if Dominic were to find out, I'm afraid I might lose my job. I really can't afford that."

I suspected Dominic already knew about Nina's gossiping.

I hummed in sympathy and hoped she'd tell me how it came to be that the two women had talked about Brad. My patience was rewarded.

"You see, Zara came over to my apartment about two weeks ago. My teenaged son was playing a video game in the family room. It's one of Mr. Ruller's most popular games, and I mentioned I was creating bespoke tuxes for Mr. Ruller and his groom." She shrugged. "I didn't take Zara for a video game type of person, but she seemed very impressed and asked a lot of questions."

"Did she drop the subject of Mr. Ruller after you answered her questions?"

"She did at first, but then out of the blue, she asked when he'd be coming back to the shop. She even asked once if I could introduce her to him next time he came in for a fitting." Nina lowered her eyes, and her long lashes swept her cheeks. "I told her I could lose my job if I did that. Our clients expect privacy, and I'd already gone beyond the limit of propriety."

"What did she say to that?"

"Zara threw a little hissy fit, which surprised me. I guess she really was fangirling over Mr. Ruller." Nina bit her lower lip. "It's my fault she died, isn't it?"

"Unless you were the one who killed her, absolutely not." I reached out to touch her arm. "Zara is the one who chose to go into that house. You didn't make her, nor did you encourage her to take that path."

"Thank you for saying that. I still feel so guilty for telling her about Mr. Ruller, but I swear, it wasn't me who killed her." Nina smoothed her hand over the tux and took a deep inhalation. "Do you want to examine the garments more closely, or shall I return them to the bags?"

I had just opened my mouth to ask if she knew who might have wanted to kill Zara when the bells jingled, and another customer entered the shop.

Nina pasted a smile on her face then turned toward the new customer. "I'll be right with you."

She hurriedly zipped up the bag and shoved it into my hands. "I wish nothing but the best for Mr. Ruller and his groom. My congratulations to them both."

Without another word, she swiftly walked over to the waiting customer without a backward glance my way. I looked at the workroom door to see if Dominic would reappear. He didn't, so I gave Nina a half-hearted wave and left.

Chapter 11

Carefully, I hung the garment bags on the clothes hook in the backseat of my SUV. I didn't want to be the one responsible for wrinkling them, nor did I want to risk having to iron anything before the ceremony. It would be my luck I'd scorch one of the custom-made pieces.

I lived low maintenance, from my hair to my makeup to my clothing. Fortunately, Brad had allowed me to pick out my own "best person" dress, and I'd chosen, much to my mother's horror, an off-the-rack nondesigner black jersey-knit dress. Not only was it comfortable, but it actually complemented my figure as well, so I didn't look like a lumpy pear stuffed into a sausage casing.

Gabe's best man, Colin, would be wearing his own black suit, and a tie was optional. Brad had confided in me that they'd originally planned on wearing casual wear for the ceremony, but Gabe's grandmother had had a conniption. To pacify her, bespoke tuxes had been ordered, but the grooms drew the line at making anyone in their wedding party cough up money to purchase formal attire.

My nieces, the flower girls, were different, though. They

adored the satin-and-tulle dresses Brad had picked out for them, and they looked like princesses. Of course, he paid for the dresses himself and refused to take a cent from Carrie for them. My mother had purchased pearl necklaces—fake, but they looked genuine, to my undiscerning eyes—for my nieces to wear. And little Tommy would wear a long-sleeved button-down shirt, black slacks, and red suspenders. I just hoped we'd be able to keep his clothes clean before he trotted down the aisle.

I climbed into my SUV and checked the dashboard clock. It was only ten thirty, which meant I still had time to visit Zara's apartment. There were no messages from Brad, so I sent him a quick text.

Heading to Zara's apt complex. Send me text when yr free to chat. SO much to tell u!!!

If I was being honest with myself, I'd expected Brad to have already been blowing up our text message stream. Since he hadn't, did that mean Detective Hawkins was still grilling him? Had he been arrested? I resisted the temptation to call. Brad didn't need me interrupting the detective's questions, nor did I want to draw attention to myself. Before I started driving, I removed Ethan's pages from my purse and extracted Zara's photo.

I examined her features closely, since I hadn't seen her aside from the crime scene. And I'd just as soon forget that memory, if I could. Up close, I could see that her dark-brown eyes were flecked with gold. Shoulder-length dark brown hair framed her heart-shaped, almost-chubby face. A scar led from the top of her thin lips almost to her nose. If I had to guess, I'd put her age in her early thirties, although a few fine lines were already forming around her eyes.

I placed the photo in my purse then the remaining pages in the glovebox. As I began to shut the glovebox, it occurred to me that if Nina knew where Zara had lived, then she would be the perfect solution to get the information to Detective

Hawkins without confessing to the hacking Brad's employee had done.

After locking the SUV, I hurried back into the shop. The customer was nowhere in sight, and Nina stood at the counter.

"Do you have a moment? I have a quick question for you." I rapidly strode over to Nina.

She warily looked around the shop. "My client is in the fitting room, so please be quick."

"Did you ever visit Zara at her apartment? Do you know the address?"

She chewed her lower lip then nodded. "Yes, but why do you want to know?"

"The police are going to need the info, and sometimes I help track down information. As far as I know, they think she still resides in Half Moon Bay." I wondered if I should tell her Brad and Gabe were suspects. I decided against it. "Please? Mr. Ruller's wedding is less than two weeks away, and since he, you know, found Zara, he's super stressed. I think having the case solved before the wedding will help him recover."

Nina appeared to consider my request for a moment. "Stay here. I'll get my phone from my locker and give you the address."

Once she returned, iPhone in hand, I jotted the address down on a slip of the shop's note paper. "Did you ever visit her at her apartment?"

"I dropped by once but didn't stay. I took her over a bottle of wine and some flowers as a housewarming gift right after she moved in."

"But you never visited her again?"

"She was a bit odd that way and said she was still living in a disaster zone with all the unpacked boxes and such. When I offered to help, she shut me down."

"So you met either at your apartment or at a restaurant?"

"After her first couple of trips down here, I couldn't afford to keep meeting for dinner, so we usually met up for a quick cup of coffee or a glass of wine." She motioned around the shop. "I work long hours, and even though my son is a teen, I still like to be around for him. I don't have much free time to socialize."

The customer emerged from the changing room, dressed in a tux. The trousers were much too long, and I assumed he was there to have them altered to fit.

"Thanks for talking to me. I won't keep you from your client." I inclined my head toward the man then made my way out of the shop.

I returned to my vehicle and considered my options. I knew I should call Detective Hawkins right away with the information. But I really wanted to check out Zara's dwelling first. It would be my only opportunity. My curiosity got the best of me, and I started my vehicle and made my way east on Culver Drive.

Zara's apartment was about a ten-minute drive from Signore Bespoke Studio, which included traffic-light stops. As I drove, I considered everything Nina had told me. It was apparent that Zara had found Brad through an unfortunate coincidence. However, I suspected Zara had narrowed down Orange County as Brad's place of residence, which was why she'd been in the area for the last two months.

I slowed down when the sassy navigation voice told me I was approaching the address. The older three-story building looked like it could use a fresh coat of paint and new land-scaping that didn't include dying or dead shrubs and grass. Crammed next to a brand-new multistory modern apartment complex, Zara's home looked depressing. Despite its appearance, I was sure she'd been paying a ridiculous sum of money to live there.

A driveway with unpatched jagged cracks crisscrossing the asphalt led down the side of the building. Numbered parking spaces sat perpendicular to the wall that sepa-rated the old complex from the new. I found a spot that had a rusty sign stuck on a wobbly pole indicating it was for visitors only. I pulled into the space—and only had to back out twice to straighten my vehicle between the narrow lines—and parked. After making sure that my vehicle was locked, I made my way to the double glass doors that I hoped led to a lobby and perhaps a manager or at least information on how to contact a manager.

I pulled the door open and stepped inside the lobby. It was a study in beige—dingy beige, at that. The beige linoleum flooring might have had a pattern once, but it was scuffed and worn and quite dirty. The beige walls appeared as if they hadn't seen a paintbrush in decades. Nails stuck out where outlines of frames used to hang. A teeny-tiny elevator, with its door wide open, sat on the far side of the room, next to a set of stairs. Both the elevator flooring and the stairs had beige carpet covered with indeterminate stains. On the opposite wall, a bank of locked vertical mailboxes took up most of the space.

The door opened, and a timeworn woman stepped in. Her face was wrinkled, and her lank shoulder-length hair was a yellowing gray. She was hunched over with age, and her overly large tunic almost reached her knees. She appeared to be in her seventies. She tugged on a rusty wire shopping trolly when the wheels caught on the threshold. I rushed to hold the door open for her.

"Thank you. I'm not as strong as I used to be." The woman turned her rheumy faded-blue eyes toward me. "You must be new here. No one else takes the time to help an old woman like me."

"I'm actually trying to find out if anyone knows this woman." I pulled Zara's photo from my purse and tried to smooth the crinkles before showing it to her.

"Oh, her. She's a rude one." The woman snorted. "She lives a few doors down from me, and several times, she's refused to hold the elevator for me. Instead, she sneers and jams the buttons to make the door close."

"I'm so sorry to hear that." It was obvious the police hadn't found Zara's residence yet and hadn't notified anyone there of Zara's demise.

The woman peered closely at my face. "She's not your relative or something, is she?"

"Not at all."

"Then what do you want with someone like that?" The woman shifted her handbag to her other shoulder.

I needed to be careful about how to word it. I didn't want to be the one to break the news of the murder. "I'm wondering if you've seen anyone visiting Zara or hanging around her apartment when she's not home."

"Are you an investigator or something? Did she commit a crime?" The woman almost looked gleeful.

"Or something." I held the photo up again. "Have you seen anyone visiting her?"

"No. Sorry, I can't help you. I don't get out much, and most of my days are spent with my cats, watching the soaps."

"No worries. Maybe I'll head upstairs and see if any of your other neighbors have seen anyone." I put the photo back in my purse.

"I'm in 309, and that young lady lives in 303. I can tell you that apartment 304 is empty, and 305 is in the hospital with a broken hip." She shrugged. "I can't tell you about the other people on our floor."

"Thanks so much for your help." I looked at her shopping trolly. "Would you like me to help you get that to your apartment?"

"No, thanks. I can manage, as long as the elevator doesn't break down again." She began wheeling the trolly toward the tiny box. "You might want to take the stairs. It's a tight fit in here for even one person."

I thanked her again and headed for the stairs. They were

dark, narrow, and smelly but, I was certain, preferable to that claustrophobic elevator. I reached the third floor, huffing and puffing a bit. Cupcakes and buttercream had not been my friend, fitness-goal-wise. And with the holidays upon us and the stress of the wedding, it wouldn't be anytime soon that I could remedy my untoned body and cardio stamina.

The elevator still hadn't arrived on the third floor. In fact, the light indicated it was still on the first floor. I hoped it didn't mean the elderly woman was stuck down there. I decided I'd knock on a couple of doors, and if the elevator still hadn't arrived, I'd go back downstairs and check on her. I knocked on apartment 301, and when nobody answered the door, I moved on. The woman had said Zara's apartment was 303. Even though I knew no one was there, I knocked anyway. The door swung open beneath my fist as I struck the beige-painted door.

"Hello?" I called out. When no one answered, I stepped inside and found myself in the living room. Even the interior of the apartment was a study in beige, from the carpet to the furnishings to the overhead lighting. However, plastered all over the walls, hiding every square inch of what was sure to be beige paint, were photos of Brad.

Chapter 12

A chill slithered down my spine as I stepped closer to get a better view. There were photos of a much younger Brad. Some were of him in high school, since he wore his marching band uniform. Others looked to be from his college days as he walked across the grassy commons at his university. A stab of regret hit me that I had allowed our friendship to wither all that time. I examined the older photos more closely. Since Zara hadn't known Brad in his younger years, I had to guess that she'd found the pictures from yearbooks or online.

I gazed at the more current candid photos. I had to swallow down bile when I saw I was in a few of them, my face scratched out. The only reason I knew it was me was from the frizzy red hair that framed what had been my face. Other photos were of Brad and Gabe. Gabe's face had been scratched out, the same as mine. In one photo, Gabe had been kissing Brad's cheek, and Zara had stabbed a knife into Gabe's face. The hilt of the knife still stuck out from the wall.

In none of the photos did Brad seem aware he was being photographed. I looked closely at the ones taken of me and tried to place where we'd been. There were a couple that looked like we were walking the dogs along the beach; another of us sitting on the patio at our favorite coffee shop; and two of us standing in my pool house backyard. How had she gotten that photo? I didn't recall a drone ever flying over. She had to have had a telephoto lens. Had she been peering over my wall that bordered the street to get our picture? How long had she been stalking Brad this time?

I felt sick to my stomach. Zara was beyond disturbed. If Gabe had seen these, no one could blame him for killing Zara to protect Brad. Had Gabe seen these? Or had someone else broken into Zara's apartment then left the door partially open when they'd departed? There was only one thing left to do, and that was to call Detective Hawkins. I was in way over my head.

I rushed out to the hallway, making sure the apartment door firmly closed behind me. The elevator indicated the car had reached the second floor. A door farther down the hallway slammed closed, and I started at the noise. An elderly man dressed in blue jeans and a navy cardigan headed my way.

"Are you looking to rent here?" The man was balding, and wispy strands of gray hair stuck to his mottled pate. "If I were you, I'd avoid this place like the plague. The owner's nothing but a slum lord."

"I'm sorry to hear that." I pulled Zara's photo from my purse. "I'm actually trying to find out if you've seen anyone visiting this woman. She lives in 303."

He studied the photo a moment. "A young woman with a long dark braid visited her right after she moved in. She didn't stay long."

"Did they seem to get along okay?" I assumed he was talking about Nina. She wasn't that young, but because of the man's age, it made sense he'd describe her as such.

"Oh sure. It seemed like they were friends, and the young woman brought a bottle of wine and some flowers. I heard her say it was a housewarming gift. Like I said, she dropped off the gifts and left a couple of minutes later. The only reason I saw the whole thing was because I was waiting on that darn slow elevator. I'd take the stairs, but my gimp knee won't put up with it."

"Did you notice anyone else visiting Zara over the last two weeks?"

"Are you an investigator or something?" He peered at me through smudged wire-rimmed eyeglasses.

"Or something…"

He waited a beat to see if I'd give him more information, but when I didn't, he shrugged as if my nonanswer didn't matter. "There was a guy hanging around the hallway in front of her apartment three days ago. He knocked on her door, but when she didn't answer, he took off for the stairs."

"Can you tell me what he looked like?"

"Tall, although everyone seems taller than me nowadays." He looked down at me and chuckled. "Well, present company excluded."

"I definitely know the feeling." I smiled to let him know I wasn't offended. "Did you notice anything else about the man?"

"Let's see. His hair was kind of what I'd call a strawberry-blond. I dated a girl in my youth with strawberry-blonde hair. I wonder what ever became of her?"

I gulped. Gabe had golden-blond hair, but in certain lights, an undertone of red popped out. I didn't want to ask, but I had to. "What was the man wearing?"

"He was dressed up mighty nicely. Dark slacks and a long-sleeved white shirt but no tie. I thought maybe he was an insurance salesman or something."

I opened my phone and swiped through some photos until I came across one of Brad and Gabe. I enlarged the photo with two fingers until only Gabe's face showed on the screen. "Do you think it was this man?"

He studied it a moment. "Maybe? I can't rightly say. I never got a good look at his face. As you can see, our slum lord doesn't believe in keeping the hallways well lit."

I looked down the hallway and saw that only every third sconce was lit. No wonder it was so dim in the building. "I appreciate you talking to me."

"Is that guy your young man? Is he cheating on you?" The man pointed at my phone.

"No, but he's engaged to one of my friends." I decided to let the guy think whatever he wanted. No way was I going to tell him I was tracking down a murderer. It just couldn't be Gabe. Could it?

The door of the elevator dinged open, and out stepped the elderly woman, dragging her cart behind her. I was relieved I didn't have to call the fire department to come rescue her from a broken-down elevator.

"Oh! You're still here. Did you have any luck tracking down your friend?" the woman asked.

"Not yet." I smiled and waved to them both. "I need to get going. Thanks for talking with me."

Dashing toward the stairs, I glanced back over my shoulder. The pair were chitchatting and paying me no mind. I made my way down the stairs, huffing and puffing more than I wanted to admit, and finally collapsed in my vehicle. I took a few sips of water, waited until I wasn't gasping for air, then called Detective Hawkins.

Chapter 13

Detective Hawkins answered on the second ring. "You scurried out of the office awfully quickly, Ms. Martinez. I was hoping to have a word with you."

"I had wedding errands to run." I swallowed hard, wondering why Brad hadn't texted me back yet. "You'll never believe this coincidence, but when I picked up the tuxes for the guys, the woman assisting me told me she'd been a friend of Zara's."

There was complete silence on the phone, and I thought the call had dropped. "Hello? Are you still there?"

"I'm still here. Continue with this coincidental tale." Detective Hawkins's tone was dry.

"I'm telling you the truth. I didn't track her down." I huffed out a breath. "Anyway, she said once Zara found out Nina—that's the woman from the tux shop—was working on Brad's tux, she started asking all sorts of questions about Brad. I think that's how she found him and started stalking him again."

"We've found no real evidence of stalking, aside from her showing up at the Huntington Beach wedding venue."

Had Gabe not told the detective that Zara had located his

and Brad's residence? And Colin could confirm she'd been snooping around. It wasn't my place to mention it, so I let it drop.

"Well...." I gulped. "Nina gave me Zara's address, and I just might have stopped by the apartment."

"You what?" The detective's stern voice made me cringe.

"I wasn't going to break into her apartment, but the door was ajar." I waited for him to yell at me, but when he remained silent—no doubt grinding his teeth—I continued. "You need to get to her apartment ASAP. It's beyond creepy. Zara is... or was... a twisted, sick individual."

"I have so many things to say to you, but I guess it'll need to wait until I see you in person. What's the address?"

I rattled it off, including the apartment number. "Don't take the elevator. Trust me on this."

"Where are you now?" he asked.

"Sitting in the parking lot next to the complex."

"As long as you don't feel like you're in danger, sit tight, and keep your doors locked. I'll be there in about twenty minutes." A siren sprang to life. "If you leave, send me a text on where you're going."

Before I could say anything, the phone went dead. I immediately sent Brad a text.

Urgent! Can u talk? Call me now!

Nothing. I stared at my screen, willing those three little dots to appear. Still nothing. Was Brad in jail? Wouldn't Detective Hawkins have told me if that were the case? I tossed my phone onto the seat beside me. Things weren't looking good for Gabe. Someone fitting his description was seen at Zara's apartment, although there didn't seem to have been any interaction between the two, at least at that point.

Then there was Nina. She knew Zara and knew where she lived. Could Nina have gotten so angry over Zara prying into her clients' lives and jeopardizing her livelihood that she followed her and killed the woman? I thought it wasn't likely, but I'd add Nina to my list of potential suspects. There just had to be someone else besides Gabe and Brad who wanted Zara dead.

I pulled the hacker's papers from the glovebox to study. Maybe I'd find a pattern of places Zara frequented. Then I thought better of it and put the pages back into the compartment, out of sight. I'd never be able to explain to the detective how I came across the information without ratting out Ethan and Brad.

I had just about stooped to playing Wordle to pass the time when an incoming text chimed on my phone. I snatched up my device and swiped the screen. It was from Brad.

Sorry! On client zoom meeting that I can't ditch. Maybe another hour or so?

Ugh. I needed to talk to someone about this, but I didn't want to drag Tillie into it yet. I noted the time. The detective should arrive soon. I'd have to find some patience and wait. I wanted to see his reaction when he walked into Zara's apartment, assuming he wouldn't make me sit in the SUV while he went alone.

Ok. Meeting w/det soon. I'll let you know when I'm done.

Twiddling my fingers, I watched two seagulls fight over a discarded piece of bread, the national chain sandwich wrapper still stuck to part of it. My mind drifted to Zara's motivation for stalking Brad for so long. Was she really madly —and I used the word literally—in love with him, or did she just not want him to have any affection for anyone else? Brad had mentioned that Zara had worked for his company up north for a while, but for certain, he would never have given her any indication that he was romantically interested in her. Had she misconstrued his fun banter with his employees? I wanted to pull my hair out. I had too many questions and no way to answer them.

Thankfully, a black sedan pulled up alongside me, and

Detective Hawkins exited his car. I flung my door open, narrowly missing dinging the government-issue car, and went to greet him.

"Thanks for responding so quickly." I pointed at the decrepit building. "She lived on the third floor, in number 303."

"So you said earlier." He bent down and retrieved his iPad from the front seat. "I need to have a long talk with you about what not getting involved in my investigation means, but it'll have to wait. For now, let's go see the apartment and make sure it's secure. Were you able to lock the door when you left?"

"No. It was a dead bolt only and not one of those button-lock-knob thingies." I thought I saw a corner of his lip raise a smidgen. "I should probably tell you that I chatted with two residents who live on her floor."

His lips turned downward at that news. "And their names?"

"I actually didn't catch their names. Sorry." I squinted when the sun hit me in the face as I looked up at him. "They're both elderly, and they both live a few doors down from Zara. I can't remember the apartment number of the lady."

Detective Hawkins swept his arm toward the building. "Let's go take a look."

I led the way into the lobby. There were no other residents around, so I made a beeline for the stairs, bypassing the slower-than-molasses elevator. I didn't want the detective to know how out of shape I was, so I slowed my steps down.

"Is something the matter?" he asked.

"No. Nothing's wrong." I tried to hide my wheezing, but all it did was make me feel like I was going to pass out.

"You've practically stopped moving."

"I just thought you'd want to look for clues on the way up. See if anyone dropped anything."

He grunted. "I'm more interested in reaching her apartment before Christmastime."

I scooted to the side of the narrow stairs and pointed upward. "Be my guest, and lead the way."

It took less than a handful of seconds for the detective to disappear from my sight as he bounded forward. In my defense, his legs were probably twice the length of mine. I pressed onward until I reached the second floor then took a short breather before heading up the last flight to the third floor. When I reached the landing, I inhaled gulps of air and fanned my hands over my face. I promised myself I'd get in shape after the holidays and never let another spoonful of buttercream pass my lips. Ha, who was I kidding? That'd never happen.

"Ms. Martinez? Are you okay?" Detective Hawkins stood a few feet away from me.

I tried to act as casual as I could instead of sucking in more oxygen. "Just fine. I'll be there in a sec."

"Your face is all red. Do you need to sit down, or can I get you some water?"

"No." My voice squeaked, so I cleared my throat. "No, thanks. I'm fine."

He studied me for a moment. "Would you prefer to wait out here while I enter the apartment?"

"I think I'm okay to go in now. I just needed a moment to get the courage to face it again." That was as good an excuse as any instead of confessing I was in terrible shape. And when he saw all those photos, it wouldn't be hard to sell him on the idea that I was emotionally distraught.

Chapter 14

"Galloping gremlins!" Detective Hawkins's voice boomed when he stepped into the living room and got a good look at the walls. "I've personally never seen a stalker take it to this level before. It's twisted."

I remained just inside the doorway, hesitant to step farther into the apartment. I'd seen enough of Zara's twisted adoration of Brad to last a lifetime. "She was obviously a very sick person."

"I need to get the crime scene techs in here." He gazed at me. "You're looking pale, Emory. Do you need to sit down?"

"I'll be all right. It's just a lot to take in. Especially the anger toward me and Gabe." I pointed at the knife still buried in Gabe's photo.

"I hate to think what might have happened to you if Zara hadn't been stopped." Detective Hawkins pulled his cell phone from his pocket. "It's a wonder she hadn't escalated to violence toward you or Gabe yet."

He tapped in a number then spoke into the phone and turned his back to me. His voice was quiet, so I didn't catch most of the words, but I thought it had to do with requesting crime scene techs.

Once he'd completed the phone call, he turned his attention back to me. "Can you wait here without touching anything? I want to take a look at the rest of the apartment."

"I'll stay right here."

He walked through the living room then turned right and walked through a doorway. I guessed it was the kitchen, given that a small dining table with two chairs sat just outside the doorway, against the exterior wall, which held a large window. The filthy window didn't allow much light to enter. Cupboard doors banged, and drawers slid open and closed. It didn't take long for the detective to reenter the living room and head down the hallway opposite the kitchen. I assumed it held a bathroom and a bedroom.

I thought I heard the detective utter "galloping gremlins" again. My curiosity got the best of me, and I hurried to follow him down the hallway.

Detective Hawkins stood in the middle of the room, his back toward me. The windows had the shades drawn, and a dim overhead light barely illuminated the small space. But it was light enough to make me stop in my tracks when I saw the full-size mannequin. I almost threw up.

The male mannequin reclined on a red velvet fainting couch. It wore a black-and-gold fleur-de-lis jacquard smoking jacket, and its chest was bare except for the heavy gold necklace that hung down from its neck. Black satin boxer shorts peeked out from beneath the smoking jacket. The most disturbing thing about the mannequin was that it had Brad's face and hair. Zara must've spent a small fortune on it.

"Oh em gee! This is searing my retinas!" I shivered. I'd never be able to unsee that, and I worried I'd think about this horror every time I looked at Brad.

The detective spun around to face me. "I thought I told you to stay put, Ms. Martinez."

"Sorry." And I truly was sorry I'd seen that disturbing sight.

"Whatever you do, don't touch anything. I don't need your fingerprints mixed up with the victim's." He shook his head. "I'm going to have to get a criminal psychologist involved. I didn't know you could even buy something like this."

A wave of dizziness hit me, and I leaned against the doorframe. "I think I need to go home. This is…"

"I hear you. I'm not sure there are any words to describe this." He flipped his hand over, his palm facing downward, and waggled his fingers at me. "Go on home. I know where to find you when I'm ready to take your statement."

"Thanks. I appreciate it." I turned and walked as quickly as I could then practically ran down the stairs to my SUV. I couldn't wait to get home and take a hot shower, even though I hadn't touched a thing in Zara's apartment. I needed something to scour my mind too.

With shaky hands, I pressed the button to start the engine then carefully pulled out from the parking spot. Just as I merged onto Culver Drive, my phone rang. I glanced at the screen and saw it was Brad, so I answered using the Bluetooth hands-free mode.

"Hey, Cupcake. Where ya at?" From a honking horn in the distance, I guessed Brad was in his car as well.

"I'm still in Irvine but heading home. How about you?"

"Same. I need to check on Gabe."

Our call disconnected, so I hit redial. Brad answered on the first ring. "Sorry. I just went through a dead spot. What was so urgent earlier?"

As much as I wanted a hot shower to scrub myself, I knew Brad and Gabe needed to know about Zara's apartment right away. "Listen. I just left Detective Hawkins at Zara's apartment. We need to talk. In person."

"No fair! You weren't supposed to go there without me. I'm your number-one sidekick, remember? And I need to be in on the action."

Personally, I thought it was a good thing Brad hadn't been

there. I was freaked out enough for the two of us. "I'll meet you at your house in about thirty minutes. Both you and Gabe need to know what I found."

"Don't leave me hangin' like this. Tell me what you found at the psycho's house."

Little did he know how accurate his description of Zara was. "Nuh-uh. I need to tell you and Gabe about it together."

"C'mon, Cupcake. Give me the deets."

I hissed and threw in a couple hums then whispered, "I think... breaking... up," then ended the call. Brad wouldn't fall for my ploy, but at least he'd get the message that I wasn't going to talk about it until I reached his house.

Chapter 15

It took close to forty-five minutes to reach Brad and Gabe's abode because of lunch-hour traffic. Brad stood in the front doorway, as if he'd been waiting for me. Perhaps he had.

"Sorry for taking so long. Traffic was terrible." I locked my vehicle, gave Brad a one-arm hug, then handed him the two garment bags containing the tuxes. Entering the house, I was greeted by the distinct aroma of pizza.

"We were just finishing up lunch. Do you want some pizza?"

"Not now. We need to talk."

Brad placed the back of his hand on my forehead. "You don't have a fever. Are you feeling all right? I've never seen you pass up Luigi's pizza before."

I slapped his hand away. I just wanted to get it over with and then try to forget that demented apartment. "Where's Gabe?"

"He's in the family room." Brad inclined his head. "Let me hang these up and grab some water before we talk."

He opened the door to the coat closet, which had been made by using the empty space beneath the stairs that led to the upstairs bedrooms, and hung up the tuxes. I followed Brad as he detoured through the kitchen and grabbed three bottles of chilled water from the refrigerator and handed me one.

After reaching the family room, at the far end of the great room, I curled up in the overstuffed armchair, and even though I wasn't cold, I pulled the cashmere blanket around my shoulders.

Gabe reclined on the leather sofa, his black-sock-clad feet propped up on the glass-topped coffee table. The side of his temple had turned a sickly greenish-yellow, and it still looked swollen. A cheery fire danced in the fireplace. It put out just enough warmth to make the space feel cozy.

"How are you feeling, Gabe?" I asked.

"All right."

"Humph. Don't let him fool you. He still has a horrific headache, and in the doctor's opinion, he should have an MRI to check to make sure there's nothing worse than the concussion she suspects he has." Brad sat next to Gabe and handed him the water along with two pills, which appeared to be ibuprofen.

"Stop fussing over me. I'll be okay." Gabe swallowed the pills dry then crossed his arms.

"Fine." Brad rolled his eyes then directed his gaze at me. "You've left me on pins and needles long enough, Em. Tell us what's got you so worked up."

So I did, starting with meeting Nina at the tux shop and learning that she was friends with Zara. "Somehow, Zara knew you'd moved to the area, but it was just an unfortunate coincidence that she found you. My guess, given all the photos she has, is she started following you after spotting you at the tux shop and eventually found out where you live and where the wedding is going to take place."

"What photos?" Gabe's voice was sharp.

"I'm getting to that. I asked Nina if she knew where Zara lived so we'd have legal means instead of... Well, so we could tell Detective Hawkins where she lived. I thought it would speed up the investigation if they knew she'd relocated down here instead of still residing in Half Moon Bay."

Gabe threw Brad a side-eye and mouthed the word "hacker."

Brad ignored his fiancé and waved his hand as if to tell me to continue.

"Nina gave me the address, so I went to check it out."

"By yourself? Are you nuts?" Gabe's face turned an alarming shade of red. "Why didn't you immediately call Detective Hawkins?"

"It turned out okay. Well, kind of." When Gabe bolted upright as if to stand, I hurriedly continued my story. "It's mostly senior citizens who live there, and they were very friendly and, I might add, safe. I was never in danger. Anyway, the lady who lives down the hallway from Zara told me about a couple of her visitors. I decided to have a look upstairs and see if any other neighbors were home."

Gabe was sputtering, so I held up my hand.

"They're all senior citizens. It was perfectly safe. I knocked on Zara's door, and it swung open, so I peeked inside, and well, I'm sorry to say I now know what a deranged stalker looks like." I twisted my hands together. "Her walls were covered with photos of you, Brad. From when you were a teen to just last week."

"*What?*" Gabe practically exploded. "How did this happen? You never told me she was back to stalking you again."

"I had no idea. She never revealed herself." Brad's mouth turned downward, and a deep line appeared between his eyebrows. "This isn't good. The detective is really going to think that we killed her to protect ourselves."

I pulled Zara's photo from my purse and handed it to Brad. "I don't think you had a chance to look at this before Detective Hawkins came to question you. Does she look any different from the last time you saw her up north, two years ago? Have you seen her around here or while you've been out and about over the last month?"

"She's changed her hair color and gained weight." Brad handed the photo to Gabe. "I guess I wouldn't necessarily notice her, especially if she were wearing sunglasses or a hat. I mean, I never expected to ever see her again, so I wasn't keeping a lookout for her."

Gabe examined the photo. "When I caught her here, at our house, she must've been wearing a blonde wig, because she resembled the photos from up north. It's how I immediately knew it was her."

"Or else the dark hair is the wig, and that's how she was able to get close enough to take so many photos without us knowing." I cleared my throat, not wanting to go on. "Unfortunately, it gets even worse."

Gabe gaped at me. "How can it be worse?"

"Zara took photos of both me and you standing with Brad. She showed signs of aggression, like scratching out our faces, and..." I gulped. "She stabbed your face with a knife and left it stuck in the wall."

Brad bent forward and covered his face with his hands while Gabe rubbed his back. Their quarrel over Gabe's health was forgotten.

"I'm afraid it gets even more disturbing." Tears pricked my eyes as I beheld my two sweet friends who should have been celebrating their upcoming nuptials but instead had to face the terror of being accused of murder. I quickly took a sip of water. "Zara had a mannequin made in the likeness of Brad and dressed it, ah, suggestively. The detective and I found it in her bedroom."

"I think I might get sick," Brad whispered into his hands.

Gabe growled, "If that woman weren't already dead, I'd kill her myself."

Chapter 16

I hadn't stayed long after breaking the news to the guys. They needed time together to process what the twisted discovery might mean for their legal defense, if the killer wasn't found. I felt morose. I'd not uncovered any new viable suspects but instead had found more evidence that pointed at Gabe and/or Brad having been the murderers.

Brian called me during my drive home. I tried to chase the gloom from my voice and hoped I sounded upbeat. "Hey, you! Are you getting a break from the tyrant who owns that fine dining establishment?"

"What's going on, Em?" Brian asked, his concern coming over the line.

"Why do you think anything's wrong?" I hadn't been able to contain the squeak that escaped on the word *wrong*.

"I can read your voice, and you're trying way too hard to sound chipper." He chuckled, and I could imagine him running his long fingers through his blond hair, which looked perpetually wind tousled. He'd let it grow longer than usual, and the ends curled around his face and neck. "What's happened to make you so concerned? Gram's okay, isn't she?"

I hastened to assure him that his grandmother was

perfectly well. "It's just that I've been trying to help Brad and Gabe with the investigation, and all I've managed to do is find more evidence that points their way. No matter what I do, I can't find any other suspects."

Brian remained quiet for several seconds, and I thought maybe we'd been disconnected.

"Are you still there?" I asked.

"Yeah. I'm here. Just trying to take it all in." He sighed. "Do I want to know what you've done to find new evidence?"

I shuddered, thinking about the creepy apartment. "It's too much to get into right now. Detective Hawkins has taken charge of the evidence, so at least I've gone through the proper legal channels."

"I hate to voice my concern, but is there any chance that one of them committed the murder?" He continued to talk over me when I tried to sputter my objection. "I mean, I really don't see Brad committing the crime at all, but Gabe? Yeah. I think if the right circumstances presented themselves, like he needed to protect Brad or another family member, he might be capable."

"You're not the only one voicing those concerns. I just don't want to believe it." And with all the evidence found in Zara's apartment, no one could fault Gabe for trying to protect Brad. Well, that was, aside from the legal system.

"I know." Brian muffled his phone, and I could hear him talking to someone in the background. "It's time for the tyrant to go back to work. I've called in a favor so I can get off work around nine tonight. If you're not busy, I'd love to come see you."

The hopeful tone of his voice made me smile. "I'll be home, waiting for you. I've missed you, but I also know how important your restaurant is. If you need to work, I'll understand."

"Love you, Em. You're the best. Really."

"Love you too." Except my words went into empty space. Brian had already disconnected.

By the time I made it home, it was close to two. As much as I wanted a hot shower, cozy pjs, and a cup of hot cocoa with marshmallows for comfort, I had buttercream frosting to make and cupcakes to deliver.

I texted Tillie to let her know I'd made it home but had cupcakes to attend to. She sent a message right back along with a photo of the two dogs napping on the patio, their feet stuck straight up in the air.

Having relaxing afternoon. Come over when you get back from delivery.

I sent a thumbs-up and went to work. I'd left the butter out on the countertop so it would be nice and soft for creaming. I scooped it into the bowl of a stand mixer. Next, I took cream cheese from the refrigerator and placed it on a ceramic plate. Microwaving it on fifty percent power for thirty seconds softened it enough. I added it to the butter and turned the mixer to medium speed to cream the mixture. After it had turned light and creamy, I added vanilla and some salt. While salt might not sound like it belongs in a sweet confection like buttercream, it actually enhances the flavors.

Once it was all mixed together, I slowly added confectioners' sugar, along with a tablespoon of the strained cranberry sauce I'd made the day before. I decided I wanted the buttercream to have a deeper ruby color, so I added another tablespoon of the sauce. The buttercream wasn't quite stiff enough, so I added a bit more confectioners' sugar then turned the mixer to medium-high and let it beat the buttercream until it was light and fluffy.

Once the consistency was to my liking, I filled a pastry bag fitted with an extra-large star tip and piped swirls of buttercream onto the cooled cupcakes. When the cupcakes were covered with the jewel-toned frosting, I topped each with three sugared cranberries. After setting aside four cupcakes for us, I nestled the remaining baby cakes into the cupcake pastry boxes. Once I'd loaded and started the dishwasher with the sticky dishes, I carefully packed the cupcakes into my SUV.

Knowing Vannie's day teaching English at a local high school had just ended, I sent her a text before I started up the vehicle.

Delivering cupcakes. Need anything at market for dinner?

Three pulsing dots appeared, disappeared, then reappeared again. I sat, waiting for her message. Nothing came through, so I started the engine and had just put the car into reverse when my phone pinged.

Can you get 1-1/2 lbs of shrimp and angel hair pasta? I'm in mood for shrimp scampi.

Since I hadn't eaten lunch, my mouth watered.

You got it. I have cranberry-orange cupcakes for dessert.

More dots appeared, so I waited to back out of the garage.

Teresa will be joining us.

I sent a thumbs-up, glad I'd saved four cupcakes. Brian would be none the wiser that his cupcake had been given to Teresa, nor would he mind. I considered my driving options for the cupcake delivery location in Dana Point. This time of day, there would be no getting away from traffic, whether I took the 405 to I-5 or stayed on the PCH the entire way south to the beach and the boating community. I opted for the more scenic drive and steered onto the PCH.

As I drove, I mused over Vannie and Teresa's relationship as a diversion from thinking about Zara's apartment. My sister had confided in me that while they liked each other, working at the same high school—Teresa was the Spanish teacher— made them decide to keep things platonic for the time being. I also suspected that something tragic had happened in Vannie's past that impacted her relationships, but Tillie had counseled me to not pry. I'd respected her advice, even though I wanted to help Vannie heal from whatever had happened and be truly happy.

I turned my attention to the sassy navigation voice telling me I'd missed my turn. I guessed that was what I got for letting my mind wander to problems I had no control over. It took a few minutes to find a legal U-turn lane then sit through a couple of extra red lights until traffic cleared just enough for me to squeeze in and head back in the direction I'd come from. By the time I reached the dock—the dinner party was being held on a sixty-five-foot yacht—I was ten minutes late. I hoped I hadn't held up their departure.

A uniformed crew member waved to me as I meandered down the pathway, hunting for the correct yacht amid all the other colorful boats. A stiff breeze blowing in from the ocean ruffled flags stuck to the sterns of various boats, and I could smell the tang of salt and seaweed. I shifted the tote with the cupcakes to my left hand and lifted my right hand in response. He hurried to meet me and took the tote.

"I'm so sorry I'm late. I hope I didn't hold you up."

The young man grinned, and his white teeth flashed in sharp contrast to his dark features. "No, ma'am. Guests won't arrive for another hour."

"That's a relief." I pointed at the tote bag, which had been silkscreened with a cake stand filled with stacked cupcakes along with my name, phone number, and website, which Brad had designed for me. "I don't need any of that back. It's yours to keep or pass on."

"Thank you, ma'am." He shifted his feet. "I was told you'd send a Venmo request for the balance due?"

"Of course. Should I use the same ID used for the deposit?"

"That'll be great. I'll make sure it's paid right away." He backed away from me, as if to bolt for the yacht.

I supposed he had a thousand things to do, so I gave a quick wave and hurried back to my SUV. It was a relief not to have to stay and work the dinner party cruise. The steward who had hired me to provide the cupcakes had asked if I could help serve drinks and then serve up dessert. It had been almost a year since Carrie and I had catered a party aboard a yacht. Unfortunately, the events of that night had turned out fatal. I had no desire to ever cater aboard a yacht again. Besides, cupcakes were the easiest dessert to serve. Everyone could help themselves, and they didn't need me around to tend to their every need.

Chapter 17

The traffic going home was even worse than my trip down. By the time I stopped at the market to buy the shrimp and pasta and made my way to Tillie's house, the party had started without me. I found Tillie, Vannie, and Teresa out on the patio, sipping gimlets, with the patio heaters turned to low. A pitcher of the lime-based cocktail sat in the middle of the table along with a basket of tortilla chips and a bowl of guacamole. Two citronella candles glowed with their dancing flames. Piper and Missy were both receiving their rightful adoration from Vannie and Teresa, who were stroking their ears and scratching their backs.

"I'll put the shrimp in the fridge and grab a glass for myself." I held the colorful reusable grocery tote up. "Do you need me to bring anything out?"

"I think we're good for now," Vannie answered. Piper nudged Vannie's hand when she stopped petting her to talk to me.

Once I sat at the table and had downed half my cocktail in a few hearty glugs, I let out a long breath. Tillie immediately refilled my glass. So much for my vow not to drink until the wedding reception.

"It must've been a heck of a day," Tillie observed.

"You have no idea." I took another long drink of the gimlet. I figured alcohol might scrub the images of Zara's house from my brain. At least, I could hope it would.

"Do you want to talk about it?" Vannie asked, her voice soft and tentative. As much as I tried not to pry into her life before meeting us, she also seemed to walk on eggshells when asking questions of us.

"It's just the investigation into Brad's stalker. I seem to be making it worse instead of finding actual suspects who may have killed her." I rubbed my cheek and felt something cold and slightly chunky.

Tillie reached over to me and used a napkin to wipe off the smear of guacamole I'd left behind.

Vannie and Teresa exchanged glances, and Teresa's swooping eyebrows rose toward her hairline.

"Do either of you know something that might help?" I asked.

"Sorry, but no." Teresa chewed on her lower lip then turned her amber-colored eyes toward me. "The gossip going around the teachers' lounge is that Gabe really did it. The assistant principal's cousin works at the same station as Gabe, and rumor has it Gabe's got a temper."

Personally, I'd never seen that side of him before, and Brad had never mentioned it to me either. "I don't know what to think or what to do. If it is true about Gabe, it'll kill Brad."

"I know, but better to find out now than marry a killer." Vannie placed her hand on mine and gave it a squeeze. "He'll have you and us to see him through."

"It doesn't seem possible it's Gabe, and I'm not ready to give up yet." I crunched on a chip then washed it down with another swig of gimlet. "What I'm about to tell you can't leave this table. Promise?"

All three nodded, and Missy yipped, which made me

laugh, if only momentarily. "Brad's stalker, Zara, turned out to be a sick psycho."

I proceeded to tell them about finding Nina then visiting Zara's apartment and then Detective Hawkins's discovery. By the time I'd finished sharing with them, the gimlet pitcher was empty, aside from a few lime slices. The three women all looked as green as I felt.

"As horrific as that is, what makes it even worse is that one of the senior citizens who lives a few doors down from Zara said he saw a man knocking on Zara's door the day before the murder." I paused to make sure I had their attention. "The man's description sounded like it could have been Gabe."

"Detective Hawkins has all this information, right?" Tillie asked.

"Yes. And he planned on questioning her neighbors himself." Not only did my head hurt from the implication, but my soul ached too.

"I think you're going to have to let the police handle this one, Em." Vannie's face reflected the sorrow I felt.

"As much as I hate to admit it, I think Vannie's right." Teresa stood, and the candlelight illuminated her honeyed skin tone. "Why don't y'all stay here and chat. I'll fix dinner this time."

"We can both fix it." Vannie stood and gently tugged on Teresa's long dark-brown braid, which hung almost to her waist. "Your Texan accent is showing."

Teresa laughed and deepened her Southern accent. "Cocktails will do it every time."

Vannie smiled and tore her gaze from Teresa. "Will anyone want wine with dinner?"

I shook my head. "I think I'd better switch to water. My head's getting fuzzy."

Tillie held up the empty pitcher. "If you add some ice water to this, I'll be good with that."

Vannie took the pitcher and promised to fill it and bring it back soon.

Once Vannie and Teresa were out of earshot, I leaned in toward Tillie and lowered my voice. "Brad's employee was able to track Zara's movements for the last two months. I have the printouts of it all."

"Why didn't you show us?" Tillie blotted her perfectly painted-red lips with a linen napkin. I'd long suspected she'd had the color and lipliner tattooed on, since I'd never seen her without, nor did the color ever smear or wear off when she ate.

"Brad used a hacker, and he really doesn't want it getting out to anyone. It could come back to bite him in the you-know-what." I tried to get my fuzzy mind to focus and come up with a plan. "I thought I—or maybe we—should visit some of the other spots Zara frequented to see if anyone else saw her meeting with a potential suspect."

"Dear, I think it would be best to let Detective Hawkins see the investigation to the end." She held up her hand when I began interrupting. "But I won't say no because I'd sure hate to see Brad's heart break in two."

I flung an arm around Tillie and gave her a hug. "Thank you. I hope we find something worthwhile."

"What are you two scheming about?" Vannie poured water into fresh glasses and placed them in front of us. "I hope it's nothing that will get you into trouble."

"Who? Us?" Tillie winked at me. "We're the perfect picture of propriety, and besides, we'll have Andrew with us."

Andrew was Tillie's long-time driver. He was cover-model worthy and dedicated to taking care of Tillie, even when it meant getting involved in our sometimes-hair-brained schemes.

"If you say so. Just be careful, please." Vannie blew a kiss to Tillie then returned to the kitchen.

We feasted on the garlicy shrimp scampi served over angel

hair pasta. Vannie had also prepared a fresh green salad with a light lemon vinaigrette that complemented the flavors of the scampi sauce. Our conversation turned toward the holidays, and Teresa shared her large Hispanic family's traditions for both Thanksgiving and Christmas, which included everyone pitching in to make hundreds of tamales.

Vannie had mentioned to me the previous month that Teresa asked her to fly to Texas over the holiday to meet her family, but she'd declined. It was Vannie's first Thanksgiving with our family, and she didn't want to miss it, nor did she want to rush back for Brad and Gabe's wedding.

Once our plates were empty, I cleaned up the kitchen then retrieved the cupcakes from my house. They oohed and aahed over the sugared cranberry garnish and gushed over the fresh cranberry flavor. Teresa even asked for the recipe, which I promised to email to her.

When Vannie walked Teresa to her car, Tillie took the opportunity to discuss the following day's schedule.

"What time should I have Andrew pick us up?"

"Maybe around eleven? I really need to get to David's first thing in the morning and pay bills."

David was Tillie's son and Vannie and Brian's father. I worked part-time for him at his home in Newport Beach. He allowed me to set my own hours and days, and all I had to do was go through his mail, pay bills, and do some general accounting stuff to coordinate with his company's accounting and tax department requests. It was simple work but provided me with some extra income along with health insurance through his business.

"Where is that son of mine these days?"

"He's back in New York, but I think he plans on coming home early next week." I paused for a moment. "Is he coming to our Thanksgiving dinner?"

"He is, unless he's gotten a better offer." Tillie's voice held a tinge of bitterness. Her son had a knack for entangling himself in romantic relationships with younger women who were only attracted to his money. As a result, Tillie had been the target of their machinations in getting their hands on her property and her wealth. Even knowing what had happened with at least two of his former wives, David didn't seem to be able to help himself whenever a pretty face turned their attention toward him.

"We'll hope for the best, then." I kissed her cheek. "I think I'll head home. Brian promised to take off a little early tonight and come over."

"Tell my grandson to come visit me in the morning and have breakfast with us before he leaves."

"Do you have any requests for what you'd like to eat?"

"Whatever you two come up with will be fine."

I called the dogs to come with me. They stood and stretched into downward-facing-dog poses. Missy's loud yawn sounded almost human. They followed me to the front door, where we met Vannie coming in.

"Tillie wants Brian and me to come over for breakfast in the morning, so you don't need to worry about leaving anything for her."

Vannie gave me a tight hug. "I wish I didn't have to leave so early for school, but I'll make a pot of coffee for you anyway."

My sister tried to stifle a yawn, so I took the hint and left for home. It wasn't long before Brian showed up, and we snuggled in for a cozy night together with no talk of murder.

Chapter 18

Brian spoiled Tillie and me by making crepes for breakfast. Again, he avoided bringing up the murder investigation. It wasn't because he didn't think I should be involved but I suspected it was because he knew I was upset that Gabe seemed to the one and only viable suspect. Once Brian left for a quick stop at his home and then another long day at the restaurant, I changed out of my yoga pants and a stained T-shirt into stretchy slacks and a knit tunic. I could dress as casual as I wanted when working at David's, but yoga pants seemed to be a bit too casual for the setting. Maybe if I were in better shape, I wouldn't be so self-conscious.

David lived about a mile away from Tillie, as the crow flew, but it was across the bay from her residence. There were two ways to reach his house, neither of them terribly convenient. The first was to drive a couple of miles north along the finger of land that was bordered by the Pacific Ocean on one side and the bay on the other side. Then you'd have to turn south and drive another couple of miles. Summertime and holidays meant hordes of tourists, which meant it could take thirty or even forty minutes to go the short distance, depending on the time of day. And don't even get me started on the lack of parking. It was often easier to walk to the ferry station and take the under-ten-minute ferry ride, which had been in operation for more than a hundred years, to the other side of the bay. From there, it was another reasonably short walk to David's house.

I used to take Piper with me while I worked at the house, especially on the days I walked. But once Missy came along, the two of them together made the excursion too much work. Tillie was more than happy to hang out with our dogs, and more often than not, Brian gave them a good walk on the mornings he was around. If they hadn't been walked in the morning, Vannie or I took them for a walk in the late afternoons... usually. Recalling the tightness of my clothing and how the stairs had made me huff and puff, I figured I should get in some additional exercise by walking and taking the ferry ride to work.

Of course, it was my luck that a seagull flew overhead as I sat on the open-air ferry bench. A collective "ooh" from other passengers confirmed what I already knew. The seagull had dropped a sticky white bomb onto the top of my head. Could this day get any worse?

Apparently, it could, because twenty feet from the dock, the ferry came to an abrupt halt. The engine shuddered to a stop, and then silence filled the air. It didn't take long for the ferry to start drifting with the current, and soon we were forty feet from the dock.

"Sorry for the delay, folks," the captain said on his speaker. "We'll get a tow and be on our way soon."

My scalp itched, and I longed to wash the goo from my hair. But there wasn't a bathroom on board the vessel, so I'd have to tough it out and wait.

A young woman who'd been sitting next to a man holding a toddler in his arms came and sat next to me. She handed me a pouch of diaper wipes then gestured at my hair. "I thought you could probably use these for… you know."

"Thanks, but I don't have a mirror. I'm afraid I'll only make it worse."

The woman looked at the top of my head then down at her hands. She shook her head, and her tangle of raven curls bounced. "I'd help, but I really can't get any of that poo on my hands. I worry I might transmit something terrible to my son before I have a chance to wash it off."

"Don't worry about it. We'll be docking soon, and my destination is only another ten minutes or so from the dock." Except I was worrying about it. I thought I felt a burning sensation on my scalp, although it was probably just my imagination.

"I couldn't help but overhear that you need a mirror." An elderly woman—she couldn't have been a day under seventy—dressed in eyewatering chartreuse-colored body-hugging workout gear stood in front of me. She held out a small compact mirror.

"Thanks. That's very helpful." I grabbed a couple of diaper wipes with one hand then held the mirror with my other. I couldn't get a close look at the mess in my hair, but at least I was able to dab in the right vicinity. The younger woman placed a couple of additional wipes on my knee and inched away from me. I couldn't blame her. I didn't want to be around myself either.

Knowing there wasn't much else I could do to clean my hair, I thanked them both then walked over to the trash can and disposed of the soiled wipes. The young mother retrieved a small bottle of hand sanitizer from her toddler's diaper bag and offered to squirt some onto my hands. I gratefully accepted.

By that point, we were a hundred feet from the dock, but the sound of a puttering engine gaining on us brought me some hope that we'd soon be able to disembark. I tried to contain my impatience, but at this rate, I wouldn't have time to get through the work that awaited me at David's and get back to Tillie's at eleven to start our investigation. And I desperately needed a shower and a change of clothes.

Twenty minutes later, we walked off the disabled ferry. I'd had enough of the morning's mishaps, so I pulled up the Uber app on my phone and summoned a car to take me home. While I waited impatiently, I gazed at the people waiting to board the ferry that had replaced our broken one. I squinted against the sun as I studied a man standing next to a black BMW sedan with a surfboard strapped to the roof. He looked familiar, and I thought maybe he was in his late twenties or early thirties. He wore a T-shirt and Hawaiian-print board shorts. Maybe he was one of Brian's friends I'd met in passing.

A young woman, perhaps in her early twenties, joined him and handed over a Starbucks disposable cup. The skimpy black bikini top and cutoff jean shorts she wore showed off a fit figure. Although the sun was shining, I wondered how the woman wasn't cold. She had the same fair skin as the man, but where his hair was dark brown, her hair was a dark blonde, worn in a high ponytail. I considered walking over to say hello—especially if the guy was one of Brian's friends—but then remembered the residual goo still sitting in my hair.

Just as my Uber arrived, the man caught my gaze upon him, and his mouth fell open for a second. Before I could lift a hand to wave, he spun around and placed his back toward me. He pulled the woman to stand in front of him, out of my line of sight. That was odd. I'd have to ask Brian if he knew which friend it was. Maybe he was having an affair and didn't want me to inadvertently spread the word that I'd seen him with another woman.

I guessed I'd stood there too long because the Uber driver honked at me. Startled, I jumped and looked up just in time to see the mystery man watching me. I ignored him and climbed inside the white Prius, which, although clean, looked like it'd seen better days.

The man, who looked like a recent retiree, pointed at the ferry. "It'll be faster if we take that instead of driving around the bay to your destination."

"No, thanks. I just came across, and my ferry broke down. It took twenty-five minutes for them to tow us in." I rolled the window down a crack to disseminate some of the recent cigarette smoke that had occupied the vehicle.

"Fine. Have it your way." The man's gaze fixated on the top of my head. He pointed at his own head.

"Thanks, but I'm aware. That's why I'm heading home instead of going to work."

"Hope your day turns around for you." He fixed his attention on the road ahead and slowly pulled away from the curb.

On the drive home—fortunately, traffic was light, and my driver hit mostly green lights—I thought about the surfer I'd seen waiting for the ferry. My mind went through the list of Brian's friends I'd met, including his employees. None of them matched the mystery man's description. I berated myself for not snapping a photo, although it would have been awkward if he'd caught on to what I was doing. His actions in turning his back to me and shielding the woman from my view were also suspicious.

I checked the time on my cell phone. Chances were the mystery man had already disembarked from the ferry and I wouldn't be able to find him. But if the ferry had been delayed a bit, I might still be able to catch him.

"Excuse me. Would you mind dropping me off at the ferry station?"

"Are you sure you want to do that?" He glanced around and looked pointedly at my hair.

"Yes, please."

Within a few minutes, he pulled up curbside, and I hopped out. There were two cars waiting to take the ferry to the

Newport Beach side of the bay along with a handful of people. The incoming ferry was perhaps twenty feet away from docking, so I positioned myself behind a column next to the ticket office. I wished I'd had a hat or scarf to hide my red hair, but there was nothing I could do about it.

As the cars drove off the ferry, I surreptitiously held my phone up and took several photos as the black BMW drove past me. I had no idea if I'd gotten a good picture of the driver or his passenger, but there wasn't anything else I could do without getting caught. Once the car was out of view, I flipped through the photos. They were on the blurry side, and the man had his head angled away from me. Oh well. It was worth a shot. Something about the man bugged me, and I'd done the best I could. I sent Brian a text, attaching the best photo, which was still pretty bad, and asked if he recognized the person. He immediately answered no. I'd known it was a long shot but nevertheless still felt disappointed. I tucked my phone into my purse and power walked home.

Chapter 19

Showered, shampooed—multiple times—and dressed in clean navy slacks and a lightweight blush-colored long-sleeved blouse, I made my way to Tillie's at exactly eleven. Andrew stood by the Town Car, holding the back passenger side door open for Tillie while I slid into the car on the opposite side. I didn't stand on ceremony and never expected or wanted Andrew to open or close the door for me.

I gave Andrew the address of a coffee shop that Zara had frequented multiple times in the month she'd lived at the Irvine apartment. I tucked Ethan's printouts back into my purse.

"Anything new happening at my son's house?" Tillie asked once we were on the road.

"I dunno. I never made it there." I gingerly patted the top of my head. A stinging sensation still bothered me.

"Why not?" Tillie pulled a compact mirror from her handbag and handed it to me along with a tube of lipstick.

"I must've had a target on my head, because a seagull dive-bombed me while I was on the ferry, and it hit the bull's-eye." I was pretty sure Andrew stifled a snort, but it was hard to tell because of Tillie's guffaw.

"Oh dear. That can't have been good." Tillie covered her mouth with her hand and giggled again. "What did you do?"

"Just wait. It gets better." By the time I finished my tale of Emory versus the seagull goo and the broken-down ferry, even Andrew was chuckling.

"You do have quite the mishaps, Emory." Tillie took back her lipstick and mirror after I'd applied some.

"As uncomfortable as it was, I did run into a mystery man waiting for the ferry when I disembarked."

"Oh? Do tell. Was he tall, dark, and handsome?" She patted my hand. "Not that I want you to find any competition for my grandson's affections."

"No worries there." I pulled up the photos on my cell phone. "He seemed kind of familiar to me, and at first, I thought maybe he was one of Brian's friends. But he says he doesn't know him. Plus, when the mystery man caught me staring, he turned his back to me really fast and blocked my view of the woman standing with him."

"Curiouser and curiouser." Tillie enlarged the photo using two fingers. "Can't say I've ever seen him before. Maybe he's no one and just didn't want to be caught with the woman."

"That was my thought too. It looked like they were going surfing, but still, I know I've seen him somewhere before."

The rest of the drive passed quickly as Tillie gossiped about her country club's ladies who lunch and filled me in on some of her upcoming philanthropic events. She made me promise to come up with some Valentine-themed cupcakes and cocktails for one of the committee-planning gatherings. I got the feeling that the gatherings were more of an excuse to host a party, since spouses were included, and not much planning for the charity event went on. But I'd be paid a generous sum for my cupcakes, so I couldn't complain.

Andrew pulled into a tired-looking strip mall that was only a few blocks before we'd have reached Zara's apartment complex. After finding a parking spot close to The Coffee

Klatch, he helped Tillie from the car while I climbed out the other side. Tillie and I pushed through the glass door and into the charming coffee shop. It gave off grandma's farmhouse vibes with its gingham-covered tables topped with mason jars filled with daisies. Quilts hung from blanket racks on one wall, with price tags hanging from the quilts' edges. Another wall held shelves filled with a variety of preserves, the lids covered with calico fabric and tied with raffia bows.

There were a few customers, all senior citizens, enjoying beverages and a variety of baked goods, from biscuits to scones to pie. My mouth watered at the aroma of baking bread.

"Welcome to The Coffee Klatch. Take a seat, and I'll be with you in a moment." The grandmotherly figure walked toward us, carrying a coffeepot and a plate of what looked like blueberry muffins. The full-figured woman had white hair pulled up into a tight bun. Her denim dress was covered by a pink-rose-patterned calico apron. Her cheeks were rosy, and she wore gold wire-rimmed spectacles perched halfway down her nose.

We found an empty table set a distance from other guests. I didn't need a nosy customer trying to eavesdrop on our questions.

"I'm Opal, the owner. Welcome to my establishment." She set down two empty coffee mugs then handed us each a half page of paper. "These are our offerings today, but I think we ran out of the chocolate chip scones already. Owen—he's my son and the baker—is mixing up another batch if you want to wait. Can I bring you some coffee or tea?"

"I'd like a cup of coffee, and...." I quickly scanned the list. "I'll try a piece of your apple pie."

"Would you like that a la mode?"

"Yes, please." Dessert for lunch was always the right choice, especially after all the walking I'd done that morning... or so I told myself.

"And for you, ma'am?"

"I'd like a cup of Earl Gray tea and your traditional scones with strawberry jam." Tillie handed the menu back to Opal.

"I'll have it right out for you." Opal took Tillie's coffee mug and hurried back to the kitchen.

I pulled Zara's photo from my purse and placed it on the table then pulled up Gabe's photo, which I'd zoomed in and taken a screenshot of, on my phone. In no time at all, Opal had filled my coffee mug and settled a floral china teapot in front of Tillie along with a matching teacup and saucer.

"I left the strainer in with the loose-leaf tea, so you can steep it to your desired strength." Opal tapped the top of the teapot. "I'll be right back with your food."

She stopped and chatted with a couple of senior men for a moment then disappeared into the kitchen. Opal came out a minute later, carrying a tray with our food. She set an individual apple pie—large enough for two people—in front of me with a huge scoop of vanilla ice cream perched on top. The pie must've been hot, because the bottom of the ice cream had started to melt. The fragrance of cinnamon wafted up, and I couldn't wait to dig in.

Tillie's two scones were round, the traditional shape served in Britain. The platter the scones came on contained butter, clotted cream, and what appeared to be homemade strawberry jam. I hoped Tillie would share a bite with me.

"Can I get you ladies anything else?" Opal beamed down at us.

"Do you have a moment to tell me if you've seen this woman before?" I showed her the picture of Zara.

"Why, yes. She comes in several times a week for afternoon tea and scones." Opal touched Zara's face. "Oh dear. I think I just saw her picture in the paper. She's the one who was recently killed, isn't she?"

"Unfortunately, she was," Tillie murmured.

"Can you tell us if she ever came in with anyone else, or

did anyone ever stop by her table to talk to her?" I asked.

"Why are you asking? Are you with the police or something?" Opal's brow knitted.

"Or something," I muttered. "The truth is I'm the one who found her, and I feel responsible for finding justice for her."

"Shouldn't the police be handling the investigation, dear?" Opal ran her hand over the tablecloth as if to smooth out nonexistent wrinkles.

"Yes, but they're not making much progress. Have they been by to ask about her yet?"

Opal frowned. "Why, no. They haven't."

"I'm only asking a few questions, and if I find out anything worthwhile, I can pass it along to the detective. They just don't have the manpower these days to follow unlikely clues."

"Hmm. I can see your point." Opal pulled an empty chair from a close-by table over to us and sat down. "So, you'd like to know if Zara came in with anyone or if anyone talked to her, aside from me? I'm assuming you don't think I had anything to do with her death. Right?"

"You're absolutely in the clear." I was sure that was the case. Opal was too friendly and nice to have committed murder. "We heard rumors that she loved your food, so we thought we'd stop by and see if anyone had seen or heard anything strange going on with Zara."

"Now that you mention it, she had a friend join her every once in a while." She tapped her index finger on her lips. "Nina is her name, I believe. Anyway, they were usually friendly, but a week ago, if I remember right, they got into an argument. Nina was pretty hot under the collar and stormed out of here after she told Zara she didn't ever want to see her again."

Tillie's eyes widened. "Do you know what the argument was about?"

"No. It was busy in here, so I didn't hear anything until Nina gave her parting shot and stomped out."

I found it suspicious that Nina hadn't mentioned her argument to me. I'd have to ask her about it. I opened my phone, scrolled to my photo of Gabe, and showed it to Opal. "Did this man ever come in here to talk to Zara?"

Opal twisted her mouth then backed the phone away from her face by a few inches as if to bring the photo into focus. "He seems familiar, but I'm pretty sure I never saw him with Zara."

"Who're you looking at, Grammie?" A teenaged girl with bouncy blonde locks looked over Opal's shoulder.

"These ladies are wondering if this man ever ate here or if I've seen him talking to Zara." Opal pointed at Zara's photo still sitting on the table.

"That guy's never been in here, but another dude who kinda looks like him stopped Zara in the parking lot last week. They were yellin' at each other is why I noticed." The teenager looked at Zara's photo again.

"Do you remember what day that was and what time it happened?" I asked.

"It was Wednesday at four because I came straight here to work after my dance class." The girl gave her grandmother a hug. "I'm gonna go fix myself a sandwich before I have to go back to school."

Opal watched her granddaughter skip off then stood. "I need to get back to work too. Lunch rush will be happening soon. I'll bring coffee to refill your mug, and you can let me know if I can get you anything else."

"We appreciate you taking the time to talk to us." I swept my hands over the plates. "And your food is absolutely amazing."

Once Opal left to tend to other guests, Tillie and I devoured our food. It was just as delicious as it looked and smelled.

Chapter 20

Back in the car, with my stomach straining against the waistband of my slacks, Tillie and I reviewed the printouts from Ethan. Zara had shopped at Target several times, but I didn't think we'd find any employees who could tell us if she'd shopped alone or had any contentious conversations with anyone.

She'd visited The Tuscany Room, a wine bar close to the airport, three times over the last two weeks of her life. On her last visit, four days before she died, she'd purchase two glasses of chardonnay and two glasses of merlot. The tab had been closed out at seven forty-five. All evidence pointed at Zara having been drinking wine with someone that evening.

"I say we visit the wine bar after an early dinner." I tapped the address into my phone. "We can see if Vannie, Carrie, and Mother would like to join us. We can make it a girls' night out."

"Would you like me to drive you this evening?" Andrew asked.

"There's no need. Vannie told me she's not drinking until Thanksgiving." Tillie winked at me. "You deserve an evening to yourself, Andrew."

"Thank you, Mrs. Skyler, but if you change your mind, please let me know."

"Why isn't Vannie drinking?" I asked. She'd enjoyed her share of the pitcher of gimlets the previous night, right along with the rest of us.

"I think she had a bit too much last night. This morning, she said having to deal with holiday-hyper high schoolers while suffering from a headache wasn't anything she wanted to do again." Tillie smiled. "I gave her a travel mug of coffee and ibuprofen. She should be feeling fine by now. But that gives us a good excuse to drag her out as our designated driver."

I wondered if my sister would stick to her resolution longer than I had.

"Where shall I take you next?" Andrew asked.

"I guess home." I quickly scanned the printout again. "There's nowhere else she might have socialized. I seriously doubt she'd argue with her killer at the drycleaners or the car wash place. She shopped quite a bit at high-end department stores, but again, it'll be difficult tracking down any employees who might have interacted with her, especially since she shopped at so many different stores."

"You're probably right, dear. Okay, Andrew. Home, it is."

As we drove, I studied the portions pertaining to the department stores. She'd racked up a lot of expensive charges. Unfortunately, none of the department store charges detailed what she'd purchased, unlike her charges at Target and the restaurants she'd visited. I tried to push the disturbing images of Zara's apartment out of my mind and instead think back to her furnishings.

If I recalled correctly, nothing seemed luxurious or pricy, aside from the fainting couch—ugh—and the mannequin's clothing—double ugh! What had she done with all the purchases? Granted, I hadn't seen her closet, nor had I opened any cabinets in the kitchen. Perhaps she'd had a taste for fine china and crystal along with designer clothing, shoes, and handbags. I'd have to ask Detective Hawkins about it, if I had a chance.

"What are you going to tell the detective?" Tillie asked, interrupting my musings.

"I was just thinking about him." I twisted my mouth from side to side. "I guess I need to tell him about Nina's argument with Zara."

"What about the guy who kind of resembles Gabe having an argument with Zara? That could get Gabe off the hook." Tillie rubbed her hands together. "The plot thickens."

It made me think of the man at the ferry that morning. I swiped open the photo and showed Tillie. "Does he vaguely resemble Gabe? I mean, the hair color's all wrong, but maybe the shape of his face?"

She studied my phone screen for a moment. "From that angle, it's impossible to say."

"Maybe he mistook me for someone else he didn't want to see him with that woman." I shrugged. "I think I'm so desperate to find more suspects I'm targeting random strangers on the street."

Tillie murmured her sympathy while I scrolled through my calendar and made note of upcoming cupcake orders. I'd need to spend a good part of the following day baking and frosting eight dozen mini cupcakes for a charter school's bake sale being held on Thursday. Wealthy Newport Beach mothers didn't bake sweets themselves for the fundraiser… and I was sure most of them wouldn't eat the sweets, either, given how rigorously so many strived to be a size zero. Instead, they ordered the treats from bakeries and caterers and most likely gave away any of the sweets they bought at the event or sent them to their husbands' places of employment.

"Andrew, can you drop me off at David's before taking Tillie home?" It wasn't that far out of the way. I turned to

Tillie. "I think I'd better get through all my work there, since I've got quite a few cupcake orders to make starting tomorrow."

"Of course, Emory." Andrew flicked on his blinker and switched lanes.

"You'll be back in time for an early dinner, won't you?" Tillie asked.

"I should make it. Does five thirty work?" That would give me a good three hours to dive into the mail and take care of bills and anything else that needed attention.

"I don't think you should walk home in the dark. Andrew can pick you up."

"Absolutely not. You already promised Andrew a night off, and Uber is just as convenient."

Andrew's gaze met mine when he looked in the rearview mirror. He gave an almost imperceptible nod. I took it to mean that he appreciated not being on call.

"I just want you to be safe." Tillie gave my hand a quick squeeze. "Will Hannah be there this afternoon?"

Hannah was David's live-in housekeeper and cook. When she knew ahead of time when I'd be coming in to work, she often prepared one of her Scandinavian dishes to share with me. I figured she had to be a bit lonely, living in the huge house all by herself, since David traveled so much. I tried to allow extra time to have a cup of coffee and one of her treats while chatting with her each time I was there.

"I'm assuming so. I'd better text her to let her know I'm on my way." I thumbed a quick text, telling Hannah I'd be there in about ten minutes.

She immediately responded.

David will arrive home in about an hour. He's bringing a guest.

"*What?*" My voice was louder than I'd meant it to be in the close confines of the car.

"What's wrong?" Tillie asked, leaning over to see my cell screen.

I handed her my phone.

"Well, this is troubling." She returned my phone. "Hannah didn't mention he was arriving home earlier than planned, did she?"

"No. I definitely would have told you."

Tillie pursed her lips. "Maybe I should stay and meet this new guest."

I shook my head. "Let me check it out first. Maybe it's not what we think."

I knew, without a doubt, we were both remembering the last new guest he'd introduced us to. But instead of being a guest, she'd been the new Mrs. Skyler. It hadn't been pretty.

"I'm not holding my breath," Tillie muttered. "Fine. I won't worry about it until I hear from you. But you'd better text me the second you find out anything."

"I promise I'll let you know just as soon as I can." I bit my thumbnail, worrying I'd left my office in a mess and hadn't attended to my work as diligently as I should have. I tended to leave things to the last minute, tidying up and doing the work right before David returned home. His arrival out of the blue wasn't a good sign, especially since his company's executive assistant hadn't told me about his change in itinerary. Janelle was diligent about keeping me up-to-date on David's schedule or any changes he made.

"While you've got your phone out, send Carrie, Addie, and Vannie a text and let them know what the plan is tonight. Vannie can invite Teresa to join us, if she'd like."

I did as Tillie requested. Vannie didn't immediately reply, which wasn't unexpected. After all, Vannie was a conscientious teacher and at least silenced her phone during class if not turned it off completely. My mother replied that her bridge club was meeting that evening, and Carrie declined, stating she had an early morning the next day, catering a breakfast. I read the replies out loud to Tillie.

"I hope David's arrival doesn't mess up our plans for tonight." I tried to ignore the jittery sensation in my stomach. Perhaps polishing off the apple pie and having that third cup of coffee hadn't been the smartest thing to do. "If anything changes, I'll let you know."

Chapter 21

Hannah must've been watching for me, because as soon as I let myself through the security gate, she stepped out of the house and stood at the top of the steps.

"David hasn't arrived yet, has he?"

"Not yet." Hannah held the massive front door open for me, and I stepped inside.

Once she'd closed and locked the door, I asked, "Do you have any idea who the guest is?"

"Mr. Skyler didn't say. He only asked that I make up the guest room overlooking the bay and serve filet mignon and twice-baked potatoes for dinner with chocolate cake for dessert." Hannah smoothed back strands of her gray hair that had escaped her braid. She wiped her pudgy hands on the chocolate-stained apron tied around her ample waist. "I need to run to the market for the steak just as soon as the cake comes out of the oven in five minutes."

I breathed a bit easier. If David had requested steak, potatoes, and chocolate cake along with a separate guest room prepared, then he probably wasn't bringing a romantic partner home. "Let me know if there's anything I can do to help."

"So far, I feel like I have everything under control." She pointed at the curved staircase that led to the second floor. "I put all the mail in your office and opened a window to freshen up the room. Can I bring you anything to eat or drink before I leave?"

"Tillie and I just came from lunch, so I'm fine."

Hannah tried to insist on bringing me at least some herbal tea, but I shooed her back to the kitchen. Entering my office, I opened the French doors that led out onto a small balcony. I stepped out and drank in the sight of the glimmering bay. I avoided looking down, to the right of me, where a crystalline turquoise pool took up part of the yard. The memories of finding a dead body there were still too fresh in my memory.

Hannah had thoughtfully stacked catalogs and what appeared to be junk mail into separate piles. I quickly scanned the items then dumped them into the recycling bin. Next, I separated invoices from gala events and charitable-donation requests. David and Tillie were both generous with their fortune and supported numerous charities for the less fortunate in addition to the local performing arts scene.

I quickly paid the bills along with writing checks to the charities I knew David approved of then prioritized the invitations' details according to date on a spreadsheet and printed it out. Once he reviewed the spreadsheet, David would mark the functions he'd attend. I'd RSVP for him, sending any necessary fees associated with the invite, and send regrets to the rest of the people. When David was out of town for an extended period of time, I'd email the spreadsheet to him for review.

I'd just finished filing the last of the paid invoices when I heard the alarm chime at the opening of the front door. Unsure whether I should hide out in my office or go see who David's mystery guest was, I hovered in the doorway.

Rolling suitcases and footsteps echoed as they traversed

the stone flooring. They stopped at the bottom of the staircase.

"Emory? Are you still here?" David's voice was firm but not overly loud.

I stepped onto the landing and hurried to the top of the stairs to look down. "Welcome back—" My mouth went dry when I saw the figure standing next to David. It was his eldest son, Theodore.

"You look like you just saw a ghost." Theodore chuckled and held up his arm, which seemed more muscular since the last time I'd seen him. His hair was cut short, almost in a military style, and he wore blue jeans and a white button-down shirt. "It's me. In the flesh. Out of the slammer for good behavior, as long as I perform all my community service hours and check in with a parole officer and a therapist every now and then."

A few years ago, Theodore had been involved in a vehicular high-speed accident that resulted in the death of one of his friends. He'd covered it up and then, with the help of his father, had fled the country before he could be charged. After a stint in rehab, Theodore and his father decided he should return home and turn himself in to authorities. Thanks to the best attorneys and money, David had managed to secure a reduced sentence for his eldest.

Theodore was being open and honest about his situation, a far cry from his behavior earlier in the year. Or maybe it was his new brand of sarcasm. I hastily plastered a smile onto my face. "Welcome home, Theodore. Your grandmother will be thrilled with the surprise."

"Is she home? I thought I might go visit her this afternoon." He fidgeted with the watch he wore on his left wrist.

"She should be. Vannie and I are supposed to have dinner with her around five thirty this evening."

A cloud passed over Theodore's face and just as quickly disappeared. He had been less than thrilled to discover David had a daughter who would no doubt claim a share of what he supposed was his inheritance. Not that Vannie was a money-grubbing person. Theodore just had an overly strong sense of entitlement.

"Fine. I think I'll unpack and then head over." Theodore turned to look at his dad. "Will that work for you?"

"Of course. It'll give me some time to take care of business with Emory."

I stepped back into my office as the two men climbed the stairs, luggage in hand. My phone pinged with an incoming text while I listened to David directing his son to the best guest room in the house. I checked my phone and saw Vannie had agreed to our plans but that Teresa had other commitments. Relieved it wasn't Tillie asking for an update—I wouldn't want to be the one to ruin Theodore's surprise visit—I finished tidying up the office.

A knock sounded on the doorframe, and David poked his head in. "Is this a good time to go over anything that needs my attention?"

"Sure. Come on in." I offered him the most comfortable chair in the room and then pulled a rolling stool from beneath the desk and sat down. I wanted to ask about Theodore's release but held my tongue as David scanned the items I'd marked for his review.

He quickly signed two documents his office had emailed over for me to print out and hold for his return then check marked three events he planned on attending. Once business was taken care of, David pushed his chair away from the desk and swiveled it to face me.

"As you can see, Theodore has been released." David sniffed then cleared his throat. "It might be a trying time ahead for all of us, but one of the conditions is that he must live with me."

I nodded, not having a clue what I should say.

"I hope you won't feel uncomfortable having him here at

the house while you're working." David gazed out the window. "He hasn't been kind to you in the past, but he's changed. Hopefully, as he proves himself, you'll be able to move beyond how he's treated you before."

"It's not a problem." I tried to keep any emotion from showing on my face, not that it would have mattered, since David still kept his attention focused on the window. "I'm happy for the family. It's got to be a huge relief that Theodore was able to come home."

David nodded. "It's been hard on Matilda, especially."

For some reason, David had never called his mother by any name except her given name. He wouldn't even call her by her chosen nickname, Tillie. But that was between them, and I didn't need to offer up my opinion. I nodded again.

"Are you about finished up here?" David gestured around my office, which thankfully looked clean and organized.

"I'm caught up, but is there anything else you need me to do?"

"Can you give Theodore a ride to Matilda's? His license is still revoked, and Janelle hasn't had the chance to set up a full-time driver for him yet."

Janelle probably hadn't had the chance because David probably hadn't even told her Theodore was out of prison and needed a driver.

"I would, but I don't have my car here. I'm planning on calling an Uber. Theodore is more than welcome to share the ride with me." I hated to offer a return ride home, but then I reminded myself how much David and Tillie had done for me. "Would you like for me to drive him back home this evening?"

"No need. Just have him download the Uber app, and give him my credit card number." David looked warily at me. "It's not hard to do, is it?"

"Not at all. I can set him up in two minutes flat, and I'll show him how to schedule a ride, if he doesn't already know how." Given Theodore's level of entitlement with super-expensive cars and limo service at his beck and call, I'd bet a latte he had no idea how to use Uber.

"Good. And thank you for being welcoming to Theodore." David stood and briefly touched my arm. "I'll go tell him you're ready to leave."

"Hold on a sec." I picked up my cell phone. "Let me check and see how long it'll take for an Uber to get here. We might have to wait a bit."

David's eyebrows rose. "I thought there were available cars all over the place."

"It depends. Around the airport or shopping malls, yes. Here in the residential area, I'm not sure." I quickly swiped, tapped, and looked at the offerings. "A car is ten minutes away. I'll order it now, if you can tell Theodore to meet me by the front door in ten?"

"Good. And thanks again, Emory."

David left, and I gathered up my belongings. I sent Hannah a text telling her I was leaving, but David was home, and his son was the guest, but to keep it a secret until Theodore surprised the rest of the family. I felt strongly that I should warn Vannie, since Theodore—and I had to remember not to call him Teddy, like I'd almost done earlier—had been less than kind to her as well. I thumbed a quick text, keeping an ear open for Theodore's footsteps coming down the hall.

Theodore released from jail! He's riding with me to Tillie's. He wants to surprise her, but I thot u should be warned.

She immediately sent back three exclamation points.

Chapter 22

B rian was another family member who needed to be warned. While Brian and Theodore were half brothers, there weren't any warm and fuzzy feelings between the two. I placed all the blame on Theodore and his perceived rivalry for the family fortune. I truly hoped he'd changed and wasn't trying to bamboozle his father.

I clicked on my text to Vannie and forwarded it to Brian. It wasn't a surprise when I didn't receive an answer back. He was sure to be crushed with the start of dinner service prep. The Uber map showed the car was two minutes away, so I made my way to the front door. Theodore followed close behind me.

"David said you'd enter his credit card into the Uber app for me." Theodore handed his phone to me. The Uber app was already open.

I opened Notes on my phone then entered David's credit card information into Theodore's app. I then swiped the app closed before I handed the phone back to him.

"Do you need me to show you how to use the app to summon a car?" I asked.

Theodore scoffed. "I know how to use it just fine. It was probably David who suggested I didn't."

"I think it's more that he has no idea how to use the app, so he assumes most people are in the dark, same as him."

Before he could respond, a small Toyota pulled up alongside us. The driver, a middle-aged woman, rolled down the passenger side door. "Emory Martinez?"

"That's me." I opened the front door then gestured for Theodore to sit in the back seat. I wasn't interested in getting cozy with him. I slid into the passenger seat and secured my seat belt. "It's up to you if you want to take the ferry across or take the road all the way around. But to warn you, I got stranded on a broken-down ferry this morning. It took close to twenty-five minutes for them to tow us back in."

"The road around it will be." She put the car into gear. "Those ferries kind of freak me out anyway. I feel like my car could just roll right off."

"I don't think I've heard of any accidents like that, but I know what you mean." Riding the ferries as a passenger was one thing, but driving my car onto it was a completely different feeling.

Theodore remained silent for the entire ride while our driver chitchatted about tourist sites we should visit. I didn't correct her assumption that we were tourists. But when we pulled up in front of Tillie's security gate, she looked abashed.

"I guess you're residents and not tourists. Sorry for my running dialogue."

"Not a problem. I actually forgot about the Sherman gardens, so I'll have to check it out one of these days." I climbed from the car and, after thanking her again, shut the door.

Theodore stood beside me. A bead of sweat ran down his cheek. He wiped it away with a trembling hand. "Maybe this wasn't such a good idea. David should have set up a meeting instead of my showing up with no warning."

"It'll be fine. Your grandmother loves you very much, and while she may shed some tears, they'll be happy tears."

Theodore looked horrified. "I can't do it. Please go tell her I'm here."

I punched in the security gate code, and once the gate swung open, I pulled him along, toward the house. Before I could shut the security gate, the front door opened. It was a good thing I had ahold of Theodore's arm, because he looked like he was ready to bolt.

Tillie stepped forward, raised her hand to her mouth, then ran down the steps and pulled Theodore into her arms. Piper and Missy trailed right behind her. They gave Theodore a sniff then came to greet me. Tillie stepped back, wiped her eyes, and handed me their leashes.

"They were making a fuss at the front door, so I thought I'd take them for a short walk." She grabbed hold of Theodore's arm. "How did you keep this a secret? You should have told this old woman you were coming. You almost gave me a heart attack."

"Sorry, Gram. David and I weren't sure my release would happen, so we didn't want to get anyone's hopes up." Theodore hung his head.

Tillie slung her arm around his shoulders. "Come on in. Vannie will be cooking us dinner in a while. You'll stay and eat with us, won't you?"

Theodore stopped walking. "I don't want to intrude."

"You're not. Vannie is family, and the sooner you get to know her, the sooner you'll come to love her the same as the rest of us."

Piper and Missy danced around my legs, and then Piper grabbed a leash between her teeth and tugged on it.

"I'm going to take the dogs for a walk. I'll be back soon."

Tillie gave a quick wave of her hand, but her focus remained on Theodore. I couldn't blame her. Her eldest grandson had broken her heart, and it looked like he was home, ready to reconcile with her.

I snapped the leashes on and allowed the dogs to pull me along the alleyway and onto the sidewalk. They set a brisk pace, stopping every so often to sniff the calling cards of dogs who'd passed that way before them. As daylight faded, a stiff ocean breeze began to blow, and I wished I'd thought to grab a sweatshirt.

The dogs turned onto a side street and tugged even harder. The only thing in that direction was the beach, and I wasn't about to let them romp in the sand that time of evening. Their fur acted like Velcro with the fine sand, and it would take an hour to bathe and brush the dogs to get them clean again. I didn't have the time, especially if we still planned on going to the wine bar that evening. I tugged on their leashes and urged them to turn around and head home. At first, they resisted, but then they must've realized I wouldn't change my mind, so they heeded my plea.

As I led the dogs, who'd slowed their pace to a snail's crawl, from the side street and prepared to cross the main thoroughfare, I checked for traffic. I didn't see any oncoming headlights. I'd just stepped from the curb when a black car revved its engine and sped by me at high speed, going the wrong way down the road. The vehicle was so close I felt the heat of the engine as it passed me. I jumped back, tripped over the curb, and fell to the sidewalk. My heart jackhammered in my chest. If the dogs had been pulling on their leashes like they'd been doing earlier, they would've been mowed down. Then I realized that if I'd been even another six inches into the street, it would have been my body that had been hit.

Looking around the sidewalks and streets, I didn't see anyone who was paying me any attention... which meant no one had seen the nearly disastrous accident or the sedan that had come so close to injuring me or worse. Piper licked my cheek and whined.

"It's okay, girl. We're all okay." I stroked her ears with shaky hands. I looked down the road at where the car had disappeared. The incident had happened so quickly I hadn't gotten a look at the car, the driver, or the license plate. All I knew was that it was a black vehicle or some other dark color. There wasn't any use calling the police.

Missy pawed my knee.

"Let's get home before anything else happens."

I stood and began limping toward home. The dogs kept close to me, and I continuously scanned the area, watching for another speeding car. Fortunately, no other dangers materialized, and we safely made it home.

I opened Tillie's door and removed the leashes from the dogs. They immediately scampered down the wide hallway and headed straight for the kitchen. The aroma of garlic greeted my nose as I followed behind my pets.

I'd almost turned the corner that led to the kitchen when I heard Theodore's angry voice. It stopped me midstep.

"There's something wrong with Emory. No sane person could ever find so many murder victims." A bang sounded, like Theodore had slammed his hand onto the wood farmhouse table top. "David needs to put a stop to her and start protecting you from yourself and your Miss Marple syndrome."

"That'll be enough, Theodore." Tillie's voice held steel, but I could hear hurt beneath her words. "I don't need your or David's permission to live my life like I want. Your father is fully aware of my position on things, and he has no complaints or concerns. I suggest you lose your patriarchal, entitled attitude and accept that Emory is an intelligent woman, as am I, and as is Vannie. If you can't handle that, then I suggest you seek out an enlightened therapist."

I backed down the hall, the way I'd come, then swiftly ran

up the stairs and into a bathroom. Quietly closing the door, I switched on the light and, with shaking hands, splashed water on my face. I checked my clothes for dirt after falling on the sidewalk, but I was reasonably clean, aside from a bit of dust. I dampened a disposable towelette and used it to clean my slacks then washed my still-trembling hands with hot water and foaming soap that smelled of cinnamon and apples. After drying my hands, I took a deep breath and opened the door.

The front door slammed shut. Missy barked until Vannie told her to hush. I took another deep breath and cautiously made my way down the stairs, my knees feeling like jelly. All was quiet, aside from the murmurs of Tillie and Vannie. I had to hope it had been Theodore who'd slammed the front door on his way out.

Chapter 23

Stepping into the kitchen, I found Tillie sitting at the table, her mouth set in a grim line. Vannie sat beside her, bright-pink spots coloring her cheeks.

"Well, that homecoming didn't go as well as I'd hoped." Tillie's voice was steady, but I knew it took effort not to show how Theodore's outburst must've hurt her.

"Why does he have to be so...." Vannie appeared to be trying to think of the right word.

I had several words I could call his attitude and action, but I bit my tongue instead. Name calling wouldn't help the situation. I sat on the other side of Tillie.

"I'm sorry he said all those awful things to you." I wanted to touch her arm, but I was afraid my shaking hand would give away how upset Theodore had made me feel.

"My opinion, born of my old age and wisdom, is Theodore feels like an outsider. He's lashing out at people he knows I hold dear, trying to make himself feel bigger and more self-important."

"So you weren't kidding when you said he should get an enlightened therapist?" Vannie asked.

"Not at all. David's probably setting him up with one of

his stodgy society connections without any thought to what type of therapy would benefit his son the most." Tillie sighed. "All we can do is hope that once he settles in and begins to feel like an accepted member of the family, he'll get over his angst."

"Do you think I should go after Theodore and offer to drive him home?" I thought of the darkening night and the car that had tried to run me over. Its lights hadn't been on, and even though I didn't want to admit it, I feared they'd aimed for me on purpose.

"He didn't drive you both over here?" Tillie asked.

"Uh-uh. His license is still revoked. David's having Janelle set up a full-time driver, but it's not a done deal yet." I chewed my lower lip. "I set up David's credit card on his Uber app, so he's probably already scheduled a car pickup."

"Theodore is a grown man. He can manage to get home on his own." Tillie tried to smile but failed.

The oven timer dinged, and Vannie jumped up. "Dinner will be ready in a few minutes. Can you toss the salad and pour glasses of water for us, Em?"

I sniffed the air. "What's smelling so delicious?"

"Roasted pork tenderloin with fingerling potatoes. I made a port wine sauce to go with the meat."

I hopped up from the table and got the salad and dressing from the refrigerator. While I tossed the salad, Tillie added kibble to the dogs' bowls then snitched a piece of pork from the chopping board. She tore it in half and gave both dogs a piece.

She grinned when she caught me watching her. Her voice went into babytalk mode. "They deserve a treat. Don't you, sweet girls?"

"I barely put any salt on the pork and saved the garlic and pepper for the sauce." Vannie, who was used to Tillie's antics and determination to spoil our dogs, quickly covered the sliced pork with a sheet of tin foil. "Do you hear me,

Gram? No sauce for the dogs. Garlic is dangerous for them."

"I hear you." She tugged at a corner of the tin foil, pulled out another slice of meat, and tore into tiny pieces before sprinkling it on top of the dog kibble in each bowl. "Would you want to eat that dry, tasteless cardboard? I think not. Dogs need protein and real meat."

After our close call with the speeding car, I wasn't going to argue and instead agreed the dogs deserved to be spoiled once in a while. Although Tillie's definition of once in a while meant several times a day.

We ate our dinner quickly, and I considered telling them about the close call with the black car. In the end, I decided against it. It would only worry them, and besides, there wasn't anything anyone could do about it.

While Vannie and I cleaned up the kitchen after dinner, Tillie went upstairs to freshen up. Or so she said. She looked just fine to me after eating, with her hair and makeup impeccably in place. I, on the other hand, knew my hair must look a fright. Instead of worrying about it, I tugged an elastic out of my pocket and pulled it up into a messy bun. Tillie would be sure to give me her lipstick tube on the drive, so I wasn't worried about that either.

THE TUSCANY ROOM wine bar was what you'd expect, since it was close to the Santa Ana airport—not lavish but not a dive bar either. The lighting was dim, and a dark-brown counter held ten barstools. There were also fifteen round glass-topped cocktail tables with the same barstools, and only half the tables were being used. I sniffed the air. It smelled like the aroma of a winery, a bit yeasty and a bit fruity.

"Let's sit at the bar. It'll make it easier to ask the bartender about Zara," I said.

When we'd settled ourselves, the bartender, an attractive

man in his thirties, handed us each a large leather-bound binder along with a single sheet of appetizers available. "Hi. I'm Umberto, your sommelier this evening. Take a look at our offerings. We have a nice selection of wines by the glass, or if you prefer by the bottle, we have more than five hundred labels from Italy and California wineries to choose from."

"Oh my goodness. That's a lot of wine!" Tillie opened the binder. "I'm not even sure where to start."

"Will you ladies be wanting to order a bottle of wine or by the glass?" Umberto's long black lashes framed his mesmerizing blue-green eyes. A wavy hank of black hair fell over his right eyebrow, giving him a rakish look.

I glanced over at Vannie, who sat on the opposite side of Tillie. "Vannie, are you going to have a glass?"

"I'd better stick to water, since I'm your designated driver. Next time, though, we'll take an Uber." She thumbed through a few pages. "You have some fabulous wines here."

"Thank you. I've enjoyed working directly with California vineyards to get a nice selection for my establishment. It's been a challenge to narrow it down, since there are more than seventeen hundred wineries in Napa Valley alone. My cousin in Italy sources our wine selections on that end and arranges for the bottles to be imported." Umberto filled a water glass with chilled water from a carafe and set it in front of Vannie. "He also runs a wine bar in Florence, and I arrange for the bottles I source here in California to be shipped to him."

He reached over and flipped Vannie's binder to the last page and pointed with his long, slender forefinger. "I have five different nonalcoholic wines you might want to try. They're a little sweeter than traditional wine or sparkling wine, but they're not bad."

"I'll try the sparkling chardonnay, then." Vannie handed him the binder.

"I think we'd better stick to just glasses of wine." I turned to the first page to browse. There were several varietals to choose from, and I decided to try something new. I typically stuck to chardonnay or merlot, and depending on the meal, once in a while, I sipped cabernet sauvignon. "Can you suggest a red wine, light bodied but not overly fruity?"

"I have a nice Paso Robles pinot noir. That's one of my favorites. It's a bit peppery, but it still retains its light body."

"That sounds good. I'll try it." I handed my binder to him, and he brushed his fingers across the back of my hand before he took it. Was he flirting with me, or had it been an accidental touch?

Umberto smiled at Tillie. A dimple appeared in his left cheek. "And for you, miss?"

"I'd like a glass of your Napa Valley sparkling chardonnay. The real stuff, if you please." Tillie beamed up at the sommelier and winked. Pink blushed his olive-tone complexion.

"Would you ladies like to order a cheese plate or any other appetizers?"

"I think we're fine with the wine. We just finished having dinner," I said.

"Then allow me to bring you a small dish of olives from my family's estate in Italy to go with your wine. It's on the house." Before we could reply, Umberto headed to the back, to where I assumed a kitchen was.

"Isn't he handsome?" Tillie fluffed her hair. "And that adorable accent of his."

Vannie twisted in her seat and looked around. "I had no idea this wine bar even existed. From the wine list offered, I'm surprised it's not busier."

Umberto chose that moment to return, and he overheard Vannie's remark. "Thank you for your concern. Tuesdays and Wednesdays are our slow nights. The rest of the time, you'd have to wait for a table."

"I'm glad to hear it. You have a remarkable place." Tillie skewered an olive from the dish he'd placed in front of her.

"I appreciate hearing that and hope you'll visit us again."

Umberto gazed at me as he wiped his hands on a bar towel. "If you give me a moment, I'll bring your wine out."

As soon as the sommelier was out of earshot, Tillie elbowed me. "Get Zara's picture out before he comes back. We need to question him before he gets busy with other customers."

I did as she said, knowing she was right. We might have wasted valuable time talking about wine instead of getting to Zara first.

Umberto returned, carrying a tray with two champagne flutes and a long-stemmed goblet containing my red wine. He carefully placed the glasses down and began talking about the characteristics of Tillie's sparkling wine.

"Young man, let me interrupt your wonderful spiel about this wine, even though I could listen to your delightful accent all day long." Tillie practically batted her eyelashes at him. "We're actually here to see if you know this woman."

I slid Zara's photo across to him.

"Yes, she's come in a few times. Why do you ask?" Umberto wasn't exactly scowling, but he didn't look terribly happy either.

I fiddled with the stem of my wineglass then looked up to meet his gaze. "You see, she, uh, passed away recently. We're trying to track her movements and see if she met with anyone or had an argument with anyone."

"Why are you asking? Are you with the police or something?"

Again with that question. I chose to ignore it. "Unfortunately, I'm the one who found her. I kind of feel a responsibility to find justice for her, since the police haven't made any progress."

That I knew of anyway. But I didn't need to go into that with the sommelier.

He seemed to consider it for a moment. "She was murdered, then. Is that right?"

"That's correct." I took a sip of the wine, waiting to see if Umberto would give us any information about Zara. When he remained silent, I continued, "Did she come in with anyone?"

"No one else. She was always alone."

He'd stated it so matter-of-factly I wondered if perhaps he hadn't been around the last time Zara had visited. I double-checked the notes I'd scribbled with the dates she'd visited. "Were you here a week ago? Last Tuesday evening?"

"Of course. I'm always here." He wiped down the bar with the towel then tossed it beneath the counter.

"And she came in alone and remained alone?"

"Yes. I already told you that." Umberto seemed to think for a moment. "She had two glasses of Temecula Vineyards chardonnay with a cheese plate, and then she switched to Stone River merlot—from the Grass Valley region in Northern California. She ordered a small wood-fired chorizo pizza to go with the red. As soon as she finished, she left."

"You've got a remarkable memory, young man." Tillie raised her bubbling glass of sparkling wine in a salute then took a sip.

"I don't always remember all my customers, but her attitude was one of anger." He shrugged. "She didn't take it out on me or any of my staff or customers. It was just the way she was hunched over her phone, muttering, then slamming the phone down. Plus, with the four glasses of wine she drank in a relatively short time, I worried about her driving. I offered to call a taxi when I brought her bill, but she said she'd already ordered an Uber."

"Thanks for talking to us. We really appreciate it." I slid my credit card over. "You can go ahead and close out our check."

"Of course. And I meant it when I said I hoped you'd come back and try us again." Umberto held my gaze much longer than necessary, and I felt my cheeks warm.

"I'm sure we will," Tillie said. "We'll bring the rest of our posse for a girls' night out."

He took the hint and picked up my card then ran it through the reader at the far end of the counter. When he returned, he handed the card to me and laid a leather case containing the credit card slip on the countertop. "Let me know if you'd like to try anything else."

Once we'd climbed into Vannie's car, I couldn't contain myself any longer. "What a bust. I was certain we'd find another suspect to look into."

"It wasn't a complete bust," Tillie said. "We found a charming wine bar and an equally charming sommelier who seems to find you irresistible."

"Gah. That doesn't help with our investigation." I buckled my seat belt. "I'm going to have to resort to pestering Detective Hawkins and see if he's made any headway in finding a suspect other than Brad and Gabe. I'll call him tomorrow morning."

Chapter 24

I'd just snuggled into bed for the night when Brian called.
"I hope I didn't wake you." Banging pots and pans echoed over the phone. It was clean-up time in Oceana's kitchen. "I meant to call you earlier, but we were slammed tonight."

"It's no problem. I just got into bed." I switched my bedside lamp on and propped myself up on pillows. "That's good you had another busy night."

"It definitely is." Brian sighed. "The reason I'm calling is that Theodore stopped by the restaurant a while ago. He was totally blitzed and then got argumentative when I refused to serve him any more alcohol."

"Oh no. That's not good." I wondered if Theodore had complained about me and my murder investigating to his brother.

"He got so bad I made him sit in my office to drink coffee and eat some dinner."

That explained why Brian was talking to me in the noisy kitchen instead of in his relatively quiet office.

"I'm going to have to drive him to David's and make sure he gets safely to bed."

"He's really that bad off?"

"He's in no condition to walk without falling down." Brian uttered a curse. "I'll probably be able to leave here in about thirty minutes. Do you mind if I stay with you once I get Theodore settled? It could be another hour or longer before I get there."

"I'd love for you to stay, and don't worry about how late it might be. I'll be waiting for you." My heart broke for Brian and the unsettling relationship he had with his older brother.

"Thanks. You have no idea how much I appreciate having you in my life."

"Did you call David and let him know where Theodore is?"

"I did as soon as Theodore stumbled into Oceana. He asked me to deal with the situation." Brian blew out a breath. "Is this what it's going to be like for the foreseeable future? I just can't..."

"Give him some time to adjust, Brian. We can talk more, if you want, when you get here."

"Thanks. I gotta go, or I'll never get out of here."

After he disconnected the call, I couldn't help but think about how Theodore had seemed so contrite and humble after returning from his stint at a rehab center in Switzerland. Even though he more than deserved his time in prison after returning to the US, the gains he'd made while in rehab seemed to have been wiped away. I wondered if there was any way Theodore's community service could be postponed until he completed another stint at a rehab program. If he kept up the same behavior he'd displayed this evening, I feared he'd tear his family apart and break their hearts all over again.

Brian stumbled in around one thirty in the morning. Exhausted, he didn't want to talk, and it didn't take long for him to fall into a deep sleep. I, on the other hand, tossed and turned while my mind went over and over every single clue that might point to a new suspect. It was no use. I couldn't find a connection between Zara's murder and anyone besides Gabe and Brad.

My phone chirped with a text and woke me from an unsettled slumber. Brian and the dogs were gone, hopefully out for a restorative run. I checked the screen to see it was already seven thirty. Brian had sent me a text at seven, letting me know he and the dogs were already at Tillie's. He'd keep breakfast warm for me. The new text that had woken me was from Brad.

Gabe's been commanded to meet Det Hawkins at PD for formal interview this a.m. Please tell me u found evidence someone else killed her!!!!

Brad had included several teary-eye emojis.

I immediately called him.

Brad jumped in without a hello or anything. "Please tell me you've found out something new. This is getting unbearable."

"I'm so sorry. I haven't found much of anything that leads to a new suspect. Whoever did it covered their tracks well."

"I don't want to hear that, Em." Brad's voice took on a whining tone. "Gabe didn't do it, and there's no way someone else could've been that invisible. He's out there somewhere."

"There are a couple things I found out, but they really don't provide any evidence. Nina from your tux shop was arguing with Zara just a few days before the murder. I'll call Detective Hawkins this morning, even though I'm sure it'll pan out to be nothing."

"You can tell him, but it won't do any good. Nina has a rock-solid alibi for the time of the murder."

"How'd you find that out?" My heart sank. Nina was the only other suspect I'd managed to come up with.

"One of Gabe's buddies is feeding him bits of information on the investigation. Turns out Nina was at a concert at the Hollywood Bowl with her sister and eight other women. Afterward, they went out for dessert, and then she spent the night at her sister's up in LA." Brad groaned. "What else have you got?"

"Well…"

"C'mon. Throw me a life preserver. I'm drowning here."

"Tillie and I visited the Coffee Klatch down the street from where Zara lived. According to the owner's teenaged granddaughter, some guy was arguing with Zara out in the parking lot last week."

"That's great news. Does the kid know who the man is?"

"No, but don't get too excited." I didn't know how to word it without Brad getting upset. "He, uh, kind of resembles Gabe."

Nothing but silence filled my ear. "Brad? Are you still there?"

"You. Showed. Her. A. Photo. Of. Gabe." He overly enunciated each word. "What are you trying to do? Put another nail in his coffin?"

"Of course not, but I think we can agree that someone is working hard on framing Gabe. It stands to reason that they might take it a step further and have someone disguised as your fiancé interacting or arguing with Zara so people would notice him." I wish I could take back my words. It sounded lame even to me.

"Yeah. Right."

"Brad, I'm so sorry that Gabe's got all this stacked against him. I'm doing my best to find even the tiniest scrap of evidence that might give us a clue who this other person is." I waited a beat. "Just remember the girl definitely said it wasn't Gabe, just someone similar. I'll make sure I pass the information to Detective Hawkins, and maybe it'll be enough to make him back off Gabe for the time being."

Brad's snort of derision made me uneasy. It was time to redirect our conversation.

"Okay, there might be one more thing I can tell you, but I have no idea if this relates to the case or not. Yesterday, I saw a man who looked kind of familiar at the ferry. He freaked when he caught me staring and immediately turned his back on me. There was a young woman with him, but before I could get a good look, he shielded her." I took a breath before I continued. "I got a pic with my phone as they drove by, but you really can't tell who he is. So far, no one I've asked recognizes him. Give me a sec, and I'll send it to you."

I attached the photo to a text and sent it off to Brad. "Did you get it?"

"Yep. I'm opening it now."

I waited impatiently. Maybe it was the break we needed, although I knew I was unreasonably getting my hopes up.

"Em. That's the worst pic ever. What were you doing? Running alongside the car while you were taking it?"

"Ha ha. I was trying to hide behind a column so he wouldn't see me. I was blindly pressing the photo button."

"Blindly is right. This guy's features are so blurry he could be anyone."

"I knew it was a long shot."

"Do you have anything else to give me hope?" Brad's voice cracked.

"Again, I have no idea if it's connected, nor do I have any evidence that could even identify the person—"

"That's not going to cut it with the detective. We need proof."

"Let me finish telling you what happened."

"All right. Sorry I interrupted."

"I was out walking the dogs before dinner last night, and we were just getting ready to cross Balboa Boulevard to head home when a black car with no lights on came out from who knows where and almost mowed me down."

"Em! Are you okay?"

"I fell down when I jumped out of the way, but I'm fine. I

didn't even get a scratch."

"Tell me you called the police or Detective Hawkins."

"And tell them what? That I have no idea what make or model the car was, that I have no idea who was driving it, and that I have no idea why someone would have wanted to run me over? They'd laugh and send me on my way."

"Do you think it was connected to your mystery man at the ferry?"

"I have no idea. It could just be a coincidence, except something about that mystery man bugged me." One of these days, I'd have to tell Brad about the bomb the seagull dropped on me while I rode the ferry. He had a juvenile sense of humor and would get a good laugh out of it. But it wasn't the right time.

"I appreciate your trying. I'd hoped for something concrete that we could give the detective so he'd stop looking at Gabe." Brad sighed heavily. "I guess you should tell him about the coffee place and what the kid said."

"I'll do that. However, I'm guessing that maybe the person who tried to hit me with their car thinks I'm getting close to finding out about their involvement in Zara's death. Or is that too much of a reach?"

"What I think is that we're both willing to grasp at straws at this point," he said. "I'd better go check on Gabe. He's having a rough morning."

"Let me know how his interview goes." My heart sank. What if they arrested Gabe?

"I will as long as you let me know the second you find out anything new with the case."

Brad disconnected the call, and I got dressed. Before I left for Tillie's house for breakfast, I called Detective Hawkins. He didn't answer, but I left him a long, drawn-out voice mail. I got cut off midway through, so I called back and finished my ramblings on what I'd found out and ended by giving the address of the Coffee Klatch. It would be in his hands to track down the man who'd been seen arguing with Zara. I didn't bother telling him about the man at the ferry or my close call the night before. There wasn't a thing he could do with that information.

Chapter 25

The smells of waffles and coffee met me when I let myself into Tillie's house. The dogs ran to greet me then flopped onto their backs so I could give them belly rubs. As soon as I stood, they ran back to the kitchen, where, no doubt, Tillie was spoiling them rotten.

Brian kissed me then handed me a cup of coffee made just the way I liked it, with a splash of milk. He had dark circles beneath his eyes, and his hair stood on end, like he'd been running his fingers through it.

"I hope you slept better than I did." Brian gave me a warm waffle with fresh sliced strawberries on top. "I woke up at five and took the dogs for a run, then I've been hanging out over here with Gram and Vannie, until she had to leave for work. I didn't want to wake you after I got in so late."

"I slept okay once I finally fell asleep around two thirty. But you needn't have worried about waking me up. I never even heard you getting up, nor did I hear your text." Before I sat down to eat, I poured more coffee into Tillie's dainty teacup. She preferred to drink it that way instead of using a larger mug. "I talked to Brad this morning."

"Oh? Anything new going on with the boys?" Tillie asked as she added cream to her coffee.

"Gabe was commanded, according to Brad, to formally appear for an interview with Detective Hawkins this morning."

"That can't be good," Brian said. "Have you made any progress in finding any more suspects?"

"Maybe one or two, but their identities are completely unknown. And it's a guess on my part if they're even associated with Zara's death." I wanted to pull my hair out. The last murders I'd been involved with seemed to have too many suspects to weed through. This time, there were pretty much zero, because in my heart of hearts, I knew Gabe didn't do it. Right? No. I couldn't let my mind even consider the possibility. "The only other potential person was the woman who works at the place they got their tuxes. But it turns out she has an ironclad alibi."

"You told the detective what you've found, haven't you?" Brian asked.

"I left him a voice mail, but I haven't heard anything back." Nor did I expect to either.

Tillie twisted the buttercup-yellow linen napkin in her hands. "I know Brian gave you a quick update on Theodore late last night. David called me at six. Theodore borrowed David's Mercedes without asking and took off sometime before then. He hasn't been able to track Theodore's cell phone either."

"You mean he *stole* David's Mercedes." Brian's words were bitter. "It's just like him to come home and wreak havoc on our lives then disappear."

My heart fell. If Theodore had been falling down drunk at one that morning, he wouldn't have been in any condition to drive anytime soon. And if he got caught violating his parole by driving with a suspended license, he'd end up right back in prison, no matter what strings David might try to pull. I had no idea what to say.

Tillie patted my hand. "We're all speechless too."

"I'm not. I've got plenty I'd like to say to him." Brian clenched his fists. "And I'd start by telling him to go crawl back to whatever rock he's been hiding under."

I rose, walked to Brian's side, and wrapped my arms around his waist. "I know he's hurt you, Tillie, and David. But striking back will only hurt you more."

I felt him relax a little, and his body shuddered. When a tear dropped onto my arm, I hugged him even tighter.

"It's not right that he can do this to our family again."

I glanced over at Tillie. She held her napkin to the corner of her eye. I needed to try to help. "I thought of this late last night. Theodore seemed so contrite and humble when he came home from Switzerland. It seems that if David could pull strings to get an early parole for him, he could surely make it possible to get Theodore into rehab before doing his community service hours."

"That's a great suggestion, Emory. I'll call David now." Tillie grabbed her cell phone then left the kitchen.

"I hope he's okay and doesn't do anything reckless that'll put him back in jail." I released Brian and went to grab the tissue box for him.

"I know you're right, but I can't help but be angry with him for hurting Gram like this." He pulled a few from the container, dabbed at his eyes, then sat. "He was even raging about you last night and about Vannie too. I felt powerless trying to protect you both because nothing I said calmed him down."

"I wish I knew what to say to make it better." I sat beside him and placed my head on his shoulder.

He kissed the top of my head. "David is going to have to figure it out. Gram will help, but David's the one who keeps bailing Theodore out of his messes. At this point, I think Theodore expects others to clean up after him and never face any consequences." Brian kissed the top of my head again then stood. "I've got to go home for a change of clothes and get to work. We have the chamber of commerce coming in for a lunch meeting."

"That's good for business but bad for making your day even longer."

"Truer words never spoken." Brian flexed his fingers together, causing his knuckles to crack. "It'll be a good trial run to decide whether we want to expand our hours to include lunch."

My face fell. It had been hard enough when the restaurant started offering Sunday brunch, but if they were open every day for lunch, I'd never see him except in passing. Brian must've sensed my concerns.

"You don't need to worry. If we do, we'll bring a lunch chef on board." He crossed his fingers. "And if we get lucky, I might even be able to have him or her cover a dinner shift every now and then so I get some time off. I've missed you."

"I've missed you too."

"Now, don't you two be getting all mushy." Tillie swept into the room, looking a lot more cheerful than when she'd left. "I know you've got to get to work, Brian, but I thought you'd like to know Theodore's been found. He checked himself into a rehab facility near Palm Springs. Your father will work with the parole officer to see what needs to be done to make this work out."

Brian's shoulders lowered, and his eyes glittered beneath the overhead lights. "That's such a huge relief."

"Yes, it is." Tillie kissed her grandson on his cheek. "Now go to work so Emory can get busy baking her cupcakes."

Chapter 26

Depending on the number of cupcakes I had to bake, I often used Tillie's industrial-size kitchen. With a huge stainless-steel island and full-size double ovens, it was much easier to produce multiple batches at the same time. If I only needed to make one or two dozen cupcakes, I liked spending time in my cozy pool house's kitchen. Because the bake sale order required eight dozen mini cupcakes, two dozen each of vanilla, chocolate, lemon, and pumpkin spice, I needed all the space I could get.

Tillie took the dogs upstairs with her, and I put a dog gate across the entrance to the kitchen. Next, I quickly mopped the floor and disinfected every surface. Even though neither of the dogs shed, I took every precaution to make sure no fluff ended up in my cupcakes. In between bites of my cold waffle and sips of scalding-hot coffee, I got out all the ingredients and chopped the cold butter into small pieces so it would soften quickly.

I started mixing the vanilla cupcakes first. Once they were baking, I could mix the lemon cupcakes in the same bowl without washing it out first. Every shortcut I took would mean time saved. The fragrance of the floral vanilla imbued the air as I mixed the batter. I'd use the seeds from a whole vanilla bean in the buttercream frosting to give it an even stronger punch of vanilla flavor.

With jazzy music playing on my iPhone, I finished baking all four flavors before noon. The tiny cakes sat on wire racks, waiting to be frosted. I'd just put the last sticky dish in the dishwasher when my phone alerted me to a text. It was Brad.

Are u home? I'm at yr door. I need to talk to u.

I hoped he wasn't still mad at me, but then I shivered. Had Gabe been arrested? Was that why Brad had shown up in person instead of texting or calling?

At Tillie's. I'll meet u at gate.

I stepped over the dog fence and rushed to the door. Brad's head peeked over the top of the security gate. He didn't look happy. The second I opened the gate, Brad strode inside and headed for the house. I followed close behind.

"Is everything all right? Did Gabe talk to Detective Hawkins?"

"I need coffee with something strong added to it." Brad picked up his pace and headed to the kitchen.

"Sure. Just watch out for the doggie fence, though. I'm in the middle of baking cupcakes for a school bake sale."

Brad's long legs easily cleared it. I had to use a bit more caution, with my short legs not wanting to stretch that far up.

I poured a mug of coffee and set it in front of him then retrieved Tillie's medicinal bottle of brandy. He poured a few healthy glugs into his hot brew then took a large swallow.

"Better?" I slid a couple extra mini cupcakes onto a napkin and handed them to Brad. "I haven't gotten around to making the buttercream yet."

"These will do just fine." He popped a whole one into his mouth, gave a few chomps, and swallowed.

"Are you ready to talk about what's eating you up?" I took a long look at my best friend. He hadn't shaved for a few days, and the scruff on his face glinted golden red. There were bags beneath his eyes, and when he raised the coffee mug up to his lips, the odor that wafted from his armpits made it apparent he hadn't showered in a couple of days either. I scooted away as inconspicuously as I could.

"I don't even know where to start. My life is falling apart on all fronts." He took another large swallow of coffee then polished off the second mini cupcake. "Let's see. Shall I start with the wedding?"

I nodded, unable to tear my gaze away from him.

"Detective Hawkins released Gabe's grandparents' house on Monday. Did you know that?"

"No. He never called or texted." I berated myself for getting too busy and not following up myself.

"The detective told Gabe. On Monday morning." Brad narrowed his eyes. "Guess how I found out today."

"I don't know, and I'm kind of afraid to ask." I considered pouring myself a shot of brandy to calm my nerves. I'd never, ever seen Brad so worked up.

"I happened to 'accidentally' hear Gabe talking to Colin on the phone this morning." Brad scowled and used his index and middle fingers to form a quote. "I've had to resort to eavesdropping on my fiancé to find out anything. Anyway, he told Colin that the house had been released on Monday but that he wasn't sure we would be using the venue now."

"What the…" My mouth hung open.

"Exactly. As soon as Gabe ended the call, I said the same thing." Brad covered his face with his palms. "He wants to postpone the wedding until the murder is resolved one way or another. And if for some reason he's convicted, he's insisting we break off our relationship."

"Oh, Brad. I'm so, so sorry."

"I tried telling Gabe that I'm a stand-by-your-man type of guy and no matter what happens, I'll remain dedicated to him." He poured more brandy into his mug then abruptly stood and retrieved the coffeepot. He added hot coffee to his mug then refilled mine. "No matter what I said or how I begged, he wouldn't listen to me. All he kept saying was that he wasn't going to be the one to ruin my life."

My eyes stung with the tears that were gathering along my lashes. "There's got to be a way to change his mind."

"I don't think I can, which means we've got to try harder to solve the case."

"How did Gabe's interview with Detective Hawkins go? I'm assuming he met with him this morning." I resisted the urge to add brandy to my coffee and took a sip of the black brew. I knew Brad had to have been really distraught, since he'd forgotten to add milk to my mug.

Brad shrugged. "Gabe wouldn't talk to me about it, but I guess the fact that he hasn't been arrested and locked up means they don't have enough evidence for that yet."

"I left a detailed voice mail for Detective Hawkins about the mysterious man at the Coffee Klatch, but I haven't heard back from him yet. I'll call him in a bit." I caught Brad chewing on his thumbnail and slapped his hand away. "Is there more that's happened to make you so anxious?"

If possible, Brad's face fell even more. "I'm afraid so. This next part is making me angry, hurt, and worried."

I kept still and allowed Brad to collect his thoughts.

"It seems Colin and his sister are flying back from the wine country tomorrow and are dying to get a reservation at Oceana for dinner." Brad rolled his eyes.

I snorted. "It's impossible. They should have made reservations last month."

"Exactly what I told Gabe when he asked me to ask you to get them a table."

I choked on the sip of coffee I'd just taken. "They *what*? They have a lot of nerve. Just tell him or them it's impossible."

"Gabe suspected that's what your response would be, so he

told me, and I quote, 'If you have to get on your knees and beg Emory, then do it for me.'"

"You have got to be kidding." Something was seriously wrong with Colin's sway over Gabe, and I said as much. "These are not the actions of the Gabe I know."

"Exactly. But, Em, given how tenuous things are between Gabe and me, would you please, please call Brian and see if he can fit them in tomorrow night? Pretty please?"

"Oh good galloping gremlins." I handed Brad another napkin when he snorted coffee from his nose.

"Ouch. Why did you have to make me laugh when I had a huge mouthful of coffee?" Brad went to the sink and tried to wash the coffee stains from his T-shirt. "Where in the heck did galloping gremlins come from? That's hysterical."

"From Detective Hawkins. And sorry, I wasn't paying attention to you when I said it." I retrieved a clean dish towel from a drawer and handed it to him. "Let me call Brian and see what he can finagle. It's just a table for two?"

Brad slowly dried his hands, his gaze lowered to the floor. A flush crept up his neck. "It's a table for three. Gabe's invited. I am not."

"No way! Uh-uh, I will not let Colin or Gabe treat you that way. They can find another restaurant, for all I care." I hugged my best friend, remembering not to breathe in, then returned to my seat. "We've got to find out what hold Colin has over Gabe. He'd never treat you like this in a million years if something weren't terribly wrong."

"At this point, I'm willing to do whatever it takes to make Gabe happy and take his mind off the investigation. Even if it excludes me."

"You kids, there's an easy solution to this." Tillie slid the doggie gate aside, stepped into the kitchen, then closed the gate. Piper and Missy plopped down on the floor and pressed their noses between the slats of the gate.

"Ugh. You heard me talking about the disaster my life has become?" Brad gave Tillie a peck on her cheek.

"Poor boy. I have to agree that something is going on with the way Colin is trying to kick you out of Gabe's life." She took two steps away from him. "But I have a plan that we'll discuss just as soon as you take a shower."

Chapter 27

B rad, freshly showered, shaved, and wearing a pair of Brian's clean sweatpants and one of his T-shirts, leaned toward my phone, as did Tillie.

Brian, sounding a bit tinny on the speakerphone, was clearly exasperated. "You want me to do what, Gram?"

"We need to indispose Colin and get him out of the way for a couple of days until we can find out what he's holding over Gabe's head." Tillie pushed up the volume on the phone.

"I get that Colin is insisting that I get them a table for dinner tomorrow night, and I've already promised you I'd rearrange the dining room and stick another table next to the kitchen, but..." Brian coughed and cleared his throat. "You cannot be serious about me adding a laxative to his food."

"Whyever not?" Tillie swiveled her lips to one side. "It seems like a foolproof plan. What could go wrong?"

"Oh, I don't know." There was no mistaking Brian's sarcasm. "Maybe a one-star rating on Yelp for food poisoning? Or maybe an employee sees me and decides to complain to the health department?"

"You're overreacting, Brian," Tillie chided him. "He'd never be able to prove it was your food if we all ate the same thing. Set up a prix fixe dinner for our group. Colin won't be able to blame your food, since the rest of us won't be sick."

"What's with this 'we' business?" I asked.

"You don't think we'd let this Colin person shut Brad out, do you? And naturally, you and I will have to join him to make sure Colin doesn't chase Brad out of Oceana." Tillie patted my cheek. "Trust me. You and I are going to set this right."

"Gram, you are one devious character." Brian chuckled. "But I will not be a part of the laxative business. If you want to drop something into his drink or somehow get him to ingest it otherwise, be my guest. I just don't want to know about it."

"You're no fun." Tillie stuck her tongue out at the phone, even though Brian wouldn't be able to see her. "I'll have the medication in my purse, should you change your mind. All you need to do is serve something spicy with a thick sauce, like shrimp diablo. He'll never detect the ground-up pills in something like that."

"I won't be changing my mind. Tell me again how many will be coming for dinner tomorrow."

"There will be six of us, and expect Emory, Brad, and me at seven fifteen. The rest of them will be there at seven thirty," Tillie said.

"Gram, you're killing me. Let's make the reservations for eight forty-five, since that's the tail end of my second seating."

"That'll be fine, Brian. If Colin or Gabe want to complain, they can go eat hamburgers at McDonald's, for all I care," Brad said. "I want you to know how much I appreciate your doing this for me."

"You got it, bro. I wouldn't do this for anyone I didn't consider family." A chime sounded. "I've got to run, but I'm assuming you'll trust me to come up with the prix fixe menu without running it by you?"

"Anything you want to serve is fine with us." I picked up the phone and turned it off as soon as Brian disconnected.

"See how easy that was?" Tillie rubbed her hands

together. "If my grandson won't put laxatives in Colin's food, I'll have to think up another means to get him out of the way for a couple of days."

"I don't know, Tillie. He might think we're trying to poison him." Brad pondered for a moment. "I think I'll have my hacker do a deep dive on him, and maybe there's something in his past I can threaten to expose if he doesn't back off."

"Ooohhh, blackmail is always a good idea." Tillie leaned into Brad and lowered her voice. "Can I go watch your hacker at work?"

"Sorry, Tillie, but he'd like to remain anonymous, aside from me." Brad glanced my way. "And Em."

"Spoilsport, but no matter. At least we have a plan, and hopefully you won't be so stressed." She looked deep in thought. "You know, you should tell Gabe the reservations are for their group of three at eight forty-five. Then you, Emory, and I can meet at eight thirty and be sitting at the table already. That'll catch them off guard and won't give this Colin person an opportunity to ditch us and spirit Gabe away to somewhere else."

"Yeah, that's a good plan." Brad rubbed the back of his neck. "I think that's exactly what Colin would do if he suspected I was going to crash his dinner with Gabe."

The mini cupcakes sitting on the counter reminded me I still needed to whip up buttercream and frost them. But my stomach growled, reminding me it was past lunchtime. "Can I make us quesadillas for lunch before I get back to my cupcake order?"

"That would be great. I'll take the dogs for a quick walk while you make them. I'll call Ethan while I'm out." Brad stepped over the gate, where Piper and Missy pranced around. They'd jumped up at the word *walk*. He knew where their leashes were and where the dogs liked to sniff most.

"That sounds good." Tillie sat back down and eyed the

brandy bottle. "Brad is sure wound up. I hope we can help him."

"Me too." I chuckled. "Thanks for getting him to take a shower. I was a bit worried for my cupcakes and my olfactory senses."

"You're welcome, dear. Sometimes it's useful being an old biddy."

"You are not an old biddy, and I forbid you from ever saying that again." I grated the cheddar and jack cheese blend. "Should we have included Vannie in our dinner tomorrow?"

"I don't think it's necessary, and with the drama that's sure to unfold, she'll probably be most grateful that she got to stay out of it."

Tillie began playing a game of Candy Crush on her phone, and I quickly layered the filling into burrito-sized flour tortillas and placed them on a hot griddle. By the time Brad returned, with tired pups trailing behind him, the quesadillas had cooled to warm instead of molten-lava hot. With sides of guacamole, sour cream, and salsa, we demolished lunch. Brad swiped another two cupcakes and headed home, while Tillie said she needed to head upstairs and finish the book she was reading.

I'd just turned the mixer onto high to whip the double batch of vanilla buttercream—I'd use it to frost the vanilla cupcakes and then add some cinnamon to the remaining buttercream to pipe onto the pumpkin spice cupcakes—when my phone rang. It was Detective Hawkins.

I stopped the mixer and answered. "Hi, Detective. I'm assuming you got my voice mail?"

"I did receive your two voice mails and wanted to let you know that I followed up with the owner of the Coffee Klatch and her granddaughter."

"Did you find out who the man was?" I tapped my foot, hoping for an affirmative answer.

"Until proven otherwise, I'm afraid it appears it was Gabe. The girl admitted she didn't really get a good-enough look at his face, which is why she was mistaken about another person."

My stomach dropped, and the quesadilla felt like a lump of lead. "That's... unfortunate."

"Yes, it is." He waited a few beats then continued. "I understand you have something else to tell me?"

"Oh?" I wondered what he'd heard and who he'd heard it from.

"You didn't think it important to tell me that someone tried to run you down?" His voice was stern and carried a hint of exasperation.

"I never saw the driver, nor did I catch the make of the car, so it didn't seem useful to inform you. For all I know, it was a misfortunate happenstance and they just didn't see me as they drove by."

"We could have searched camera footage from businesses in the area to see if they caught anything." He sighed. "We might still be able to do so, but right after it happened would have been so much easier."

"I never thought of that. With it being dark and the car not having lights on, I didn't think anyone else would see enough to get a good description."

"Now tell me about the man you saw at the ferry. I hear you were able to get a photo of him."

"It's a really blurry photo, and honestly, you won't be able to tell if it looks like anyone of interest." I had to assume it had been Gabe who told the detective about my misadventures. If Brad had done so, he would have warned me. Wouldn't he? "I'll send it to you right now, if you still want it."

"Yes. Go ahead and text it to me."

I quickly opened the text app, attached the photo, and sent it. "It's on its way."

"Describe the man for me, and explain the circumstances in which you saw him."

I quickly did so. There wasn't all that much to tell.

"Hmm. I just looked at the photo. You're right. It's worthless." The detective chuckled. "Thanks for trying, though."

"While I have you on the phone, can you tell me if you've found any new evidence that will exonerate Gabe and Brad?"

"You know I can't divulge what I have."

"But you have to know they're both innocent and someone went out of their way to implicate Gabe."

"My investigation isn't over, Emory. You should know that I'm doing everything in my power to follow leads and make sure the right person is brought to justice." He sighed. "You're going to have to trust me, and I'm going to have to trust you to bring any tiny little shred of potential evidence to me, no matter whether you think it's connected to the case or not. Can I count on your doing that?"

"Yes. I won't downplay anything, especially if there's another incident like with the black car."

"That reminds me. Text me the street and cross street of where it happened along with the date and the time. I'll see if any businesses in the vicinity have cameras. Maybe we'll get lucky."

I looked at my unfrosted cupcakes and the clock that reminded me I was running out of time to get my delivery done. "I'm not sure I know the exact time it happened, but I'll send my best guestimate in a little while. I'm kind of in the middle of trying to frost eight dozen cupcakes and get them delivered this afternoon."

"Fine. As long as you get that information to me before close of business today."

The second the detective disconnected, I sprang over to the mixer and pushed the power lever to high. Ten minutes later, I had a bulging piping bag of buttercream fitted with a medium-sized star tip and began piping mounds of frosting onto the little cakes. I added coarse sparkling white sugar to the tops of the vanilla swirls to add a glittery effect. The pumpkin spice cupcakes would each receive an orange candy pumpkin nestled on top of the cinnamon frosting; the lemon cupcakes would have a small wedge of lemon jelly fruit slice tucked into lemony frosting; and the chocolate cupcakes would get a generous amount of chocolate sprinkles to accent the chocolate frosting.

While the lemon frosting whipped into a light and creamy confection, I thought back to the evening before, when the car had almost struck me. With everything going on, it seemed like it had happened a week ago rather than less than twenty-four hours ago. The sun had been setting when I left the house with the dogs, and by the time we turned around to head back, it was twilight. My best guess was that it was somewhere between five and five fifteen, and I hoped the detective could work with it.

I quickly sent Detective Hawkins a text then switched off the mixer and went to work on the lemon cupcakes. I'd almost completed frosting the two dozen when he sent a thumbs-up emoji, acknowledging receipt. I wasn't about to hold my breath and hope something came of it. I knew better than that.

Chapter 28

During the drive to deliver the mini cupcakes, I'd mulled over Gabe's desire to call off the wedding. I'd been negligent in following up with all the vendors as I'd waited for the house to be released from the crime scene. I decided that I needed to focus on performing my duties as the best person and the de facto wedding planner and assume the wedding would go forward as planned—at least until Brad told me otherwise.

It was almost five when I pulled into the garage. I sent Tillie a text telling her I wouldn't be joining her and Vannie for dinner and asked that she keep Piper and Missy for the evening.

Her text came almost immediately.

Hot date, cupcake? You're missing carne asada fajitas for dinner. Vannie is happy she'll miss the fireworks at THE dinner tomorrow night.

I thumbed my reply back.

No date. No matter what Gabe says, I'm still planning wedding. Have SO many calls to make to vendors.

When no dots appeared, I climbed from my vehicle and

went inside. I switched on all the lights in the kitchen, dining area, and living room, hoping the cheeriness would lighten my mood. After fixing hot tea, I opened the wedding planning binder and began making calls.

I'd just disconnected my call with the florist—who'd promised me that she'd found pale blush rose petals that would complement the cranberry-colored rose petals and boutonnieres as well as my bouquet—when a knock sounded on my door. It was Vannie, and she came bearing a plate of food.

"You're a godsend. I thought I might have to resort to eating cupcakes or cookies for dinner." I took the plate and gave my sister a one-arm hug.

"You know I always make too much when I cook." Vannie stepped into my house. "Can I help you make any calls or do anything to get you organized?"

"I think we're in good shape right now. I just have to call the bakery and the rental company tonight and then tomorrow touch base with the temp agency to confirm the number of house staff I think we'll need."

Vannie sat and brushed a crumb off my table. I just might have been snacking on some chocolate chip cookies earlier. "Do you think Gabe will really go through with his plan to cancel the wedding?"

"Honestly, I'm not sure. I hope we can solve this murder soon so he can relax and enjoy what's supposed to be the happiest time of his life."

"Brad has got to be devastated."

"He is." I wasn't sure I should share Brad's embarrassing lack of personal hygiene, but it would give Vannie an idea of how low he was. "He's day drinking and even neglected show-ering, shaving, and who knows what. Tillie told him in no uncertain terms to go shower, and I gave him some of Brian's clean clothes to change into."

"Poor guy. I'll let you get back to work, but I wanted to tell you that I want to be useful in helping. Whatever you need me to do, I'll be happy to do it." Vannie stood, and I followed suit. She gave me a long hug. "Good luck at your dinner tomorrow. I'm glad to be missing that one."

Once Vannie departed, I devoured the fajita along with the rice and beans on the plate. Eyeing the clock, I realized I'd missed my window of opportunity to call the bakery by twenty minutes. I'd try them in the morning. I lucked out and found the manager still working at the rental place. It took twenty minutes to go over all the details and confirm I'd meet them at the venue the Friday after Thanksgiving at noon.

"Did you hear that there might be a rain storm coming in around Thanksgiving?" the manager asked.

"No! It can't be." I shuddered, wondering how we'd manage all the guests if we had to move the wedding and reception indoors. "The Santa Ana winds always blow on Thanksgiving, so it's warm enough to barbecue and eat outdoors."

"I hear you. I'm not sure when I last ate roast turkey. We always barbecue it on the grill with lots of limes, jalapeños, and cilantro to season it."

"Yum. I want your recipe!"

"I'll email a copy to you. But back to the rain forecast. I'd suggest renting a tent that will cover a good portion of the backyard. We can set it up so that guests can enter the tent directly from the outdoor room, accessible via the media room and the retractable sliding doors."

"That's a good plan. And if the weather cooperates, we won't set up the tent." I wondered how much the tent would cost but then ignored my inclination to worry about money. Brad and Gabe had told me from the beginning of taking over the planning that money was no object. Better to be prepared than have a hundred soaked guests.

"Exactly. What I'll need from you by tomorrow are the dimensions of the backyard. As soon as I have that, I can let you know what the fee will be." Computer keys clacked over the phone. "I'll track down the right size of tent when I hear from you and will have it delivered by our set-up date."

I made a note on my pad of paper to rope Brad into going to the house with me the following morning. "Thanks. You're a lifesaver, especially if it ends up raining."

I immediately sent Brad a text, telling him we had to visit the grandparents' house the following morning, and asked what time he'd be free to go. The screen remained black, and I didn't receive a response.

Putting the planning binder aside, I decided I'd better start working on Oceana's standing order of six dozen cupcakes that I delivered every Thursday afternoon, since I had to visit the wedding venue in the morning. This week, Brian and I had settled on pumpkin pie cupcakes, which were basic pumpkin spice cupcakes, but with stabilized whipped cream instead of frosting, and for the garnish, small pumpkin cut-outs made from pie dough along with cinnamon and sugar.

For the following week, Brian asked me to deliver twelve dozen mini cranberry cupcakes for the restaurant's Thanksgiving dessert buffet table. I'd also make extra to serve for our own Thanksgiving dessert hosted by Tillie. I'd have to get the cupcakes to Brian by Wednesday afternoon, so I made a calendar reminder to start them on Tuesday. Between investigating a murder, Thanksgiving brunch and dinner, the wedding, and cupcake obligations, I wondered if I'd ever have a chance to sleep.

Chapter 29

I t was nearly midnight by the time I'd stored the cooled cupcakes, cleaned up the kitchen, and tumbled into bed. I feared I probably had some sticky batter left on my skin somewhere I couldn't see, but I was too exhausted to care. Sleep had finally claimed me, and I was dreaming of mounds of whipped cream snow when my phone rang.

I shoved off the covers and snatched the phone off the nightstand. When I squinted at the screen with bleary eyes, Brad's name finally came into focus.

"What time is it?" I fumbled with the bedside lamp and toggled it on.

"Oh, sorry. Did I wake you?" Brad's voice was jittery.

"Uh, yeah. It's the middle of the night. I think." I flopped back onto my pillow.

"It's one. But I have something important to tell you."

"And it couldn't wait until tomorrow morning? Hey, you never answered my text about going to the grandparents' house."

"Okay. Nine."

"Nine what?" My sleep-deprived brain wasn't keeping up with Brad. "How much coffee have you had tonight?"

"Too much, but that's not the point." He chuckled. "I'll slow down so you can keep up. How about I pick you up at nine to go to the house if it's important."

"Of course it's important. Otherwise, I wouldn't have said we needed to go. We have to measure for a tent."

Crickets....

"Uh, Brad? Did you hear me?"

"Yeah, I heard you. Did you fall back to sleep and start dreaming? I thought you said something about a tent. This is a wedding. Not a campout."

"No, I'm not sleeping. If you'd paid any attention to the weather forecast, you'd know it's supposed to rain next week. The tent is to cover the backyard so your guests don't get soaked." Not that I'd been paying attention to the forecast either, but I couldn't help but poke him a bit. After all, he'd woken me up at one in the morning. "Enough about that. Why in the heck did you wake me up, and why are you so hyper?"

"Oh, that. I guess you threw me off track."

"Argh... Just spit it out already, or let me go back to sleep."

"Sorry. I just got a text from Gabe and got distracted."

"You're not home?"

"No. I'm at my office with Ethan. I'm kind of not on speaking terms with my fiancé right now, if you must know, so I'm hiding out here."

Maybe I should cancel the tent. The way things were heading, there wouldn't be a wedding. "I'm assuming you called me because Ethan found something. Should I assume it has something to do with Colin?"

"Bingo!" Brad's enthusiastic exclamation made me jump.

"It must be a bombshell for you to be so excited." My tone was much less enthusiastic. "Again, I have to ask, couldn't it have waited until the morning to share with me?"

"I'm a little overcaffeinated, if you haven't been able to tell. I had to talk to someone, since Ethan's heading out soon."

"I hope he's well paid," I said dryly.

"Naturally, and he'll get a big bonus from me for doing off-the-books research."

"I wouldn't expect less from you." I sat up. "Spill it, Brad. What did Ethan find out, so I can go back to sleep?"

"You know Colin and Gabe were roommates back in college." He blew out a breath. "I'm not sure what to do with this information, because it could impact Gabe too."

"I'm not kidding. Stop ramping up the suspense and spill it, Ruller."

"Okay, okay. Back when Gabe and Colin were nineteen, they got into a single-car accident. Both were over the legal blood-alcohol level of point zero eight, which doesn't really matter because they weren't of legal drinking age anyway."

"Oh no! Was anyone hurt?"

"Colin's seventeen-year-old sister, Paityn, was in the car, even more intoxicated than they were, and she ended up with a broken arm."

I moved to sit on the edge of the bed. "Don't tell me Gabe was driving and Colin is still guilting him over injuring his sister."

"It's much worse." A hint of fatigue, or it could have been resignation, tinged Brad's voice. "You need to understand that all these records and interviews are buried deep. It's taken Ethan hours upon hours to uncover them."

"Go on."

"Some of the witnesses who'd attended the party said it was Colin driving when they left. Unfortunately, just as many said it was Gabe. When emergency responders arrived at the scene of the crash, it was Colin behind the wheel."

"So maybe they pulled over somewhere and switched drivers before that."

"Paityn told the police that it was Gabe driving and not her brother. But she was way, way blitzed, and Colin told authorities she was mistaken. Apparently, most of the party attendees were unreliable witnesses because of the illicit drugs and booze consumed." He coughed. "Colin's family are ultra-wealthy—they make Gabe's family look like paupers—plus, they have connections. His father was able to get the incident buried with no repercussions for Colin. It's like it never happened, and none of them were even charged with under-aged drinking."

"It makes sense that if Colin covered for Gabe's accident, then Gabe would forever be in his debt."

"Exactly. Ethan also uncovered several photos from that time period." He hesitated. "I know it was a long time ago, and I was far from his first relationship, but from all appearances, it looks as if Gabe was involved with Colin's sister."

"I wouldn't read too much into that. They were kids, and it obviously didn't last long." Weariness overcame me, so I lay back down.

"But why, after all these years, would Colin want to drive a wedge between me and Gabe? His sister couldn't be the one trying to stop the wedding, could she?"

"I highly doubt it." I yawned, and even though I tried to keep it quiet, a squeak escaped. "Look, we're going to have dinner with all three of them tomorrow. We'll be able to judge then whether Paityn has any designs on Gabe."

"You're right."

I yawned again but not so quietly. "Go home to Gabe, and talk to him. Maybe there's nothing to this buried report about the accident, and he might be able to set your mind at ease."

"You know I can't do that. He's going to blow a gasket if he finds out I paid my hacker to look into his past and then dug up something that might cost him his career."

Brad had a good point.

"Well, go home anyway. You don't need to deepen the divide between the two of you. Show him your support and care, and let him know you've got his back. We'll see Colin and Paityn tomorrow night, and we'll figure out what their endgame is."

Long after Brad ended the call, after promising he'd go home and pretend he knew nothing of Gabe's past, I stared at the ceiling. Colin was definitely up to something, but no matter how many scenarios I hashed over, I couldn't figure it out. I'd do anything to protect my best friend. Colin would soon find out he was no match for me and my family.

Chapter 30

A morose Brad parked in front of the grandparents' house. I'd questioned him on the drive over about how it had gone with Gabe that morning. Most of his answers were monosyllabic, but from what I gathered, Gabe was picking Colin and Paityn up from the airport and then spending the day with them. Brad had told Gabe he was spending the day with me and Tillie and not to expect him home until late that night or maybe not until the following day. I'd done my best to try to get him out of his mood but to no avail. I couldn't blame him for feeling miserable anyway.

We both stared at the house with trepidation. After finding out the crime scene team had released the house, I should have immediately called in a cleaning crew to scour the home. I shuddered to think what we might find in there. I pulled out my phone and tapped through my contacts.

"Who are you calling?" Brad asked.

"I forgot to call the cleaning crew yesterday. They specialize in crime scene cleanup."

The phone rang, and a friendly voice answered and told me to leave a message after the beep. I did with a plea to schedule a team as quickly as possible because a wedding was going to take place in the home soon. I put the phone back into my purse.

"Let's get this over with, shall we?" Brad opened his car door.

"You've got the measuring tape, right?" I checked to make sure I had a pad of paper and a pen in my purse to jot down the measurements.

"It's right here in my pocket." He patted his hooded sweatshirt. The morning had turned chilly, and a cold breeze blew off the nearby ocean.

"All right. Let's do this, then." I hopped out of the car and headed for the front door. When I reached the entrance, I spun around to face Brad. "Maybe we should go through the side gate. We only need the backyard measurements."

"It'll be okay, Em. We need to see if there's any damage, and if there is, we need to figure out what needs to be done to repair it."

"I hate when you're right." I batted his arm then stepped aside so he could unlock the door.

The house was dim and had a musty, unpleasant odor. Black powder clung to the inside door handle, dead bolt, and doorframe. We walked down the hallway and found the alarm panel coated with the same black powder. It was messy but wouldn't be difficult to clean up. As we surveyed each room, I made notes on my pad of paper to pass on to the cleaning service. I purposely steered clear of the scene of the crime, determined to make that the last stop before we visited the backyard. Nothing seemed amiss in the rest of the house, aside from general dust and a few cobwebs.

"This shouldn't take too long for the service to clean up." I tapped the pen on the pad.

"You're overlooking the obvious." Brad pulled me toward the great room.

"What's that?" I hesitated long enough that he tugged even harder on my arm.

"This is marble flooring. It's super porous, and well, with the, uh, blood pooling on the surface, I'm not sure it will come clean."

Of course it was real marble and not an easy-to-care-for printed ceramic tile. "That's not good. Do Gabe's grandparents have any extra tiles, perhaps in the garage, that can replace the stained ones?"

"Even if they do, that process isn't without its own issues." Brad tugged on me again when I stopped walking. "Worst-case scenario, we can get rugs to lay over the stain and decide on a more permanent solution after the holidays."

"I have a feeling Gabe's family isn't going to be happy about this."

"You've got that right." Brad cautiously approached the corner that led to the wet bar. "Are we ready for this?"

"No."

"Too bad. We've got to ascertain the damage." He tugged on my arm again and pulled me into the crime scene area.

Even though I could see the smudges of black powder, my gaze fixated on the dried puddle of blood. I'd heard somewhere that head wounds bled a lot, and the scene before me bore that out. If the stain didn't come out, then they'd need to replace at least four large tiles. My head felt a little woozy. Brad must've noticed, because he wrapped his arm around my waist.

"I think we've seen enough. Let's go outside and get some fresh air." He led me to the glass wall and hit a button hidden behind draperies that framed the glass. The glass began retracting until it disappeared into a pocket cleverly designed inside the supporting wall. The open doorway, around twelve feet wide, led onto the covered outdoor living space and out to the spacious backyard.

I gulped in some fresh air then walked to the middle of the yard, which was thick with lush green grass. Obviously, Gabe's grandparents didn't worry about water conservation or the drought conditions that constantly plagued California.

When Brad came to stand next to me, I pointed at the upstairs master bedroom's balcony, which had been built on top of the outdoor living area's roof. "I'd planned on positioning the string quartet up there to play while people arrive before the ceremony and then right after, until we sit for dinner. But if it rains, I think we can make space and have them sit next to the outdoor room fireplace."

"That should work. They'll be a little cramped, but at least they'll be dry."

"Good." I surveyed the yard. "Let's measure the grass area. I think we should leave the patio area by the pool uncovered for smokers or for anyone who needs a breath of fresh air after imbibing or dancing too much. Maybe we should set up cocktail tables with over-large umbrellas for protection from the elements."

"Another great idea." Brad took the tape measure and began extending it.

I jotted more notes on my pad.

"You should have told me we needed a hundred-foot tape measurer. This is only twelve feet." Brad began dragging the extended metal strip across the lawn. "This won't be very accurate."

"I'll help. Besides, if we're off a few inches, I doubt it'll matter."

"As long as we don't destroy the flower beds. Gabe and I were duly notified that it wouldn't be tolerated by his grandmother."

I looked at the planted beds. Lush green plants that looked mature and thriving crowded the space between the house and the grass. Even in the middle of November, several varieties were flowering in shades of orange, yellow, and burgundy.

"Then we'll measure twice and then reduce the tent size by a foot on all sides. Will that work?"

"It'll have to." Brad held out the end of the tape measure to me, and I grabbed it and walked over and stood a foot from the edge of the flower beds.

When we finished, I sat down on one of the patio chairs. "I should have brought something to drink. That wasn't the easiest thing to do."

"Want me to check the kitchen and see what I can find?"

"I'll be fine." I studied the back of the house and envisioned the layout of the tent. "From my calculations, we should easily be able to set up the ten table rounds with ten chairs at each with a sweetheart table for you and Gabe. There'll still be room to place the wood dance floor at one end of the tent, and we can position the arbor there for the ceremony. I know it won't be as traditional as rows of chairs for the ceremony, but I don't know what to do with the guests when we need to set up the tables and chairs for dinner."

"You should know by now that we don't stand on tradition. Do whatever makes the most sense."

I made a quick sketch in my notepad of how I thought the layout made the most sense. I'd make a better sketch later and give it to the rental company. "I think it would be best if you and Gabe stayed upstairs while the guests arrive, and then when everyone's seated you can come down the stairs, in through the great room, and make your way to the arbor."

"Should we skip the flower petals, since it'll basically be indoors now? I'd hate for them to get tracked into the house."

I thought about how disappointed my nieces would be if they couldn't toss the petals for the grooms. "I think it should still work. Nothing's changing except that the outdoor area will be covered. Maybe I can conscript Brian and Thomas into rolling up the runner after the recession. That'll capture most of the petals and keep them out of the house."

"Em?"

"Brad?"

"Why am I torturing myself by going through this?" He flung his arm out to encompass the house. "Maybe I need to ask Gabe to tell me once and for all if he wants to cancel the wedding. And if so, then let's end it. This not knowing is killing me."

I clasped my friend's hand. "Give it a few more days. I have a feeling we're closing in on finding the truth on who killed Zara. And once that stress isn't hanging over Gabe's head, we can find a way to deal with Colin. Agreed?"

"I don't exactly agree, but I guess we can see how dinner goes with Colin and his sister tonight."

For Brad's sake, I hoped Gabe didn't side with Colin and blow up when we crashed their dinner party.

Chapter 31

"I feel like a penguin," Brad complained as I tied the red silk tie around his neck. "This is Southern California. People don't dress for dinner."

"You look dashing." Tillie swatted Brad's hand down when he tried to loosen the knot. I'd spent way too much time trying to get it perfect. "You'll make quite the impression on your young man when he sees you. Even Emory is dressed nice so as not to embarrass you."

I harrumphed. It had been Tillie's idea to dress as formally as we could. She, naturally, had a closet full of designer dresses and knit suits. If I wasn't mistaking the label, she'd chosen a vintage Chanel number for the evening. The black knit two-piece dress was trimmed with cream-colored lace down the front of the bodice and the sleeves. She'd completed the look with sheer black stockings and heels.

Not knowing if the wedding would go forward, I decided to get some wear out of the dress I'd planned for Brad's big day. My mother would be horrified, but since Brad didn't care, I didn't either. I refused, though, to stuff myself into panty hose. Brad was right. It was Southern California, and close to half the guests at Oceana would be wearing resort casual.

During the summer months, more than half would be in shorts and flip-flops, which was more Brad's and my style. I'd conceded on footwear, though, and had forced my feet into open-toed sling-back heels. The salty hot dogs from a beach stand that Brad and I had consumed for lunch hadn't done my ankles or feet any favors. They were swollen, thanks to water retention.

"Hurry up, you two. We want to be seated at the table before the crew arrives." Tillie handed me her trademark lipstick. "You really should carry some in your purse, Emory."

"Why? You're always there when I need it." I smiled and blew her a kiss, which she caught.

"Why are we doing this? It's going to be a disaster." Brad's shoulders drooped. "Gabe doesn't care if I'm dressed in a suit."

"Think of it as a power play. Outshine Colin, and let him know you're not giving up on Gabe without a fight." Tillie hooked her hand through Brad's arm. "It's time to face the enemy, so forward march."

"Have you been watching the history channel again?" Brad asked.

"You know it, sweetie pie."

I followed the pair to where Andrew waited with the car. I told Brad to sit in back with Tillie, and I took the front with Andrew. Brad needed to be distracted from what we were heading to, and Tillie was the best person for it.

When we arrived at Oceana, Brad seemed a bit less stressed. Tillie had kept us thoroughly entertained with stories of her youth. She'd been quite the card when young, but it saddened me that her husband had tried to stamp out her independent spirit. At least she was getting to live large in her later years.

The maître d' knew Tillie and me on sight but kept his tone formal when he welcomed us. He led us through the tables, where guests chattered away while dining on sumptuous food. Not one table or chair was empty. How Brian had managed to fit in another circular table for six was beyond me, but I was grateful nonetheless. We took the three chairs that faced the front of the restaurant.

"Mrs. Skyler and Ms. Martinez, I hope the meal meets with your and your guests' expectations. Chef will be with you as soon as the remainder of your party arrives." He turned to leave but then swiveled to face us again. "He's ordered a bottle of champagne for the table. The server will bring it momentarily."

"Thank you, Pete," Tillie said. As soon as the maître d' was out of earshot, she leaned across Brad, toward me. "Quick. Let's change seats so Brad is sitting on the end. That way, Gabe can sit next to him."

I jumped up to swap seats with Brad, who'd sandwiched himself between us.

"What if he won't sit next to me? I'll be utterly horrified." Brad tugged at his tie.

"You know that's not going to happen. There's no way Gabe will try to humiliate you in public." I crossed my fingers, hoping I was right.

The server, Tracey My, brought the champagne and an ice bucket and set it up next to the table. "Thanks for joining us, Mrs. Skyler, Emory, and Brad. I'll be your server tonight."

"Hi, Tracey. I am so glad to see you're assisting us tonight," I said as I extended my hand for a fist bump, which she obliged.

I'd met Tracey on numerous occasions, both at the restaurant and at Oceana's employee social events that she and Brian set up quarterly. I really enjoyed her wicked sense of humor when customers weren't around. When the restaurant was open, she was nothing but professional, and the customers all seemed to appreciate her friendly service. As Brian's most seasoned and long-term employee, she was in charge of all the waitstaff and helped Brian come up with different ways to keep the employees happy, like the social events. She'd managed to put together a great crew and retained the employees instead of having a high turnover, as usually happened in the restaurant business.

In her mid-thirties, Tracey was extremely fit, thanks to her constant training for marathons. Her short-cropped black hair highlighted her piercing blue eyes, and a diamond nose stud glittered beneath the lighting. With deft experience, she poured some champagne into a flute and handed it to Tillie. Once Tillie declared it delicious, she filled all three flutes without spilling a drop and handed us each one.

"Brian filled me in on some of the issues that you might be facing with your other guests. Let me know if there's anything I can do to make the dinner successful." Tracey nestled the bottle back in the ice bucket.

"Thank you, Tracey." Tillie nodded toward Brad. "We're not exactly sure what we'll face, but perhaps making sure the libations are plentiful will help smooth things over."

"You can count on me, Mrs. Skyler. I'll be back to check on you in a few minutes."

As soon as Tracey left the table, Tillie raised her glass and clinked it with Brad's glass. "To happier days."

I agreed and took a sip. We'd no sooner put our flutes back onto the table when the front door opened, and in walked Gabe, Colin, and Paityn. Or at least, that was who I assumed they were, since I'd never met either of them.

Gabe looked washed out and dejected. He wore blue jeans that had seen better times with a faded flannel shirt. And from the look of the scruff that grew on his cheeks and chin, he hadn't shaved for several days. Even with his shoulders hunched over and his gaze fixed downward, the bruises from his attacker were visible. Not once did he look around as they followed the maître d'.

"He doesn't look well," Tillie said.

"I know. It's breaking my heart." Brad clasped my hand and held it tight.

Colin, on the other hand, look self-assured and almost cocky. His dark-brown hair swooped over his brow, and he casually brushed it back with a flick of his wrist. He wore a light-blue button-down long-sleeve shirt with black slacks.

Paityn had long, flowing dark-blonde hair that she'd styled into tousled waves—the kind of style that deceived a person into thinking no effort has been made when in actuality, a considerable amount of time and product had been used. She wore a skimpy black halter dress that showed off her well-toned arms and legs. As they neared, I could see she wore four-inch red stilettos that made her close to her brother's height of about six feet.

The maître d' stopped in front of our table. "Please have a seat, and the server will be with you shortly to take your drink order."

It was then that Colin noticed us. "No way. We're not sitting here. I demand you take us to another table."

"I'm sorry, sir, but this is the only table available."

"This is outrageous. We had reservations. I'll be letting my Yelp followers know about this." Colin practically pounded his clenched fist into his palm.

"No, sir, you did not have reservations. Our tables have been booked for a full month, and Ms. Martinez was gracious enough to share her table with you." The maître d' held his arm out and swept his palm around the table. "If you'd be so kind as to have a seat, I'll send the server over."

I was relieved that Brian had schooled Pete in the dynamics of our dinner arrangements.

"I demand to speak with the owner." Colin glared at us.

"Thank you, Pete. You may return to your station." Tillie stood and extended her hand. "You're speaking to the owner. I'm Mrs. Skyler, and you're welcome to join us."

I knew Tillie had invested in Brian's restaurant, but I

hadn't realized she was a silent partner. I supposed it shouldn't have surprised me.

"As if." Colin practically spit the words out and ignored Tillie's outstretched hand. "I want to speak to the real owner. Not some hanger-on."

Gabe looked as if he were ready to crawl beneath a rock, and Paityn tried to get her brother's attention. But he was having none of it.

"Is there a problem here?" Brian's voice came out as a low growl.

Colin looked at Brian, who wore his chef's whites. His lip curled into a sneer. "And who are you?"

"Brian Skyler. Owner and chef."

"I should have known you'd be in on this fiasco. We want our own table."

"Then make a reservation, and come back after the first of the year. Which, by the way, is the next availability." Brian flexed his hands. "Now, I suggest you sit down and stop causing a scene, or leave."

Paityn brushed by Brian, and it seemed to me she intentionally wiggled her hips as she did so. She plopped down onto the chair next to Brad. "Colin, I don't care what you do, but I'm staying."

Gabe kept his head lowered but sat next to Tillie. So much for our musical chairs to get Brad and Gabe sitting together. Colin huffed one more time then slithered into the chair between Gabe and Paityn.

Brian glared at Colin, nodded at me and his grandmother, then returned to the kitchen. Thankfully, Tracey chose that moment to appear.

"I'm Tracey My, and I'll be your server tonight. Can I start you off with some cocktails?"

Tillie gestured at the bottle of champagne then focused her gaze on Gabe. "You're more than welcome to share a glass with us."

"No, thank you, Tillie." Gabe rubbed the back of his neck.

Tracey moved to stand at Gabe's shoulder. "And for you, sir?"

He muttered his answer so quietly I wasn't sure how the server heard him.

"Would you prefer still or sparkling?"

"Tap is fine. No ice."

"And for you, ma'am?" Tracey pointed her pen at Paityn.

Paityn didn't look happy about being called ma'am, but she rallied. "I'll have a cosmopolitan but with a double shot of Grey Goose. And a lemon twist instead of a lime."

Colin seemed to pout for a moment, then a smirk appeared on his face. "I'll have your most expensive Scotch. Neat."

"That would be the twenty-five-year Macallan, sir."

Colin tapped his fingers on the snow-white tablecloth. "Fine. Make it a double."

Tracey picked up the bottle of champagne and carefully refilled our flutes. "I'll be right back with your drinks."

From the smirk on Colin's face, I worried he was going to stiff Tillie with the dinner bill. It wouldn't surprise me in the least. However, I recalled Brad telling me that Colin's family was excessively wealthy, so perhaps I was looking for trouble where none was to be had.

Tillie turned her attention to Paityn. "I understand you've been wine tasting. Were you in Napa, or did you have the chance to visit Sonoma as well?"

Paityn flashed her brother a nervous glance. "Just Napa."

"What wineries did you visit?" Tillie took a sip of her champagne.

"Uh, just the usual ones."

Brad covered his snort with a cough then swallowed the remaining champagne in his flute. While I might not be a wine connoisseur, I did know that there were more than seventeen hundred wineries in Napa Valley, thanks to Umberto's tutelage.

"That's nice, dear." Tillie refilled our champagne flutes—given the uncomfortable interaction, we'd all guzzled the champagne the minute Tracey had filled them. "And you flew back today? Was it commercial or general aviation?"

Again, Paityn flashed her brother a nervous glance. "Uh, commercial?"

"Ah. Which city did you go in and out of? I've found them all to be quite inconvenient, so I'm wondering what your experience was."

Tracey returned with the water, the cosmo, and the Scotch and placed each in the appropriate location according to who had ordered what. She met my gaze and gave me a small nod, which I took to mean she was closely monitoring the dynamics of our group.

"We flew in and out of Sacramento." Colin furrowed his brow. "And you're right. None of the airports are convenient for reaching Napa in an easy manner."

"Which airline? The last time I checked, it was only Southwest that flew nonstop to Sacramento from Orange County, but then maybe you young people don't mind being on the plane longer than necessary. You always seem to have so many electronic devices to keep you entertained."

Colin didn't answer and instead angled his body toward his sister and whispered in her ear. She lowered her eyes to the table, and her cheeks turned red. She nodded once then gulped down half her cocktail.

"Well. Apparently, some people don't know how to partici-pate in polite dinner conversations." Tillie, a leading matron in Newport Beach society, wasn't about to hide her opinion on those she deemed rude. She huffed and turned toward Gabe. "Dear, I can't tell you how excited I am to meet your parents and grandparents. Did they tell you you're all coming to my house for brunch Thanksgiving morning?"

"Yes. And thank you for including them in your generous hospitality." Gabe's voice was monotone, but at least he'd answered and wasn't being rude.

Several times, Paityn tried to draw Gabe's attention to herself by gazing at him over the rim of her cocktail glass and fluttering her fake lashes, which looked like spider legs, in my opinion. Gabe didn't seem to notice and instead remained hunched in on himself. She pouted her lips then gave up and went back to whispering to her brother. I inwardly groaned. It was going to be the longest, most uncomfortable dinner I'd ever sat through.

Tracey returned with the menus. Instead of turning his body to face the server, Colin half turned his head and let his eyes follow her. A sense of familiarity hit me all at once. Had I met Colin before?

Chapter 32

T racey handed us each a leather portfolio that had a single sheet of vellum attached to the right of the inside. Instead of having a list of dishes to choose from, Brian had done as Tillie had asked and prepared a prix fixe dinner for us. The elegant script told us what each dish would be for the four courses.

"The chef, as you can see, has prepared a special four-course prix fixe dinner for your group. Take a look at the items he plans on serving, and if you have any dietary concerns or need to substitute an item…"

Paityn interrupted Tracey and held up her empty cocktail glass. "I'll take another one of these."

"Of course, ma'am." She took the empty glass. "As I was saying, let me know if you need to substitute anything, and the chef will be happy to do so."

I'd never seen any brats who were as self-entitled as Colin and Paityn. How did Gabe ever get mixed up with the pair?

"Can I get cocktails for anyone else?"

Colin held up his empty glass. "I'll take another double. Neat."

"Of course, sir." She deftly took the empty glass from his hand. "I'll be right back."

I had to wonder who was driving, the way the siblings were drinking. Then I realized Gabe had stuck to water. He must be the lucky one—not.

While the rest of the group studied the menu, I surreptitiously watched Colin. There was something about the way he moved and his mannerisms that made me think I'd met him before.

"Are you going to stare at me all night?" Colin rolled his eyes. "Isn't it enough that you crashed our dinner, and now you're trying to make us feel uncomfortable?"

I could feel my face warm, but I wasn't going to let him bully me. "That's not it. I'm sure we've met before, but I can't place where it could have been."

"We haven't, so you can stop looking at me." He turned to his sister again.

And that was when it hit me. They were the couple I'd seen at the ferry. In the dim, ambient lighting of the restaurant, Paityn's hair looked much darker than it had in the sunlight, but she definitely had the same toned body. The amount of makeup she'd troweled on for the evening made her face appear different, but she had the same facial structure. Why had they lied and said they were in Napa, wine tasting? It explained why Paityn stumbled over answering Tillie's questions, though.

"I said we've never met, so you can stop staring at me." Colin's eyes turned dark, and his glower looked menacing.

"You're right. I must've seen a photo of you somewhere. Maybe at Gabe and Brad's? Or have you been in the newspaper recently?" Not that I ever read newspapers, but I was clutching at excuses because I didn't want to tell him the truth of where I'd seen him.

"That's probably it. The *New York Times* did a feature on my family a month ago." He puffed out his chest. "I'll be taking over as president of our family's business when my father retires next year."

"How about you, Paityn? Will you be stepping in to run your family's business?" Tillie asked.

Paityn scowled. Her brother stopped her before she could answer. "Don't be ridiculous. The company is handed down from father to son. Paityn's sole purpose is to get involved in social committees and make our family look good."

Tillie almost choked on the sip of champagne she'd just taken. "Oh my. That is, well, to be honest, quite misogynistic, isn't it? What are we? Still living in the nineteenth or twentieth century?"

"We've managed to amass quite a fortune and grow our financial company so that we're competitive with the top. Why would we want to change something that's worked for almost a hundred years?" Colin's sneer grew. "Paityn knows her place and as such is rewarded with a nice little trust."

I wanted to lean across the table and smack that sneer right off his face. It was a good thing we were interrupted by Tracey again, because I wasn't sure I could've controlled myself. Tracey must've overheard his insulting remarks as well, because she placed his Scotch glass down more forcefully than usual. Her normally cheerful countenance looked almost thunderous. Colin seemed oblivious.

"Whoa, there, Em," Brad whispered to me. "I have no doubt you could take him in a throw down, but think of Brian's restaurant and reputation."

"You're right. Someone would video it, and it'd go viral, and then Colin would sue me, Brian, and everyone else at Oceana." I kept my voice to a whisper and tried to relax my tense jaw, but it was no use. "What an entitled piece of garbage."

"If no one has any questions about the menu, I'll bring out your starter." Without waiting for an answer, Tracey spun on her heel and headed for the kitchen. I had a feeling she needed a moment to cool off in private, and I was a bit envious that I couldn't leave the table, and especially Colin, and follow her.

Tillie leaned in toward Gabe and murmured to him. Her voice was quiet, so I couldn't hear what she said. But from the look of Gabe's jaw softening and his shoulders lowering from around his ears, she was getting him to relax, for which I was grateful.

I eyed Paityn's cosmo as she chugged it down and wondered if I should do the same to help blur the edges of the awful dinner party. But I immediately talked myself out of it. I needed to be sharp and figure out Colin's game and how it pertained to Gabe.

Tracey brought out the appetizer and placed three golden-brown pan-seared scallops artfully arranged on scallop shells in front of each of us. I dipped my fork into the sauce and tasted it. The tartness of the lemon was tempered with capers and butter. A hint of garlic rounded out the flavor. The scallops were perfectly cooked, and my fork slid through the opaque piece like it was a pat of butter. I would have been happy to have another half dozen scallops and call it dinner.

Colin took a small bite, pushed his plate away, and snapped his fingers at Tracey. "I'll take a bottle of whatever your best grand cru Chablis is."

"We only serve California wines, in keeping with our locally sourced ingredients mission." It appeared Tracey was biting the inside of her lip at Colin's rude manner. I'd have to apologize to her later and make sure we left a very generous tip for putting up with him.

Colin looked put out. "What a ridiculous thing to do. Whatever. Bring me your best chardonnay, then."

She nodded and hurried to the bar. Within a few minutes, the bartender returned with a bottle of wine. I hadn't even heard of the label, Marcassin, and I wondered how much it cost.

The bartender expertly opened the bottle, poured a small amount into the wineglass, and waited for Colin to sample. "This vintage received a hundred from Wine Advocate."

"It's fine." Colin made *fine* sound like he meant *passable*.

"Shall I pour for the table?"

"No. My sister and I will be the only ones imbibing." Colin swept his hand toward Paityn. "Please see that the bottle is properly chilled."

"Of course." The bartender filled Colin and Paityn's wineglasses then retrieved a marble wine chiller. He placed the bottle in the chiller then set it in front of Colin.

Brad rumbled deep in his throat but didn't say anything about the audacity of Colin's behavior. Would this meal never end?

Next came the salad with farm-fresh greens that Brian purchased from a local organic farmer. He'd added roasted beets and goat cheese, all locally sourced as well. The vinaigrette had a hint of orange but didn't overwhelm the taste of the greens and beets. Again, Colin took a bite, pushed his plate away, and took several gulps of wine.

While all I wanted to do was scowl, I couldn't help but smile when Brian brought out our main course alongside Tracey. He'd made shrimp with some kind of buttery sauce served over a bed of jasmine rice, obviously not the dish Tillie had suggested. The hint of citrus and the scent of ocean filled the air with its mouthwatering aroma. Brian had arranged a fist-sized ball of rice in the middle of a shallow bowl then made a well in the rice and added the sauce to the center. The five grilled prawns—heads removed, thankfully—were arranged around the rice, tails draping over the top of the rice and touching the sauce. More sauce had been artfully dotted around the sides of the bowl.

I watched as he placed the bowl in front of Colin, and I wondered if Tillie had talked him into adding a laxative to the dish. After spending just forty-five minutes with Colin, I was all for putting him out of action for a day or two... or even longer.

Brian placed his hand on my shoulder. "I've prepared California spot prawns in a citrus butter sauce. The prawns were flown down live from Santa Barbara this morning by a good friend. The spot prawns are only available from February to November, in certain locations off the western coastline, so I feel lucky to have procured some this late in the season. You'll find the spot prawns are a bit sweet with a buttery mouthfeel, which is why I chose this sauce to complement them. I hope you enjoy."

I happened to know that the good friend was the other investor and sometime chef for Oceana. He owned a private plane that he often used to source fresh seafood from up and down the coast for the restaurant. Brian had told me that sourcing the seafood was just an excuse for his friend to go flying. But it did give them the ability to bring in seafood that otherwise might not be available to them.

Brian returned to the kitchen after he'd squeezed my shoulder, and we dug in. Our stilted conversations ended as we savored the sweet prawns with the citrus sauce. I could've licked the bowl clean, had I not been in public. Colin, on the other hand, ate two of the prawns but nothing else. Tillie's idea to incapacitate him wouldn't have worked even if Brian had spiked the dish.

Once our main course dishes were whisked away, Tracey returned to our table. She focused her attention on me and avoided looking at Colin. "Would anyone like a cup of coffee or tea with dessert?"

We all declined, and Tracey was about to head back to the kitchen when Colin snapped his fingers again to get her attention. "Girl, bring me a glass of your most expensive port."

"That would be the Taylor Fladgate Scion Vintage port." Tracey pressed her lips into a flat line. "Will that meet with your approval?"

"As long as it's the most expensive, it'll be fine." Colin waved her away.

Tillie looked at me and whispered, "Poor Tracey."

I nodded in agreement. I so wanted to verbally berate Colin, but I held my tongue, worried it would only add more conflict. There was enough ill will going around as it was.

The bartender delivered the small wineglass of port for Colin just as Tracey brought dessert. The blood orange tart—a fruit currently in season—was a stunning work of art on each plate. The base was a crumbly almond crust, and it had a creamy orange filling. The vivid dark-red glaze set off the garnish of tiny slices of blood oranges, tangerines, sugared cranberries, dark blueberries, and sprigs of rosemary. The second she placed the plates in front of us and finished giving us the description of the dessert, she hurried back to the kitchen.

I forked a taste into my mouth and almost groaned. The creamy orange filling held hints of ginger and the woody undertone of rosemary. The blood orange glaze was intensely flavorful. I'd have to ask Brian to bring home any leftovers. I'd be more than happy to eat it for breakfast.

"Oh my gawd," Brad said after swallowing the huge piece he'd forked into his mouth. "Forget cake for the wedding. I want this tart served instead or at least in addition to."

I saw Gabe flinch. Unfortunately, Brad saw it too. He pushed his plate away and stood. "I'll catch you later, Em, Tillie." And with that, he marched out of the restaurant. I wanted to go after him, but Tillie placed a hand on my arm.

I glanced up and saw Colin's face held a sense of satisfaction. What was he up to? And why did he want to break up Gabe and Brad?

Gabe glowered at the siblings then shoved his chair back and ran after Brad. I hoped they'd be able to talk honestly, especially about Colin's hold over Gabe, and work it out.

My gaze followed Gabe until he pushed through the front

door of the restaurant, and then I turned my attention back to Colin. His face was thunderous. He threw his napkin onto the table and shoved back his chair. He took hold of Paityn's arm and yanked her to make her stand. She grimaced as if in pain but followed his lead and stood. They began leaving, but Tillie stood and reached out her hand to stop them.

"Where do you think you're going, young man? You haven't paid for your meal or your drinks." Tillie's voice held steel, and if I'd been them, I'd be paying attention.

"I'm sure the owners"—Colin's voice sneered on the word —"would want to comp our meal. After all, they screwed us over on the reservations and served subpar food. If not, I'm happy to take my complaints to the LA Times and post a review on Yelp."

At that point, I was almost seeing red. How dare he threaten Brian's livelihood and reputation just because we were trying to save Brad and Gabe's relationship from his clutches.

"You can make all the threats you want, but I've got photos and video of you ordering and drinking the most expensive items on the menu. You can at least pay for your booze." Tillie stood straight, holding her ground.

I had to give it to Tillie and her ability to bluff. Not once had I seen her with her phone out.

Colin reached into his back pocket and extracted a wallet. He took out several one-hundred-dollar bills and threw them onto the table. He looked furious as he pushed past Tillie, his sister in tow, and made his way to the front door.

"This barely covers the wine he drank, much less the Scotch and the port." Tillie tsked. "What a piece of work. We have to get Gabe away from him, no matter what that man is holding over his head."

Tracey returned to our table just as Colin and Paityn rushed out the door and into the night. "Was it something I said?"

I gazed at her, wondering what she meant, then she laughed. "I'm kidding. I'm sorry those two ruined your dinner."

"And I'm sorry Colin was so rude to you." Tillie picked up the hundred-dollar bills and pressed them into Tracey's hand. "There's no excuse for that kind of behavior."

"Thanks, Mrs. Skyler. I'll be sure to put it in the communal tip jar." Tracey placed the bills in her pocket. "Believe it or not, I've seen worse behavior several times."

"Brian's lucky to have you, since I probably would've thrown his drinks into his face several times tonight," I said.

"Trust me—I've been tempted on more than one occasion." Tracey pointed at our half-eaten desserts. "Do you want to finish, or shall I box it up for you?"

I looked toward the front door and worried about Brad. I needed to call him as soon as possible and make sure he was all right. "Box it up, please. We need to leave and check on Brad."

Tillie handed her American Express Centurion card to Tracey, who pushed it back at Tillie. "Brian said the meal is on the house."

"Absolutely not." Tillie thrust the card out toward the server again.

"Sorry, Mrs. Skyler, I can't accept that. You'll have to take it up with Brian." Tracey picked up our two desserts and stepped away from the table. "I'll be right back with your desserts for you. I'll have the chef add an extra slice to the boxes as well."

Chapter 33

Tillie and I couldn't stop discussing Colin's horrible behavior on the drive home. The atrocious dinner had practically made me forget about Zara's murder. No wonder Gabe appeared to be crumbling between Colin's pressures and then the detective practically breathing down his neck. I'd half expected Brad to show up on my doorstep by the time Tillie and I returned from Oceana, but he didn't. Nor did he respond to my texts. Worried, I stared at the ceiling for half the night, my mind too busy replaying what had transpired at dinner and trying to find a way to get Colin and his sister to go back to New York and leave my guys alone.

Despite the lack of sleep, I rose early and took the dogs for a walk to clear my head. I still had to get the cupcakes finished for Brian, and I'd gotten so busy the day before I hadn't called the bakery for the wedding cake. Had Brad been serious when he said he'd like to have the blood orange tart served at the wedding? If so, I'd need to check with Brian to see if it was doable.

I allowed Piper and Missy to pull me along, but I kept them on the main thoroughfare. I didn't have time to take them to the beach, nor did I want to wander where there was little traffic or few people. The incident with the black car almost hitting me was worrisome. I kept my attention focused on my surroundings instead of letting my mind wander.

Returning home, we entered the alleyway that separated my pool house from Tillie's home. My gaze landed on the gate that led to my backyard. It was wide open. I knew for a fact that I'd closed and locked it. Maybe Brian or Brad was waiting to see me. But wouldn't they have sent me a text? And I hadn't noticed either of their cars parked nearby.

I pulled my phone from my pocket, ready to call for help if need be. I cautiously approached the open gate. As I stepped into the entrance, the sight of a knife protruding from the wood caused me to stumble back. A sheet of paper with bold red print was held in place by the knife. It only took a quick glance to read the print.

STOP MEDDLING OR YOU'LL BE SORRY

I tugged on the leashes to get the dogs to follow. They'd been busy sniffing the ground around the gate and didn't seem to be concerned about any possible danger. I hustled to Tillie's security gate, punched in the code, pulled the dogs in after me, shut the gate securely, then sprinted up the steps to Tillie's door. My key to her house was still at the pool house, so I rang the doorbell then knocked. Despite the fairly early hour, I was sure she'd been up with Vannie before my sister had to leave for work.

I rang the doorbell again and sent Tillie a text.

I hope yr home. Am at door. Don't have key.

A minute later, her response came.

Just out of shower. Give me a minute.

While I waited, I called Detective Hawkins. Naturally, my call went straight to voice mail. I left a message, albeit a bit of a breathless one, then reopened the security gate. Since neither of the dogs had barked or seemed concerned about a stranger, I decided the culprit had gone. I tiptoed across the alleyway and took a photo of the note and knife.

Tillie called out, "Em, are you coming in?"

Missy and Piper wagged their tails with excitement and practically yanked me all the way across the alley. I locked the security gate and unclipped the leashes. They dashed up to Tillie, who bent down and gave them attention. She was dressed in a white plush terry cotton robe that reached all the way down to her high-heeled, marabou-feather-embellished slippers. For just getting out of the shower, Tillie's hair and makeup looked flawless.

"Hang on. I need to text a photo to Detective Hawkins." I attached the photo, typed a quick note, and hit Send.

"Hurry up, dear. It's chilly out here." Tillie led the dogs into the house, and I climbed the steps and followed them down to the kitchen.

Piper and Missy went straight to the cupboard that contained their food and pawed at it. I obliged and filled their bowls with kibble and refreshed the water dish.

"Did you lose my key?" Tillie filled a teakettle with water and placed it on the stovetop to heat.

"No. It's still at my place, but I didn't want to go in until Detective Hawkins comes over."

Tillie's eyes widened, and her eyebrows shot upward. "What's happened? You're okay, aren't you?"

"I'm fine." I pulled teacups out of the cabinet along with the box of assorted teas. "Someone decided to leave me a menacing note attached to my gate with a knife."

"What did the note say?" Tillie pulled an Earl Gray teabag from the box and placed it in her teacup.

I showed her the photo.

"It appears we must be getting closer to finding out who killed Zara." Tillie pulled the brandy down.

"I don't think we need brandy this morning. At least, I don't." I examined the flavors of teas and chose cinnamon.

"Are you sure you're not in shock?"

"I'm good, but thanks for checking." I put the brandy back

up as Tillie made herself comfortable at the table. "But I'm not one hundred percent certain it pertains to Zara's death. I wouldn't put it past Colin to do something like this. He was really angry that Gabe left with Brad, and I'm sure he blames me for crashing their dinner."

"You may have a point. Have you heard from Brad this morning?" The dogs, their breakfast already inhaled, went to sit next to Tillie. They nudged her to give them some attention or maybe treats, which she obliged with both.

"No. I haven't texted him since last night which he still hasn't responded to. I have to assume he's with Gabe. If he's not, I'm sure I would have heard from him one way or another." I practically slapped my hand to my forehead. "I forgot about the security cameras out front. Let me pull up the recordings and see if we can figure out who left the note. He came by when I was on a walk with the dogs."

I logged into the security camera app and pulled up the camera that sat on Tillie's front wall. It faced my garage and the gate. I scrolled back through the saved recording until I saw me leaving with the dogs for our walk. I used my forefinger to fast forward a bit then paused the recording when a figure came into view at the end of the alley.

He—or it could have been a tall she—was dressed from head to toe in black, their face obscured by what was presumably a mask and dark sunglasses. As he walked closer to my gate, he lifted his head and stared straight at the camera. The mask was a monkey face, its mouth opened in a cheesy grin. A black gloved hand rose and gave the camera a middle-finger wave.

"Well, I never..." Tillie huffed.

The person nonchalantly strolled over to my gate and fiddled with the lock. Once the gate swung open, he pulled the knife and paper from the oversize coat he wore, and plunged the knife into the page and gate with great force. I shuddered. The person was not only brazen but had some rage behind his actions too. As fast as the person arrived on scene, he just as quickly spun on his heel and retreated the way he'd come.

"You need to give this footage to Detective Hawkins. I think that person has a lot of suppressed anger." Tillie's hand shook as she stroked Piper's head. "Maybe we do need that brandy after all."

The teakettle chose that moment to emit its loud, insistent whistle. I startled and almost dropped my phone. "You might be right."

I filled our teacups with hot water and added a couple of drops of brandy.

"That's it? I think we need more."

I poured a capful into Tillie's cup and returned the bottle to the cupboard. "I still have cupcakes to bake and wedding vendors to finalize. Not to mention needing to remain coherent when the detective calls me back. I can't deal with a fuzzy head on top of it all."

"Hmm. You could be right." Tillie pulled her robe tighter around her. "Did I mention John is flying in today? He should be arriving around noon. Andrew's picking me up, and we'll pick John up from the airport and then go out to lunch."

"No, you didn't tell me. How long is he staying?"

"At least until the week after the wedding. He's agreed to be my plus one."

John was not only a British citizen but also an actual English baron. He and Tillie had an on-again, off-again romance, dependent on John's visits to California. John wasn't anything special to look at and barely reached a little over five and a half feet tall. When Tillie wore heels, she was an inch or so taller than he was. His roly-poly stature also contrasted with Tillie's svelte figure, yet the two of them were as thick as thieves when together. What I loved most about John was his sense of humor, made all the more appealing by his BBC-broadcaster-worthy upper-crust British accent.

"Do you have plans for dinner, or would you like Vannie

and me to pull out all the stops and cook a romantic dinner for you?"

"I'm not sure what our plans are, but you girls certainly don't need to do a thing for us." Tillie's cheeks turned a beguiling pink. "You know John. He always likes to surprise me with an over-the-top romantic gesture the first night he gets into town."

I giggled. "And every day that he's in town. He likes to spoil you."

"True." Tillie fluffed her hair. "I'm worth it, though."

My phone chimed with a text. It was Detective Hawkins informing me he'd arrive at my house in twenty minutes. I told Tillie as much.

"I think you should stay the night here at my house, at least until the perpetrator is caught. They obviously know where you live and probably had been watching until you left the house to leave their calling card."

"They know where you live too. Otherwise, they wouldn't have flipped the bird at the camera," I countered. Although I knew if I stayed at Tillie's, I'd sleep easier.

"It's safety in numbers. John's staying here, too, and perhaps Brian should consider coming every night for the time being." Tillie didn't press me on when we were going to move in together, but I could tell she wanted to.

"I'll mention it to Brian, but he's swamped at the restaurant with the holiday and then catering the wedding." I toyed with my nearly empty teacup. "If he stays at his house, he'll get at least another hour of sleep instead of spending it driving back and forth. He's practically running on fumes as it is."

"That's a good point. I'd never forgive myself if he fell asleep at the wheel."

"You and me both."

Tillie went back upstairs to get dressed and finish

primping for John. I'd just dried the last teacup and saucer when the detective's text came through.

I'm at your gate. Come see me.

I sent a thumbs-up emoji then sent Tillie a text that I was leaving and the dogs would stay with her. She didn't respond, so I left.

Chapter 34

The detective's sedan was parked parallel to my garage, and he stood in front of my gate, cell phone in hand. He swiveled when he heard me approaching.

"Ah, Ms. Martinez. I see you've been busy stirring up the hornet's nest again."

"It does appear that way, although I'm not certain this is associated with Zara's murder."

"You do get around." The detective changed the angle of his phone and snapped some more photos. "What other intrigue have you gotten yourself involved in?"

"It's the case of 'Will the wedding proceed, or will the villain keep the lovers apart?'"

Detective Hawkins jerked his head in my direction. I thought I heard a bone pop. "Are you insinuating I'm the villain?"

My hand flew to my warming cheek. "No. That's not it at all."

"Well, then, let me get the knife and note in evidence bags, and then we can go inside and talk about your meddling over a cup of tea."

The detective went to his car and extracted two evidence bags. Since he was already wearing gloves, he gingerly tugged on the knife. It wouldn't budge. He tugged harder, but the knife still wouldn't give way. He handed the evidence bags to me, then using both hands to pull and bracing his foot against the gate to hold it steady, he gave a mighty heave. The knife came free, and the note fluttered to the ground. He took the bags from me and secured the evidence. After placing them in the trunk of his vehicle, he wiped his forehead.

"I think I'm ready for the tea. You wouldn't happen to have any cookies, would you?"

"Of course. How do cranberry white chocolate cookies sound?" I'd swiped a few from Vannie's stash and brought them over to my house after getting home from dinner the evening before. I'd planned on having them for breakfast, but with the latest threat, I'd lost my appetite.

"Perfect. Lead the way, please." He swept his arm in front of him.

I walked through the backyard patio and unlocked the French doors. The sweet smell of sugar greeted me. While the water heated for the tea, I played the security video for the detective.

"I'd suggest you stay with Mrs. Skyler for a minimum of a few days or, better yet, until this perp is caught. From all appearances, he's got some rage going on."

"I agree and have already made plans to sleep over at Tillie's house."

"Emory, this happened in broad daylight." He tapped my phone screen, which had gone black. "You shouldn't be over here alone, even in the daytime."

"You make a good point." I hated conceding, but I still shivered, thinking about the way he'd plunged the knife into the gate with great force.

"Now tell me about the wedding fiasco and why there's a villain involved."

I explained what I could without divulging what the hacker had uncovered about how Colin seemed to be trying to break up Gabe and Brad. Describing the horrible dinner from the previous evening and Colin's atrocious behavior made me shudder all over again.

"While we were sitting there, I realized Colin and his sister are the people I saw at the ferry. Except they said they were up in Napa, wine tasting, that day, which isn't possible." I broke a cookie in half. "I told Colin I thought we'd met before, but he insisted we hadn't. You have to wonder why they'd lie about being in Napa and about never meeting me."

"He was telling the truth if you take the word *meet* literally. You never did actually meet at the ferry, did you? It was more that you noticed each other, and he or you possibly recognized each other."

"If you put it that way, yes, but Colin knew what I meant."

"While it sounds suspicious, you really don't have any proof this Colin person could have been the perp with the knife."

"No." Except I wanted it to be Colin to prove once and for all to Gabe that he needed to break free from the toxic friendship.

Detective Hawkins intently studied me over the rim of the mug of steaming tea. He took a sip and set it down. "I get the feeling you're leaving something out."

I shook my head, knowing I was lying, and it wasn't an innocent white lie either. I couldn't throw Brad and Ethan under the bus. "I don't think so, except from what I observed, Paityn has a thing for Gabe, even though he's engaged to Brad."

"It doesn't seem likely that her brother would try to break the engagement so his sister stood a chance with Gabe, does it?"

"You're probably right."

"If you can obtain a recognizable photo of Colin, send that to me, and I'll have our techs see if they can find any similarities between him and your blurry picture of the man from the ferry." He gobbled a cookie then took a sip of tea. "I'd like to have a copy of the video footage as well, showing the culprit. Even though there are no discerning characteristics to make an identification."

"Yeah. I don't think it was a deranged monkey who shoved a knife into my gate." I tapped on the security app, found the video feed clip, and forwarded it to the detective's number. "I just sent the video to you. This updated app makes it easy."

He opened the text and played the video clip through to make sure it worked. "I need to be on my way. If there's anything else you can think of, or if you decide you want to share what it is you're holding back, you have my number."

Instead of answering, I handed him the remaining bag of cookies. "Thanks for responding so quickly. I'll head over to Tillie's soon."

Before he stepped into the alley, Detective Hawkins turned to me. "You haven't happened to have heard from Mr. O'Neill or Mr. Ruller, have you?"

"Not since dinner ended last night." I wanted to ask why, but I held my tongue.

"Hmm. If you do hear from them, I'd like to speak to them both. Neither is answering their phone, nor are they at home." He gave me a curt nod, got into his car, and drove off.

With the gate securely locked, I hurried to my kitchen and bagged up the ingredients I needed for baking Brian's cupcakes. I threw some clean clothes and toiletries into a tote, picked up the sack of ingredients, and made my way to Tillie's house.

Before I started baking the cupcakes, I sent Brad a text.

Call me! Detective looking for you.

No answer appeared, so I called him. The call went

straight to voice mail. Why had Brad turned off his phone? Was he trying to avoid Detective Hawkins finding him? Had he and Gabe gone on the lam to avoid arrest? I pushed those thoughts away. Brad and Gabe were both innocent. They had no need to escape.

Chapter 35

I mixed up and baked Brian's pumpkin pie cupcakes and, while the cupcakes cooled, went to work on the pie crust pumpkins. The first attempt gave me some trouble when the first baking sheet of mini pumpkins burned. The cinnamon-sugar mixture I'd sprinkled over the raw cutouts burned before the crust cooked through. I cut out more of the mini pumpkin crusts and baked them until they were just starting to turn golden then sprinkled the cinnamon and sugar over them and finished baking a few more minutes. But with the first baking sheet's worth of pumpkins ending up in the trash, I spent extra time I didn't have mixing up more pie crust dough.

Stretching my back after being hunched over while piping the stabilized whipped cream, I checked the time. It was already three, and I should have had the cupcakes delivered by now. I sent Brian a text, telling him I'd be there by five. I'd be cutting it close. Before I set my phone down, it pinged with an incoming text. It was Brad. Finally.

At your gate. Let us in.

I wondered if that meant Gabe was with him.

At Tillie's. Be right there.

I hurried to the security gate, where I found Brad and Gabe waiting. While there were still bruises of exhaustion beneath their eyes, I could immediately tell that a burden had been lifted from their shoulders. They were more relaxed, and both were actually grinning.

"Hey, cupcake!" Brad wrapped his arms around me and gave me a tight hug. "You can be the first to congratulate the new Mr. and Mr. O'Neill-Ruller!"

I stepped back. "What? No way! Congratulations, you two!"

Brad flashed his left-hand ring finger. A ring of swirled forged carbon encircled by platinum sat on it. Gabe waved, and I caught sight of the matching ring sitting on his left hand as well.

"Come inside, and tell me all about it." I hugged Gabe. "I'm so happy for both of you."

I was also greatly relieved that Colin hadn't come between them. Just then, a black Town Car slid up next to us and came to a stop. Andrew popped from the driver's seat and ran around to open the back passenger door. Tillie stepped out beaming, and John followed her.

"It's our welcoming committee!" Tillie reached back and pulled John next to her. "Why are you all standing out in the alleyway? Was Emory showing you where that person stabbed her gate?"

Gabe and Brad exchanged looks, then Gabe stepped closer to me. "What happened?"

"Someone with anger-management issues stabbed a knife and a warning note into my gate this morning. I'll show you the photo, and there's video on the security app too."

"Let's all get inside and talk about this." Gabe pushed open the gate and hurried us in.

Tillie waved goodbye to Andrew then pulled John in behind her.

"Brad, do you want to park your car in my garage? I'd

hate for whoever did the knife thing to come back and vandalize it." Brad's car had been shot before, while sitting in front of my garage.

"It's not a bad idea," Gabe said. "I'll park it."

"The garage code is the same as the gate code." I'd had a key pad opener attached to the garage so Brian could come and go without having to remember to bring the handheld garage-opener device. He had two vehicles—a sedan, luxury, of course, thanks to Tillie, and a pickup truck for hauling his surfboard back and forth to the beach.

Brad and I entered the house and followed Tillie and John into the kitchen. Piper and Missy came barreling down the hallway, yipping with happiness at seeing all their best friends together.

Tillie ruffled the dogs' ears then took a long look at Brad. "You look better than yesterday, even if you're not wearing your penguin suit."

Brad waved his ring finger, the platinum flashing in the chandelier light.

"Oh, darling, I'm so happy for you." Tillie gave Brad a hug, and then John shook his hand.

Brad tucked Tillie's arm into the crook of his elbow and led her to the table. "Whaddaya say we break out a bottle of champagne, and we can show you the photos of our matrimonial nuptials."

"That sounds splendid." Tillie tilted her head toward me. "Emory, break out the 2012 bottle of the La Grande Dame, and Brad can get down the Waterford crystal flutes for us."

I did as she asked and then sent Brian a text, telling him I hoped to bring him the cupcakes by six. He sent back a kissy emoji.

Despite knowing that Detective Hawkins wanted to talk to both Brad and Gabe right away, I wasn't going to spoil their wedded bliss anytime soon. The detective could wait until we'd toasted with champagne and enjoyed looking through their photos.

Once Gabe joined us in the kitchen, Brad popped the champagne cork and filled the crystal flutes.

"Congratulations to you both." I raised my flute and tapped it against the happy couple's glasses.

"To happiness throughout your life." Tillie raised her flute then reached over and kissed each of their cheeks.

"I'll tell you the secret to a long and happy marriage." John raised his flute. "A good sense of humor and a short memory."

We drank to the couple.

"Tell us about your wedding. I assume you went to Vegas?" Tillie refilled our flutes.

Gabe actually blushed. "I know it wasn't the plan, but Brad finally convinced me it would ease up some of the pressure we've been experiencing because of the wedding plans."

"You should have listened to me from the start." Brad bumped Gabe's shoulder. "Not that I'd ever say I told you so."

"When you rushed out of the restaurant, did you immediately head over to Vegas?" I asked.

"Not right away. We took a walk on the beach, hoping no one would track us down." Gabe rubbed his jaw.

I assumed he meant Colin and Paityn.

"We walked and talked for about an hour then decided 'why not?' So we hopped into the car and went." Brad took another sip of champagne. "We didn't want to get married looking like slobs, so we stopped at the Forum Shops at Caesars, got outfitted in tuxes, and then tossed a coin to see which one of us got to choose the wedding chapel."

Gabe laughed. "I've never been so grateful to see heads win. Otherwise, Elvis would have been our officiant. I'm not sure I could have allowed photos if that had happened."

"Hey! What's wrong with Elvis?" Brad flashed a cheesy grin as Gabe rolled his eyes.

"Let's see those photos, boys." Tillie patted the bench beside her, and Brad took a seat.

Brad opened his photo app, and we gathered around as he swiped through the pictures. They were elegantly dressed in white full-dress tail coats with white vests and white bowties. A single red rose boutonniere was pinned to each of their lapels.

"Don't you two look dashing!" Tillie squeezed Gabe's arm.

"We'll download the professional photographer's photos when we get home to our computers." Brad swiped through a few more photos. A couple of them were blurry, and their heads were cropped off. "We made a deal with the couple waiting behind us to get married. They took pictures with our cell phones, then we stayed for their ceremony and did the same for them."

"Did you get married last night?" John asked. "I've heard some of those chapels stay open twenty-four seven."

"We had to pick up our marriage license first, and the office was already closed by the time we made it to Vegas." Brad closed his phone and placed it on the table. "We were there right when the bureau opened at eight this morning then headed over to the Simple Weddings chapel and were married by nine."

"Simple Weddings?" Tillie raised her eyebrows.

"I know, right?" Brad shot Gabe a pouty face. "And we could've had Elvis."

"As fun as it's been talking about our whirlwind wedding, I want to hear about the threatening note and knife." Gabe crossed his arms.

I showed him the photos and the security video. "Detective Hawkins took the items and will process for fingerprints or whatever else the crime lab does."

"I doubt they'll find anything." Gabe played the video again and seemed to scrutinize it more closely.

"Speaking of the detective, he wanted to know if I'd seen

or heard from you this morning. He's wanting to talk to you both."

Brad blew out a huff of air. "We turned off our phones not long after leaving the restaurant last night. Colin called Gabe at least a hundred times and left at least that many texts."

"That's kind of an exaggeration." Gabe's brow furrowed, and his shoulders slumped.

"Not by much. So we turned off our phones." Brad leaned across the table to where I sat. "I suspected Colin may have somehow put an app on Gabe's phone to track him, and I wasn't about to have him crash our ceremony."

"We don't have proof of that."

I couldn't help but notice that Gabe didn't jump in to vigorously defend his friend. "Speaking of Colin, do you have a photo of him? Detective Hawkins would like to compare it to the photo I took of the man at the ferry. I'm almost certain it was Colin and Paityn I saw at the time they both said they were in Napa."

Gabe jerked his head up. "Are you certain about that, Emory?"

"Maybe ninety percent? It's one of the reasons the detective would like to do a computer comparison."

Gabe pulled his phone out and turned it on. He flinched at the sounds of dings and chimes as message notifications alerted him. He ignored scrolling through or opening any of them and instead went to his photos and scrolled down. He found a photo and showed it to me. It was Gabe standing next to Colin. Both had their arms crossed and stood with their shoulders touching. I recognized it as the picture I'd seen framed and displayed on a bookcase in Gabe's home office. No wonder Colin had looked familiar to me.

"How long ago was this taken?" I examined it closely. Colin was about twenty pounds heavier in the photo, and his hair was the same golden-blond as Gabe's. If I squinted, I could see a resemblance between the two men.

"I think that was three years ago. We met up in New York when I flew in for a few days to catch up with friends." He looked at Brad and smiled. "Pre-Brad."

"When did he change his hair color?"

"What? He didn't, that I know of."

"He's blond in this picture, but when I met him at dinner last night, his hair was dark brown."

Gabe took the phone from my hand and enlarged it using two fingers. "Huh. I didn't even notice."

Brad leaned over Gabe's arm and looked at the photo. "You know, I can see a slight resemblance between you two, especially when his hair was light."

"When you call Detective Hawkins, can you tell him you'll send him the photo?" I asked.

"Yeah, but I doubt it'll be of any consequence. If Colin said he was in Napa, then I'm sure that's where he was. He had no reason to keep his whereabouts a secret." Gabe closed the app and shoved his phone into his pocket.

I wasn't so sure about that. After seeing Colin's photo with his golden hair, I wondered if it had just been recently that Colin had colored his hair dark brown. What if he had been the one Opal's granddaughter had seen arguing with Zara in the parking lot? And if that were the case, could Colin have killed Zara? Except I had no idea what the motivation could have been, especially since the evidence all pointed at Gabe being the murderer. And Colin wouldn't try to frame his best friend for murder. Would he?

Chapter 36

"Enough talk about murder." Tillie beamed at John. "This is supposed to be a happy celebration, right?"

"You're absolutely right." Brad poured the remaining champagne into Tillie's flute. It was barely a dribble. "Oops. I thought there was a bit more than that left."

"No worries. We can open another bottle." Tillie stood. "I have several more in my wine refrigerator."

"None for me. I promised Brian I'd deliver the cupcakes to him by six at the latest." I looked at my phone. I still had another hour before I had to leave.

"And no more for us either," Gabe said. "We only wanted to stop by and give you our news in person. Plus, we thought we'd better start canceling all the wedding plans. Do you have the wedding binder, Em?"

"It's at my house, but why cancel?" I retrieved the piping bag from the refrigerator and started adding swirls of whipped cream to the remaining bare cupcakes.

"Because we're already married. There's no reason to go through with the wedding, which was the entire point of going to Vegas." Gabe tapped his foot as if impatient with my question.

"Very true. But you can still host the reception. Make it a casual open-house party without the stress. Everything has been done, so all you have to do is show up and enjoy yourselves." I thought for a moment. "I can send out an email letting people know the wedding has already happened and it's now just a party. Dress can be casual and the hours open from maybe six to ten or whatever hours you'd like."

Brad and Gabe exchanged meaningful looks before Gabe spoke for them both. "Okay. That sounds like a much better plan, although my parents and grandparents are going to disinherit me. If we're lucky, most of my family will be no-shows."

"I'll make sure to ask people to let me know if they're not going to attend the party." My mind was darting around the logistics, and I knew I needed to start making notes so nothing fell through the cracks. "I'll cancel the officiant and the string quartet. I think we can manage with the DJ playing jazzy music during the dinner portion—which I need to change to buffet style—and then he can switch to dance music later on."

Gabe held up his two index fingers crossed at the knuckles. "I don't need to know the details. Plan it however you want, and tell me what time to show up. That's all I want to know."

Brad slung an arm around his new husband. "No stressing. Em will make it amazing."

I would make it amazing if I didn't keel over from my to-do list first. "I need to go get the binder. The officiant and musicians need to be canceled right away, in case they get another booking inquiry."

"I've got a great idea. Why don't you guys stay for dinner, and we can continue our celebration?" Tillie pointed her finger at me. "Em can pick up dinner from Brian for all of us when she delivers the cupcakes."

"Are you sure that won't be a bother?" Brad asked.

"Of course not. We'd love to have you," I said. "And

Vannie will be very disappointed if she doesn't get to help you celebrate today. She should be home any moment."

The dogs raised their heads at the mention of Vannie. I bent to pet them. "Maybe she can take you for a W-A-L-K later."

"I'll get the menu from Brian while Emory gets the wedding planning binder." Tillie already had her phone out and was typing out a text.

"We can take the dogs for a walk, if you want," Brad offered.

At the word *walk*, both Missy and Piper jumped to their feet and started winding around Brad.

"I think you have takers." I chuckled. "It's why we always spell the word. Let me get the leashes and T-R-E-A-T-S for you on my way out."

I looked at my cell phone. If I left within forty minutes, I just might make it to Oceana by six. I set a timer and placed the phone by the remaining bare cupcakes so I could keep track of how fast I needed to work once I retrieved the binder. I put the pastry bag and the whipped-cream-topped cupcakes into Tillie's industrial-sized refrigerator.

I couldn't help but wonder where Vannie was. She generally got home between four and five, depending on whether she decided to stay at school and correct homework or work on lesson plans or do it later that night at home. Maybe she'd met up with Teresa for a drink after a hard day of dealing with high school students. If so, she deserved to let off a little steam.

Brad and Gabe followed me to the entryway, where I stopped in front of a mahogany console. Tillie's florist brought a large, artfully arranged bouquet of fresh flowers every week. It added elegance and often fragrance to the space. I pushed on the front panel of the console, and a hidden drawer popped out. I retrieved the two leashes, extra doggie bags, and a small sack of treats and handed them to Brad.

"Don't feel like you have to go for a long walk. And whatever you do, don't let the dogs talk you into taking them to the beach. I don't have time to bathe them."

Brad handed a leash to Gabe, and they clipped them onto the prancing dogs. I followed as Piper and Missy tugged the two men down the stairs, toward the security gate. After we exited, I made sure the gate was closed tightly and locked. I crossed the alleyway to my pool house, while the rest of the crew headed left, toward the road. I hoped they heeded my advice and avoided the beach.

I punched in the code to my security gate and had my keys in hand to unlock the French door. I'd just inserted the key when a figure darted from the corner of the house, grabbed me around the waist with an arm, and placed their free hand across my mouth. I tried bucking and twisting to get free. When his grip only tightened, I pulled the key from the doorknob and jabbed the end into the assailant's arm.

He cursed, his voice low and guttural. Unfortunately, the jab was more of a glancing blow against the black sweatshirt he wore instead of impaling him. He violently shoved me against the door, and my head struck one of the glass panes. A crack echoed in my ears, and stars swirled in front of my eyes. The man pushed the door open, and I fell to my hands and knees. After grabbing my ponytail, he pulled me all the way inside then slammed the door shut and snicked the lock to engage.

Chapter 37

I tried to bring the room into focus, but it remained blurry. Something warm dripped from my forehead and down my cheek. I reached up to feel, and my hand came away sticky, while my forehead stung where my fingers had touched.

"*Where is he?*" the man roared behind me.

"I don't know who you're talking about."

"Liar." He kicked my leg, which sent shooting pain up to my hip. "If you hadn't meddled, none of this would have happened."

I twisted my neck and finally got a good look at my attacker. Dressed all in black, from the hoodie sweatshirt pulled tight around his head to black gloves to black pants to black shoes, it still didn't hide the fact that it was Colin. His lips were pulled back in a rictus grin, and his eyes were wild, like they weren't even seeing me. He waved a black gun at me then stuck it into the holster secured around his waist.

I wanted to pretend I didn't know who he was talking about and keep Gabe and Brad safe for as long as possible. But I knew it was only a matter of time before he tired of beating me and would go on to kill me. He'd find out anyway that Gabe and Brad were right across the street. I needed to somehow defuse the situation. "Are you talking about Gabe?"

"Don't be an imbecile. Who else would I be talking about?" Colin muttered to himself and circled around me.

"Don't you think he'll call you when he's ready to talk? The police are breathing down his neck, and it's only a matter of time before they arrest him." I recoiled when his foot shot out and connected with my arm. I shrieked in pain and tried to curl into a ball to protect my extremities.

"If you hadn't stuck your nose in where it didn't belong, that pretty boy would've been arrested and spent the rest of his life in prison." He brought his foot back as if to kick me again. I rolled away, and his shoe glanced off my hip. Colin didn't seem to notice, and he went back to circling the room.

It took me a moment to think past my pain and focus on what I thought he was implying. "Wait. Brad was supposed to have killed Zara?"

"The stalker? Yeah. She was a sick cow, and that pretty boy had had enough."

"So you killed her to frame Brad and get him out of the picture."

"Are you dense or what? Do I have to spell it out for you in neon letters?" Colin slung his hand out and backhanded my head. More stars danced before my eyes, and tears trickled down my cheeks, mingled with blood. "What am I going to do with you?"

"Nothing?"

"That was a rhetorical question. Stupid cows who stick their noses in where they don't belong deserve their fates."

Unless I came up with a way to escape soon, I needed to keep him talking. Maybe the guys would come back with the dogs, and they'd notice something was amiss and come find me. Gabe had his gun, hopefully, or perhaps he'd be able to calm his former friend down long enough to handcuff him.

"Since I'm just a stupid cow, can you tell me how you did

it? Got Zara to show up at Gabe's grandparents' home and got Gabe out of the area?"

"You really don't have a clue either, do you?" He started to kick me again but stopped at the last second before he connected with my leg. "Where's Gabe?"

"He and Brad went to Vegas." I flinched when his hands balled into fists. "I told you—the detective is close to arresting Gabe, and he wanted to get out of the area for a while."

"Where is he staying?"

"They didn't tell me because they knew if Detective Hawkins questioned me, I wouldn't lie for them." Well, I would lie for them, under the right circumstances, like I was currently in, but Colin didn't need to know that.

He seemed to think about it. "Call him. Find out where he is."

I reached into my leggings' side pocket and came up empty. I patted the other side and didn't find my phone. My mouth went dry when I remembered I'd set it down by the cupcakes after turning on the timer.

"I left it at Tillie's."

Colin grabbed me by the arms and yanked me to my feet. With rough gestures, he patted me down, hunting for my phone. When he didn't find it, he shoved me back to the floor. I fell hard and knew the huge bruise forming on my hip would be the least of my worries.

He circled the kitchen, yanking open drawers so aggressively the contents fell to the floor.

"What are you looking for?" I didn't really want to ask. I was afraid he'd say a butcher's knife to kill me with since a gunshot might draw attention. But if I could stall him by getting him to talk, I'd have to take the risk.

"Where do you keep twine or rope?" He flung open a cabinet door. The knob crashed into the wall with a bang. There was sure to be a huge indentation in the drywall.

"There's some rope in the garage." Would he attempt to

go find it, giving me an opportunity to run out the door and get to safety?

"Right…" He yanked me back up and forced me toward the door that led to the garage.

I flicked the light switch on in the kitchen before opening the door. The interior of the garage was dark, so I fumbled for its switch as well. Before I turned on the light, I tried to see if there was anything close at hand I could use as a weapon. There wasn't. Tillie's garage had built-in cabinets, and everything was pristinely kept in place.

Once light flooded the space, I stepped down and walked over to the quartz-topped counter then slid open a drawer. I couldn't quite remember which held lengths of rope. The first held several screwdrivers and a large wrench. Before I could bring my hand up to grab one to use as a weapon, Colin grabbed a fistful of hair and yanked me away.

More stars darted in front of my eyes as pain seared across my scalp.

"Don't even think about it," he growled. He kept hold of my hair with his left hand and used his right hand to open the remaining drawers. The far-right one held carefully rolled lengths of rope. After grabbing one of them, he unfurled it and roughly tied my hands behind my back.

"Get back to the house. If you make any sudden moves, you'll be sorry."

Chapter 38

C olin marched me into the house and shoved me into a kitchen chair. He eyed the second length of rope he'd brought in from the garage then lifted his gaze to mine.

"Why are you doing this? Is it because Paityn wants Gabe all to herself?" I tried to control the shaking in my voice.

"Shut up, and let me think." Colin paced in front of me. He stayed close enough to keep me from making a move to run for the door but far enough away that I couldn't trip him.

"I didn't want to involve that old bird across the way, but it can't be helped." He yanked me to my feet. "We're going to get your phone."

I stumbled when he shoved me to the door. My mind raced. I couldn't let him barge into Tillie's house and take her and John hostage. I had to stall and give Gabe time to realize I was in trouble. "She's leaving for dinner at six. Can't you wait a little longer and keep her out of the picture?"

Colin roared in frustration but jerked me away from the door and shoved me back into the chair. Using the second length of rope, he secured my torso to the chair. With my hands tied behind my back, I had to sit in an awkward position. My hands were already going numb, and my lower back developed a dull ache. I glanced at the clock built into the oven. It was only five fifteen. Would Colin be patient enough to wait? I decided to try asking more questions and see if I could get him talking.

"Since we have time, why don't you tell me why you're doing this? I figure Paityn has been infatuated with Gabe since your college days, but surely you both knew where his interest lay."

Colin stopped pacing for a moment and glared at me. "Gah, you're such a cliché. What is it with your Nancy Drew and that old bird's Miss Marple complex?"

I didn't want to push too hard, but I needed to keep Colin distracted and away from Tillie. My heart pounded against my chest. "It's obvious you've outsmarted us both. And let's not beat around the bush—you're going to kill me anyway, so you might as well tell me how you did it."

Colin didn't answer me. Instead, he strode to the refrigerator, rummaged around, and pulled out a cold bottle of water. He untwisted the cap then drank half the contents in several large gulps. After twisting the cap back onto the bottle, he swiped the back of his hand across his mouth. He ambled toward me, tossing the half-full bottle between his hands, the water sloshing back and forth.

"So what you're saying is you want to take my full confession to the grave with you." He cocked his head as he examined my face, then he barked out a laugh. "They say confession is good for the soul. I guess we'll see about that."

He tapped his index finger on his lips. "Let's see. Where should I start? Maybe with the fact that Gabe toyed with my sister's affections when she was a minor. Or that he caused a car accident that injured her even though I took the blame for him. And all these years, he hasn't repaid my sacrifice. I'll bet you didn't know that your precious friend's fiancé was such a cad."

I shrugged. Colin was going to put his spin on their history however he wanted. Besides, Gabe had suffered for his youthful transgressions for years.

"I guess since this is supposed to be a confessional, I should confess the whole truth and nothing but the truth, so help me God." Colin spun around and wagged his index finger in my face before pacing again. "The truth of the matter is I was the one driving and caused the accident. I'd drugged Gabe's drink, planning to let Paityn do what she wanted with him later on, but then we crashed. I saw it as an opportunity to have control over Gabe. He'd owe me a debt whenever I needed a favor. Except when I called in the debt, he refused, so now he needs to suffer."

Shivers ran up and down my fatigued spine, and I shifted in my chair, as much as the ropes around my body would allow. "That's horrible…"

Before I could get the rest of the words out of my mouth, Colin backhanded me across my face. Searing pain shot across my cheekbone and nose, and warm blood began to trickle across my lips. I squeezed my eyes shut and tried not to whimper.

"When hearing a confession, you're supposed to provide absolution. Not judgment."

When I didn't answer, he yelled, "Do you hear me?"

I managed a small nod, and Colin went back to pacing.

"Now, where were we?" He unscrewed the water bottle cap and took another long drink that finished off the bottle. He tossed it onto the kitchen table, where it clattered and bounced before rolling onto the floor. "Oh yes. Gabe's betrayal."

I was confused. Why did Colin try to frame Brad when he was clearly angered by Gabe? I wanted to ask but, remembering that sharp blow to my face, kept my questions to myself.

"I needed his expertise in law enforcement to cover up a

little problem with my company. But he refused. And then when my sister went through her nasty divorce and went off the deep end, I needed Gabe to step in and become a stabilizing figure in her life. But again, he refused. Instead, he asked me to be his best man in his wedding to that pretty boy. How'd he think I'd react?"

"You set up Zara's murder to frame Brad and get him out of the picture, hoping Gabe would then comply with your wishes?" I hoped I kept the scorn from my voice. My battered body didn't need any additional injuries.

"Exactly. I'd known about that pretty boy's stalker after Gabe told me about it when they first got together. It wasn't that difficult to track her down and lure her to Orange County."

"Did you tell her where to find Brad?"

"Not at first. I gave her enough clues to track him down, but that cow was too stupid to figure it out, so I had to practically draw her a map."

Poor Nina had thought she'd led Zara to Brad. If I got out of this situation alive, I'd have to assuage her guilt.

"Then it was only a matter of time to coordinate getting her to the house and Gabe out of the way so that the pretty boy would take the fall." A frown creased his forehead.

"But you knocked Gabe out and left him stranded in the desert. He doesn't have an alibi." I didn't think Colin had thought that aspect through all the way.

"It wasn't supposed to happen like that." Colin rubbed his face. "I only wanted him out of the way for a little while. I left his keys on the ground next to the car door. I figured he'd wake up within a few minutes and drive to an ER to get checked out for a concussion, and he'd have an alibi while I was busy killing that cow."

"Gabe said the keys were at least fifteen feet away from the car, and without his cell phone flashlight, he couldn't find them until it was light enough."

"Maybe a critter picked them up and dragged them." Colin shrugged. "Anyway, I'd hidden a motorcycle out there the day before and rode back to his grandparents' house. Zara was supposed to meet me there at ten, but she didn't show until midnight."

"Back up a sec. Didn't Gabe bring ten thousand dollars in cash? What happened to the money?"

"That amount is chump change to people like Gabe and his family. I'll use it to put my sister in rehab. I need to get her away from the party scene."

"Okay, Zara showed up late?" I looked at the clock. It was five thirty. Would Brian call my cell phone to find out if I was on my way? Would Tillie tell Gabe and Brad I hadn't returned and had left my phone behind? Surely the guys were back from their walk.

"Yeah, and then she got what was coming to her. It was like killing two birds with one stone. She's dead, and Pretty Boy takes the fall." Colin went back to the refrigerator and extracted another bottle of water.

"But you overlooked the security footage, so it shows Gabe showing up at the house. Not Brad." Colin clearly hadn't thought his murderous plan out well. Brad would have had a solid alibi if Zara hadn't been late. He'd been with us all evening. Colin had either not been told about our planned celebration or else he'd forgotten about it. Or, perhaps deep down, he'd wanted Gabe to be implicated in Zara's death.

My mouth was parched, and the taste of blood lingered. But I wouldn't deign to allow myself to ask for a drink. I feared it would only give Colin more power over me, if he thought I needed something.

I jumped when the water bottle hit the wall with a crash.

"I hunted for cameras but never saw any. How was I supposed to know they were disguised? And who would have been able to predict a power outage right after I knocked

Gabe out?" Colin's face inflamed with rage. "You had to ruin everything and snoop around."

I tried to scoot the chair back, but the seat was already pressed against the table. And then I heard it—the unmistakable click of the doorknob on the interior door to the garage turning. I started coughing as hard as I could to cover up any other noise.

"I'm wasting my time here. I should shoot you now and track Gabe down another way."

"Drop the gun, and put your hands up in the air!"

Detective Hawkins and Gabe burst into the kitchen, their guns drawn and pointing at Colin.

Colin reached for the still-holstered gun, but a shrill cry stopped his movement. Paityn ran into the room and darted past the two detectives. "Colin! Please don't. I couldn't bear to lose you."

She wrapped her arms tightly around him, sobbing. Colin's body slumped, and he rested his chin on top of his sister's head.

Detective Hawkins rushed to secure Colin's gun and place handcuffs on him. Gabe gently pulled Paityn away from her brother.

The drone of Detective Hawkins's voice reciting the Miranda Rights faded into the background as the dancing stars in front of my eyes turned to black.

Chapter 39

Brad's face loomed over me right before the paramedics loaded me into a waiting ambulance.

"I'll be right behind you, and Brian will meet us at the hospital." Brad gave my hand a tight squeeze, and his eyes glittered with unshed tears. "Don't ever scare me like this again, Emory."

With the stretcher loaded, the doors slammed shut, and the ambulance took off at a gentle speed and without sirens, for which I felt thankful. My head throbbed, and every little jolt sent a searing pain through my left forearm where Colin had kicked me.

By the time I'd been carted to a private hospital room that overlooked the beach, no doubt thanks to Tillie's intervention, I'd had ten stitches in my forehead, been diagnosed with a concussion, and sported a cast on my left arm for a tiny solitary ulnar fracture. The pain meds were keeping me mostly comfortable and a bit fuzzy. Brian and Tillie hovered around my bed, while Brad arranged the several bouquets of flowers they'd brought on the windowsill.

"What can I get for you?" Brian tried to fluff up the pillow supporting my injured arm. "Do you need some water?"

"I'm fine right now. Can you find out how long I need to stay here? I really want to go home."

"That's the fifth time you've asked that, cupcake." Brad tweaked my big toe, one of the few things on my body that didn't ache. "They want you to stay overnight, and we'll be here in the morning to pick you up."

Honestly, I hadn't remembered asking. Perhaps it was the pain meds or my concussion making me loopy. "Is Vannie watching Piper and Missy?"

"They're taken care of." Brian kissed my cheek. "Your mother and Lars are here to see you. I'll wait outside until they leave, and then I'll be back to stay with you for the rest of the night."

"Wait. I want to know what happened with Colin. He's been arrested, hasn't he? He's not going to be able to hurt me anymore?" Even to my ears, my voice sounded slow, like molasses, and I had a hard time forming the words.

"He's been arrested, and both Detective Hawkins and Gabe will see to it that he never hurts anyone else again. They heard enough of his confession that he'll spend the rest of his life in prison." Tillie took Brian's place and stroked my bruised cheek. "Rest up, and we'll see you in the morning."

As soon as the three of them filed out of the room, my mother and Lars entered. Lars carried a huge bouquet of yellow roses, which he tried to fit onto a table containing several other vases, while Mother rushed to my bedside.

"Oh, darling, we've been so worried. How do you feel?"

"Pretty groggy right now. I'm sorry I worried you." I wiggled my body to try to find a more comfortable position.

"It's not your fault. Who would have thought that the best man could be so dangerous?" Mother brushed a strand of hair away from my cheek. "Just let me know what we can do for you, whether you need to stay with us while you recover, or you need me to help with the wedding plans. Don't feel like you have to do it all on your own."

"Thanks. I appreciate it." My eyelids fought to stay open. "I'll be okay."

"Of course you will, darling."

That was the last thing I heard, although I thought I felt my mother's soft lips brush my cheek. Several times during the night, a nurse came to check on my vital signs and tap in her tablet. Brian sat in the reclining chair at the side of my bed, keeping watch over me. Each time I woke, he grasped my hand and held it tightly until I fell back to sleep.

As promised, the nurse told me I'd be discharged that morning, as soon as the doctor saw me. Brian looked exhausted, with bruised bags sitting beneath his dark-green eyes. His hair, which generally looked wind tousled and a bit curly on the ends, was smashed flat on one side, while the front nearly stood on end. It looked like he'd repeatedly raked his hands through his hair and it ended up staying upright. A shadow of a beard covered his cheeks and chin, and in the light streaming through the window, there was a hint of red in the blond hair.

Undoubtedly, I looked much, much worse. I didn't bother asking for a mirror or a brush. Instead, I finger combed my hair and pulled it up into a messy bun, which was nearly impossible with the partial cast on my left arm. I accidently brushed my hand across the stitches on my forehead and nearly yelped at the pain.

"Do you want me to get the nurse to bring more pain medication?" Brian asked.

"No. The stitches just startled me is all." I also didn't want to be so groggy and out of it by taking more pain killers.

"Good morning, my dears." Tillie swept into the room with two to-go cups of coffee in hand. "I thought you'd both need an extra pick-me-up this morning."

"Thanks, Gram." Brian took both cups and placed one on the rolling table adjacent to my bed. "We actually had a couple of cups of pretty decent coffee each when they served us breakfast."

Again, I had to wonder whether Tillie had used her influence to have a decadent breakfast of eggs Benedict served to the both of us, or if she'd ordered it from somewhere and had it delivered. "Thanks, Tillie. I'll definitely need extra caffeine today. I've still got a headache."

"You're welcome." She patted Brian's cheek then rummaged in her capacious handbag. "I think you could use a bit of undereye concealer, my boy. It looks like you've had a rough night."

He swatted the offered tube of makeup. "I'm fine. Besides, don't most women like their men to look rugged?"

Tillie snorted. "There's a huge difference between rugged and ragged. I won't harm your self-esteem by telling you which category you fall into."

I couldn't help but laugh. "I'm sure Brian looks a heck of a lot better than I do. And for the record, I think he looks quite manly."

Brian stuck his tongue out at his grandmother. Before their banter could continue, the doctor swept into the room. He eyed the two cups of coffee sitting beside me.

"I hope that's decaf." He flipped through the chart he held. "You need to avoid caffeine for the next couple of weeks while you allow your brain to heal."

"But they served us coffee with breakfast." I couldn't imagine going that long without my multiple cups of coffee every day.

"It was decaf," the doctor replied.

Brian groaned then picked up both of the coffees. "No wonder I still feel exhausted."

The doctor shone a light on my stitches then looked over my cast and asked me how I felt.

"I feel as good as can be expected, but I still have a headache."

"I'll include a prescription for pain medication, but if you can tolerate it, I'd suggest you stick to alternating between acetaminophen and ibuprofen. I'll get your discharge papers signed, and you can be on your way as soon as the nurse goes over your course of action." The doctor gave a brief nod to Tillie then hurried on to his next patient.

"No coffee! Argh. How am I going to make it through all the cupcake orders I have?" I closed my eyes.

"There'll be no going back to work for a few days for you, young lady." A no-nonsense, stocky, gray-haired nurse stood in the doorway. "You need to give your brain and your body time to heal."

"But how long will it take?" I tried not to sound whiny. But it was the holiday season, and on top of all my cupcake orders for clients depending on me, there was still Thanksgiving festivities and Brad's reception to finish preparing for. I didn't have time to be an invalid.

"Take it easy, with no visual electronic devices for four or five days. Then you can start easing back into your other activities. If you feel any adverse effects, then cut back, and take it easy again." The nurse handed me a sheaf of papers and a pen. "I'll leave you to read through the forms then sign the last sheet. If your head hurts too much, one of your family members can read through it and tell you what it says."

Tears pricked my eyes as I gazed down at the papers. "I can't let my clients down, and there's Thanksgiving and Brad and Gabe's reception. There's too much to do. I don't have time to just lie around."

Tillie took the papers from my hand. "That's why you have your family and friends. We'll all pitch in and take over whatever you need done."

"But I feel so helpless." I swiped my eyes with my palms.

Brian handed me a tissue. "Look at it this way—if I were laid up with injuries, would you let my business and obligations go unattended?"

"No. Of course not."

He gently touched beneath my chin and lifted it so I'd meet his gaze. "You've got an extraordinarily talented chef for a boyfriend, a sister who owns a catering company, and another sister who is a whiz in the kitchen. And don't forget you have a mother and Tillie who would bend over backward to pitch in however they can. Don't deny us the chance to show you how much we love you."

"He's right, Emory. We want to see you heal completely, and as a team, we'll pitch in to take care of your responsibilities." Tillie snatched a tissue from the box. "Dang it, Brian. I had no idea you could be so sentimental."

Brian hugged his grandmother and kissed her temple. "I learned from the best."

"Have you signed the form yet?" The nurse stood in the doorway and watched as we dabbed at our eyes with tissues.

"Give me a sec." I picked up the pen, found the signature page, and scribbled my name. We could read through the instructions later. I handed the signed page to her.

"I'll have a wheelchair brought in, and you can meet Ms. Martinez at the loading zone out front."

Chapter 40

Over the next few days, I did as the doctor ordered and took it easy. In between bingeing on cozy mystery audiobooks and quietly chatting with visitors bearing meals and treats—while avoiding talking about my ordeal—I orchestrated getting the cupcake orders baked and delivered. Carrie and Vannie both whipped up my recipes, while Tillie had her driver, Andrew, deliver them.

My mother took over the wedding reception planning—and truth be told, she was much more proficient at it than I was—and had emails sent and responded to about the change from wedding to party only. A few declined to attend, but the majority of the invitees were enthusiastic about the casual wear recommendation. Well, aside from Gabe's parents and grandparents—they were determined that the reception should be a formal affair. Gabe finally told them to wear whatever they wanted, and their guests would do the same.

The only close meltdown that I knew of was from my two nieces. They were devastated that they wouldn't be flower girls. In the end, Brad assured them that they would still need to wear their special dresses and toss the rose petals as he and

Gabe made their grand entrance. The girls also made sure that Piper and Missy would still be the flower doggies and would cart the rose petals around as planned.

Now that it wasn't such a formal affair, I felt more comfortable about any mishaps happening because of the dogs or the girls becoming overly boisterous. And my nephew, Tommy, being a rambunctious toddler, had no idea that he would miss out on being the ring bearer.

I was starting to feel like my normal self the day before Thanksgiving. When I got home from a leisurely walk with the dogs after breakfast, Brad was sitting on a chaise lounge, waiting for me on my patio.

"How's married life treating you?" I bent over to peck his cheek.

"It's great when I get to see him, but with all the activity going on with Zara's murder and Colin's confession, he's been busy helping Detective Hawkins." Brad stood and followed me into the house.

"Can I get you a coffee or anything to drink?" I pulled a water glass down from the cupboard, filled it with cold water from the refrigerator dispenser, and poured it into the dogs' water dish. They ignored it and instead pawed at Brad to get their deserved adoration. He complied by rubbing their heads.

"Are you still drinking decaf?"

I sighed. "Unfortunately, yes. Everything I read online says I shouldn't indulge for a few weeks. A cup or two probably wouldn't hurt, but my doctor says it's better to be safe than sorry."

"Then I'll pass on the decaf. Maybe some water?"

"I can make you some regular coffee, if you'd prefer."

"No need. Water is fine."

I carefully added some ice to the glass and filled it with water. I was still getting used to having less mobility with my left hand because of the cast restricting my movement. With all my visitors and especially my nieces decorating the cast, I sported a work of colorful art. Tillie promised she was going to find me an outfit that was just as colorful to wear to the reception. Knowing her, she'd manage to find something—most likely a designer label—and I'd have no option other than wearing it.

I handed the glass to him. "You're coming by for brunch tomorrow morning, right?"

Despite everything that had happened, Tillie had insisted it was even more important to have friends and family gather together.

"Yep. My mom, sister, and her kids are coming along with Gabe's parents, sister, and a cousin. His grandparents are, well, they're being quite snotty about our elopement and casual reception. In fact, at one point, they threatened to renege on their offer for our use of the house for the party, so we didn't invite them to brunch. They'd just throw a damper on everything."

My head felt swimmy, and I hurriedly sat down at the kitchen table. "They didn't!"

"Oh, they did." Brad sat beside me. "Don't worry. My new mother-in-law—oh em gee, I won't ever get used to saying that—had to do some finessing and make some promises that I don't think she wanted to make. But in the end, we're good to go."

"The grandparents aren't going to put a damper on your reception, are they?" I gnawed at my lower lip, wondering if there was a way to mitigate any problems before they occurred.

"Not if they want their daughter to keep her promises, but between you and me, I have a feeling they won't even show up. I overheard some talk about how nice it is in Hawaii this time of the year." Brad tapped his fingers on the table. "This might be a sensitive subject to bring up, but well, Paityn wanted me to ask if she can drop by and talk to you."

I suppressed a shiver. Logically, I knew the tragedy wasn't Paityn's fault, but the terror and physical injuries that Colin had inflicted on me were going to take a long, long time to heal. I must've hesitated too long, because Brad gripped my good hand.

"I know you've avoided talking about what you went through, aside from giving your statement." He paused as a shiver ran through my body. "Are you cold? Would you like me to get you something hot to drink?"

"No. I'm all right. Go on." Piper and Missy came to sit beside me as if they knew I needed some comfort.

"I have to assume no one's told you that it was Paityn who called Detective Hawkins and warned him that Colin had made some verbal threats against you. She thought he was just blowing off steam, but when she found your address written on a notepad in his room at their Airbnb, she decided she'd better tell someone. Never in a million years did she think he was capable of that kind of violence."

"Oh. I didn't know that." My voice was quiet, and I rapidly blinked to hold back the moisture stinging my eyes.

"Gabe and I met with her yesterday. She's devastated over the destruction her brother has caused in their lives, ever since she was a teen. Colin had it in his head that she and Gabe would make the perfect couple, even though she was only mildly interested. After hanging out with Gabe for a short while, she knew they'd never hook up, no matter what her brother wanted. And she had no idea that Colin drugged Gabe and then made him believe he'd been the one driving the car and caused the accident. Paityn had apparently ingested some illegal substances on top of drinking that night and pretty much blacked out."

Brad stood and refilled my water glass. "Are you doing okay with my sharing this information?"

I nodded and wrapped my arms around my midriff.

"Maybe the sooner I face it and stop burying what happened, the sooner I'll get over it."

He placed the glass back on the table. "Avoiding things never helps, but I do understand how it takes time to overcome trauma. You're going to talk to a professional, aren't you?"

"I have an appointment next week. I wanted to wait until my headaches subsided."

"Good. That'll help in the long run."

"What happened after Paityn called Detective Hawkins?" I asked.

"He didn't tell you?"

I shook my head. "I told him I didn't want to know, so he simply took my statement and said he'd contact me if he had any more questions. So far, I haven't heard from him."

"Are you sure you're ready to hear the rest of what happened?"

"No, I'm not sure, but I think it's what I need to do."

"Detective Hawkins saw us walking back to the house with the dogs." Brad reached over and ruffled their ears. "He filled us in on what Paityn had told him, and he gave Gabe a gun. I took the dogs back toward the Fun Zone, away from any danger, and called to warn Tillie and John. They made sure the house was locked up tight with the alarm set."

"How did they get into my garage? I'm sure the side door was locked."

Brad smirked. "Just between you and me, Gabe is a wicked-smart picklock, but he doesn't like to advertise the fact. It had something to do with getting locked out of the dorm during his boarding school days. Anyway, that part was easy. Once inside the garage, they found that the door into the house was unlocked, so they stood there with their ears pressed against the door and listened. Colin was pretty frantic, and his voice carried well enough that they caught the last few minutes of his confession, and you know the rest. How did you manage to pry it out of him?"

"As you know, I left my phone at Tillie's. He wanted me to call Gabe and get him to meet up, since Gabe wasn't taking any of his calls." I ran a hand over my face and took a deep breath. "There was no way I could allow Colin to take Tillie and John hostage, no matter what he did to me. I lied and convinced him that Tillie was going out to dinner at six, and then I would take him over there to make the call from my phone. I knew Colin would kill me anyway, and since we had to wait until Tillie supposedly left, I asked him to tell me. I just hoped that the time I gained by making him wait would be enough time for Gabe to figure out something was seriously wrong."

"Oh god, Emory, we could have lost you. I can't believe how brave you were." Brad bent over and buried his face in Missy's curly fur. He straightened and swiped at his eyes. "Back to Paityn. She feels like she owes you an apology in person and wants to see that you've survived the ordeal with her own eyes."

"She doesn't owe me anything." Goose bumps broke out on my cast-free arm. Would seeing her bring back awful memories of what her brother did to me in full force?

"You may not think so, but that's how she feels." Brad looked sheepish. "Actually, she's sitting in her car right around the corner, waiting to hear your answer."

I thought for a moment. Brad was right. It was time to face my fears. "All right. You can ask her to come in."

Brad sent a quick text then went out to wait by my security gate. I ran to the bathroom and tried to fix my frizzy ponytail and dabbed on some lip-gloss. The stitches still looked like they would fit right in on Frankenstein's monster, and my bruised cheekbone and black eye had faded to a pukey-green and yellow. No amount of makeup could conceal the bruising —trust me, I'd tried—so I left it alone.

"Em? Is it okay for us to come in?" Brad asked as he knocked on the French door doorframe.

"Yes, please come in." I made my way to the family room. "Thank you for coming to see me."

Paityn looked terrible. It appeared she'd hadn't slept much in the last week, and her light-blue eyes were swollen and red rimmed. She hadn't washed her hair recently either. It hung in greasy, limp strands down her back. She thrust a gift bag toward me, and the aroma of coffee tickled my nose. "Brad and Gabe said you loved coffee but couldn't drink any for a few weeks. I bought you a pound of my favorite blend for when you can have it again."

"Thank you. I look forward to trying some." I took the bag and took another appreciative sniff. My mouth watered. Maybe I'd allow myself just one cup with brunch on Thanksgiving, since I still needed to steer clear of mimosas and any other alcoholic libations. "Please have a seat."

I settled myself at the end of the sofa, with Brad on the opposite end. Paityn chose the armchair closest to Brad. Since she was the one who requested to talk to me, I decided to let her be the one to break the silence. But instead of words, sobs filled the air, and Paityn's chest heaved with the emotion.

Brad hurried to the kitchen and poured a glass of water for Paityn while I handed her a box of tissues.

"I'm so sorry," Paityn said in between hiccupping sobs. "I should have known my brother was going to hurt you."

I knelt beside the young woman and rubbed her back. I couldn't help but notice the bruises on her upper arm, right where Colin had gripped her to yank her up from the table at Oceana. Brad stood close by, unsure what to do with the glass of water.

"It's not your fault. If it hadn't been for you, I might not be here today." I bit my lower lip, trying to contain my own emotions.

"When we lied about going to Napa, I should have

238

prodded Colin for answers." She took a handful of tissues and blew her nose. "I should've listened to my gut instead of letting him intimidate me into lying."

I had a feeling Paityn had been, at the very least, emotionally abused by her brother for years, if not physically. With Colin's description of Paityn's downward spiral of a failed marriage and embracing the party scene, it made sense that she'd turn to substance abuse to cover up her pain. "I don't blame you at all, and I hope you can learn to put the blame on your brother and not take it on yourself. Okay?"

Paityn nodded and took fresh tissues to wipe her face. Dark streaks of mascara smeared beneath her eyes.

"I don't think you should be alone. Do you have any family you can stay with in the area?" I asked.

"They're all back east." She sniffled, and Brad handed her the water. She took a large gulp and wiped the dribble from her chin. "Colin already made arrangements for me to check into rehab. Car service will pick me up in about an hour and drive me to their facility in San Juan Capistrano."

"I'm glad, and I hope it helps you come to terms with what happened so you don't blame yourself." I stood, my body stiff from the injuries I'd sustained, and sat back on the sofa.

Paityn flashed a half smile. "I came to offer you my apologies to try to make you feel better, and instead, you're the one offering me compassion and reassurance."

I smiled back. "If there's anything we can do to help you while you're still in the area, just let us know."

She lowered her head and wiped her eyes with the back of her hand. "Thanks, but I think I'll be fine. My plan is to head back to Connecticut and stay with my mom when I'm done with the two-week program. She'll keep me straight."

"You have Gabe's and my phone numbers, so please text us if you need anything." Brad rubbed his palms on his thighs.

"I appreciate all you've done for me, Brad. You and Gabe both could've let the police arrest me instead of sticking up for me." Paityn grabbed another handful of tissues then stood. "I need to finish packing and turn in the rental car before my ride shows up."

I walked toward the French doors and opened them wide. "Best of luck with everything, Paityn."

Brad gave her a quick hug, and we watched as she left to face her demons.

Chapter 41

Thanksgiving brunch was in full swing. My nieces ran in and out of the formal dining room—where I sat ensconced in a comfortable chair—chasing Piper and Missy, who were pestering the two kittens, Tigger and Patches.

Tillie had invited just about everyone we knew, including Detective Natasha Tran and her family. She came and sat down beside me. Natasha wore black skinny jeans, ankle boots, and a body-hugging off-the-shoulder burnt-orange sweater that complemented her olive skin tone and showed off her slender body. She wore her raven-black hair bobbed, and dark-blue highlights gleamed beneath the chandelier. Her black eyes beamed with joy as she watched the kids playing, and she placed a hand over her flat belly. My eyebrows rose at her gesture, especially when I noticed the diamond ring sitting on her left-hand ring finger.

"I guess congratulations are in order!" I lifted my flute of sparkling apple cider to her just as Randall—my ex-boyfriend—joined us. I expected to feel a pang of something like bitter-sweet sadness at seeing him, but instead it was more like seeing an old friend you'd grown apart from and lost touch with.

Natasha's daughter, Alyssa Mai, trailed in with my toddler nephew, Tommy. It was sweet the way the young girl held Tommy's hand as they tried to catch up with his sisters. It did much to improve my disposition after nightmares had plagued my sleep the night before.

"Thank you!" Natasha grabbed Randall's hand. "With a new little one on the way, we thought we'd better make it official."

"I'm really happy for you both." I took a sip of the apple cider. "Have you set a date yet?"

"We were thinking next month, with only our parents and Alyssa in attendance." Randall's sapphire-blue eyes sparkled as he kissed Natasha's hand then ran his long fingers through his wavy chestnut-colored hair. It brushed the tops of his ears and was longer than I'd ever seen it. When I'd dated him, it had been cut military short. Instead of the sharply creased slacks he'd generally worn when we were together, he wore jeans with a short-sleeved white polo shirt. Randall jutted his chin toward Brad and Gabe as they walked into the room. "Neither of us wants a bunch of hoopla, especially after what they went through."

"Detective and Randall." Gabe held out his hand to Natasha then pulled her from her chair and gave her a hug.

Natasha had become friends with Gabe at college, and they'd both graduated together with degrees in criminal justice. They always addressed each other as Detective in a playful manner when first meeting then reverted to their given names. I couldn't help but wonder if Natasha had known Colin and what she thought about his murderous rage. But I wasn't about to bring it up. It was over, and I didn't want to talk about such dark matters at our festive occasion.

"Detective. Congratulations on your marriage. We're looking forward to celebrating with you on Saturday." Natasha kissed Gabe's cheek then sat back down. "Who would have ever thought Colin would go off the deep end like that? Did you have any inkling?"

I guess there wasn't going to be any way to avoid the conversation without leaving the room.

"He'd been trying to pressure me into quitting the force and working for him in New York for several years. And of course, he threw me not-so-subtle hints that Paityn had a thing for me. I just blew him off and changed the subject every time he brought it up." Gabe let out a long breath then took a sip of coffee. "But to answer your question, no, I had no idea."

Brad nudged his new husband. "Tell them what's happened to Colin's company."

Gabe's mouth turned downward. "He's been running a Ponzi scheme, and it caught up with him. I think that was one of the reasons he wanted me to join his firm, so I could interact with any law enforcement agency investigating. He erroneously thought I'd be able to steer them away from evidence or assist in covering it up."

"If he thought that, he never really knew you." Natasha tsked. "You're a straight arrow, O'Neill."

Gabe shifted in his seat and licked his lips. He glanced around the room then leaned forward. He lowered his voice. "This goes no further, right?"

"Of course. Everything you say will be held in confidence." Natasha reached out her hand and gripped Gabe's.

Randall nodded in agreement.

"When we were in college, Colin drugged me and made me think I'd been behind the wheel of his car. We were in a single-car accident, and his sister ended up with a broken arm. Of course I believed him. After all, I'd been drinking heavily and was underage." Gabe spoke in a soft voice, yet he looked to make sure no one else was close to the entrance of the dining room to overhear. "He took the blame for driving under the influence and the accident but then got his father to cover it up. There were never any consequences."

"That's terrible," Natasha murmured.

"Oh, it gets worse." Brad's jaw was clenched, and his eyes narrowed.

"Yeah, Brad's right." Gabe twisted his mouth to the side. "Colin tried to blackmail me, using the accident and the injury to his sister. He said he had proof and would destroy my reputation and my career if I didn't end my engagement and move to New York to help him with both his business and his sister."

"What did you do?" Randall leaned in, toward the middle of the table, waiting to hear.

"After a miserable couple of weeks of Colin harassing me, I finally told Brad the truth of what was going on. We decided it was better to face whatever consequences came if Colin followed through on his threats."

Brad held up his left hand. "That's when we decided to head to Vegas and tie the knot."

"How did you find out that Colin had drugged you all those years ago?" Natasha's detective persona was in full force. "And what proof did he have to threaten you with?"

"I have no idea what proof he had, but Emory got him to confess to the entire thing." Gabe smiled at me, but wariness lay heavily on his features. He'd almost come undone when visiting me in the hospital, and he'd blamed himself for my injuries.

Natasha gave me an appraising gaze. "Emory, either you need some formal self-defense training, or you should stick to baking cupcakes. Which, I might add, are quite delicious. I ate two while saying hello to Tillie in the kitchen. I could eat the cranberry buttercream by the spoonful."

"I wholeheartedly agree with you," Brian said as he entered the dining room and came around the table to rest his hands on my shoulders. "Natasha, would you find some classes for Emory to take? I'll sleep a whole lot better at night, knowing she can fend off any more attacks."

"I'll make it my mission to get her signed up." Natasha winked at me.

"Signed up for what?" Mother asked as she joined us.

"Self-defense classes," Natasha and Brian said in unison.

"Oh, thank heavens." Mother sat next to Brad. "It just might lessen my worry for her safety."

"Hey, guys, I'm sitting right here." I lifted my cast. "I'm not doing anything until my arm is fully healed, so don't even think about dragging me to any classes anytime soon."

"Darling, you're here early." Tillie came around the table, holding a pitcher of mimosas. She kissed Brian's cheek. "Did you get out for good behavior?"

"I prepped everything for lunch and got the turkeys roasting in the oven. Sal will take over the rest of the duties. It's time I relinquish a little control and spend time with my family. Oceana will survive a few hours without me there." Brian smiled and kissed the top of my head before taking the pitcher from his grandmother. "Sit down, Gram. I'll take over dispensing the drinks."

While Brian refilled mimosas for those imbibing and retrieved sparkling apple cider and coffee for those who were not, the rest of the guests trickled into the dining room. Gabe and Brad's family were chatting away, and I was happy to see that they appeared not only friendly to one another but also to be enjoying their company.

My sisters, Carrie and Vannie, brought a large basket of warm cranberry-lemon muffins along with a crystal bowl containing fruit salad and sat them on the table. Thomas and John followed them in, carrying dishes of cranberry French toast casserole, while my stepdad, Lars, proudly carried the glazed ham, which they placed on the buffet. Stacks of white china plates and gleaming flatware sat on the buffet for people to help themselves.

The rest of the day flowed, with family and friends coming and going. By the time Brian, Vannie, and Carrie were ready to serve our Thanksgiving dinner, a small crowd had descended upon Tillie's home. It seemed anyone and everyone who knew me wanted to show their support for surviving the murderer's attack. Ever the gracious hostess, Tillie welcomed them all.

Brian led the parade of people pitching in to place platters of sliced cranberry-stuffed turkey breast roulade, sweet potatoes with brown butter and Parmesan cheese, brussels sprouts, salad, and pumpkin rolls on the extended dining room table. My mouth watered at the delectable aromas drifting from the platters.

Tillie stood and placed her hand on my shoulder, while my mother gripped my uninjured hand. Tillie lifted her flute of champagne. "Welcome to my home. We have so much to be thankful for, and I'm delighted you can share in our joy. And as the great Charles Dickens said, 'Reflect upon your present blessings—of which every man has many—not on your past misfortunes, of which all men have some.'"

Chapter 42

T he sun was shining brightly the day of Brad and Gabe's reception. While California might be in desperate need of rain, I was glad the weather forecasters had been wrong. Brian planned on working at Oceana until three then would swing by his place to get ready and would pick me up at four thirty to drive me to the reception. I'd wanted to help out with the setup for all the vendors, but my mother and Carrie had insisted I let them take care of it all. It was probably for the best.

At three, Vannie let herself into my pool house, styling gel and a flatiron in one hand and a black garment bag in the other. "Are you ready to get dolled up?"

I eyed the flatiron, remembering how my hair had behaved the last time Vannie had styled my hair. "I'm not sure it's worth the effort."

"Don't be silly. Your hair looked great until you started riding the mechanical bull at the Canyon Club." Vannie guffawed. "At least, I think that's what you were trying to do, since I doubt you stayed on for more than half a second."

"I don't know what you're talking about." The night she

referred to was supposed to be about celebrating Brad and Gabe two weeks ago but was quite fuzzy, thanks to some powerful margaritas. What I did know was that my hair had looked like a squirrel's nest by the time we got home afterward, and I had a large bruise on my hip.

"Come on back to your bedroom, and I'll show you the outfit Tillie picked up for you."

I groaned. "She didn't...."

"Oh yes, she did." Vannie waved the garment bag at me. "I tried it on, and it fits perfectly."

"Then maybe you should wear it." I studied my sister. Her normally frizzy hair—just like mine—fell around her face in soft curls. She had already applied her makeup. It was subtle yet gave her face a soft glow. Her dress, a cranberry shade of red, flowed around her curves, and cranberry-painted toes peeked out from her open-toed black sling-back heels. Simple gold hoop earrings, a gold chain necklace with a tassel hanging to her décolletage, and thin gold bangles completed the look. "Wow. You look beautiful."

"Thanks. I wasn't sure this dress color would go with my coloring, but I think it makes my hair look more auburn instead of clown red." She giggled. "Teresa helped me pick it out. I'll wear it again when we go to the New Year's Eve bash at her cousin's house."

"She did a great job." I was happy Vannie had someone to spend time with. I held up my casted arm. "All right. Show me the work of art Tillie bought to go with my cast."

"Close your eyes for a big surprise," Vannie demanded. "And no peeking."

I did as she said and heard the zipper slide down the garment bag. I heard a whisper of fabric slipping out and then felt cool silk as the dress was placed in my outstretched hands. I opened my eyes and was surprised to see black. Laughing, I held up the black cocktail dress. "I was expecting something wildly colorful. Tillie told me she was getting something to match my cast."

"This is perfect, and Brian's going to flip out when he sees you." Vannie took the dress from me. "Come on. Let's get you dolled up, Cinderella."

AS I HELD BACK the happy tears that threatened to spill, Brian and I stepped onto Gabe's grandparents' patio. Flickering candles illuminated centerpieces of cranberry and white roses on each of the round tables. Soft instrumental jazz played over the sound system. Waitstaff walked around, passing out flutes of champagne and hors d'oeuvres. I snatched a couple of bacon-wrapped scallops and asked the waiter for some club soda with a lime twist.

Just as I took a bite of the scallop—and oh my, was it ever delicious—Brian leaned down and placed his lips next to my ear.

"Have I mentioned how beautiful you are?" He kissed my cheek as I tried to swallow the scallop. He laughed as I gulped down the bite, and he took the second scallop from the small plate the waiter had given me.

"Only about twenty times already tonight." I bumped my hip into his. "And thank you. I owe it all to your grandmother and Vannie."

The dress Tillie had gifted me was exquisite and from a well-known designer, of course, but the dress itself wasn't fussy. The sweetheart neckline had just enough ruching to make my, ah, assets appear more generous. The wrap-style dress clung to all the good curves without making me uncomfortable, while the black silk fabric floated around the curves I'd prefer to be minimized. With every movement I made, I felt like I was walking on air. Vannie's deft hand with makeup and hair made me feel pampered. She'd even taken the time to give me a mani-pedi to match hers.

"Whaddaya say we hunt down more appetizers? I heard the restaurant catering this shindig is the best in California, if not the US." I threaded my arm through his.

Brian grinned from ear to ear. "You definitely know the way to my heart."

My heart lightened at his words. Brian had exhibited some tense feelings for a few days following my narrow escape. While he didn't blame me for Colin threatening my life, his worry for my safety made him cross with me. It had taken a long heart-to-heart talk to get to the bottom of what was going on between us, but now it seemed like all was right in the world. It was also a relief that Brad and Gabe's event was finally underway, and I could relax, knowing my mother and Carrie had everything under control.

Carrie waved for us to join her and Thomas, who stood close to the bar. We threaded our way between guests milling about to reach my sister. Some guests were in shorts and T-shirts or wore blue jeans with Hawaiian shirts, while others, like Brian, were dressed in suits. Although Brian had ditched the tie and said he was only wearing the jacket in case I got cold later on.

"You and Mother did a fantastic job setting this up." I leaned over and air kissed Carrie's cheek, careful not to smudge my lipstick on her smooth skin.

"We had plenty of help. Lars and Thomas pitched in, as did Brad's sister and Gabe's cousin." Carrie snagged a glass of champagne from a passing server.

"I haven't seen Mother and Lars yet. Are they here?" I eyed my sister's champagne enviously. But I vowed to listen to my doctor's advice and avoid alcohol for several weeks while my concussion healed. He'd assured me I could indulge by Christmastime.

"They're with the girls and the dogs, getting ready for their big rose-petal-throwing event." Carrie giggled, and I suspected that wasn't her first flute of champagne.

"And they have Tommy too?" I asked.

"No. He's around here with Alyssa Mai somewhere. Tommy is quite smitten with that darling little girl." Carrie took a sip. "Natasha and Randall promised to keep watch over him, since he's keeping their daughter entertained. They even arranged it so Tommy could eat dinner with them, although I'll be keeping close watch in case my son gets overly excited."

"That's so sweet. I hope you get some cute photos of the kids together."

"I've already alerted the photographer and told him I'd pay him extra for the shots." She pointed toward the pool area. "There they are."

I craned my neck to look beyond the gathering crowd. Leaning into each other while sitting on an extra-large Adirondack chair, Alyssa Mai and Tommy grinned at the photographer, who seemed to be snapping picture after picture from a variety of angles. Natasha and Randall stood close by, holding hands, while beaming at the cuteness of it all.

A thump on a microphone and a screech as feedback sounded caught the guests' attention. The DJ waved his arm over his head. "Sorry about that. If you'd all like to grab another drink and make your way to your tables, we'll be starting in a few minutes."

Brian and I followed Carrie and Thomas to our table and found the calligraphed place cards where we should sit. I sat next to Tillie and gave her a quick kiss then waved to John.

"Isn't this beautiful?" Tillie leaned her shoulder against mine. "I worried this would never happen."

"You and me both."

"Your parents and Vannie are sitting with us, aren't they? I haven't seen them yet." Tillie took a sip of her gimlet.

"They're helping get the girls and dogs ready for their big entrance," Brian said as he leaned around me and blew his grandmother a kiss.

"They'll steal the show." Tillie chortled then turned to

take a good look at me. "The dress suits you, and Vannie did an excellent job on your hair and makeup, not that you needed it. Our Emory looks beautiful, doesn't she, Brian?"

"Most definitely, Gram." Brian winked at me. "I think she told me I've already said so at least fifty times tonight."

"Thanks, you two." I couldn't help but smile then hoped I hadn't smeared any lipstick onto my teeth. I gazed around the patio and lawn area and was happy to see that we were close to the sweetheart table arranged for Brad and Gabe. A waiter placed my club soda on the table in front of me then took drink orders. The hum of guests chatting filled the air, while the quiet hum of patio heaters strategically placed between the tables kept us warm as the sun dipped below the horizon.

The cheerful opening strands of "All Love Everything," by Aloe Blacc, filled the air. I turned in my seat to catch a glimpse of my nieces and dogs as they entered the patio from the house. My heart caught in my throat, and moisture pricked my eyes. Brian handed me a monogrammed hanky from his suit pocket then got out his cell phone to record for me.

Piper and Missy pranced in front of the girls, side by side, as if they'd practiced their moves for days. Their matching floral wreaths sitting atop their heads appeared to be stable— I'd worried they'd slip off if the dogs shook or bobbed their heads too much. And the small baskets of rose petals riding on their backs seemed to be staying in place.

Kaylee and Sophie wore matching floral wreaths on their heads, as well, although theirs were larger than the dogs' wreaths. They seemed to float in their princess dresses, and I suspected someone, probably Vannie, had instructed them to use ballet arm moves, given the rounded position of their hands and fingers. They dipped their hands into the baskets of burgundy and blush rose petals then flung them into the air with a graceful arc of their arms.

They were about halfway to the sweetheart table, and everything was going perfectly. That was until several bursts of light from camera flashes filled the air. Piper and Missy startled and took off at a run. Rose petals dumped from the baskets as the dogs raced toward the pool.

"Oh no. Please don't jump into the pool." I bolted from the table. "No, Piper and Missy. Come back. I have treats."

Of course, they didn't listen to me and stayed on course, headed straight for the pool. An earsplitting whistle stopped the dogs—and me—in our tracks. I turned to see who had commanded our attention. It was Gabe, and he had a piece of bacon in his hand.

"Do the good doggies want some bacon?" He dangled the piece of meat in front of him.

Bacon was the magic word, and the dogs turned and ran straight for the groom. I caught them right before they lunged for the meat. Brian helped me leash them while Gabe rewarded the dogs.

"I'm so sorry about this, Gabe." My cheeks were burning with embarrassment, and I hoped my nieces weren't too upset.

"I actually counted on something like this happening, and now I'm not disappointed." Gabe's grin lit up his face. "It'll be a story to tell our kids and grandkids for decades to come. Why don't you take Piper and Missy back to the girls, and we'll start from the top again but with leashes this time."

Brian and I escorted the dogs back to the entrance of the house. Brad, Carrie, Kaylee, and Sophie had collected most of the rose petals with the help of guests. They refilled the baskets, and Carrie made sure they were still securely attached to the dog vests, as were the flower wreaths. They all were, amazingly. I shuddered, thinking about what would have happened had the dogs actually made it into the pool. With the heavy vests and baskets, I'd have had to jump in to rescue them before they sank to the bottom.

As Brian and I made our way back to the table, I heard a lot of giggles and phrases like *So cute, Adorable,* and *They'll have stories to tell for years.* Maybe Gabe was right, and I shouldn't take it so seriously.

The DJ cued up the music again, and my nieces, with the dogs attached to their leashes held by the two girls, made their way down the aisle again. When they reached the sweetheart table, they each went to a side, turned around, and waited. The rose petals made a colorful path from the table to the house.

The DJ picked up the mic again. "And now introducing the new O'Neill-Rullers!"

Brad and Gabe emerged from the house hand in hand and dressed in the tuxes I'd picked up for them. I'd never seen either of them look so happy, and once again, tears pricked my eyes. When they reached the white runner, they broke out into a choreographed dance that went with the beautiful song lyrics and melody. It was obvious they'd had the dance created for their entrance and then spent a lot of time practicing until they'd perfected the complicated moves. Applause broke out, and I joined in. Even Gabe's grandparents—who had stayed in town and attended the reception—had smiles on their faces.

As the song came to a close, Gabe and Brad ended the dance with a twirling flourish, picked up their flutes of champagne, and toasted each other.

Brad stepped forward, and the DJ handed him a mic. "Gabe and I appreciate everyone being here to help us celebrate the start of our new life together. It means the world to us."

Gabe closed the gap between them and took the mic. "As a wise man recently told us, the secret to a long and happy marriage is a good sense of humor and a short memory. So we're going to forget the obstacles that stood in our way to get to our special day, and we'll celebrate why we're all here. Drink up the champagne, and come dance the night away with us."

Cheers sounded around the tables, and Brian wrapped an arm around my shoulders. "I wouldn't want to be celebrating with anyone other than you. I love you, Emory."

I leaned into his embrace and kissed him. "And I love you, too, Brian."

RECIPES

Thanksgiving Day Menu

Brunch
Baked Ham with Cranberry Glaze
Cranberry French Toast Casserole
Cranberry-Lemon Muffins
Fruit Salad

Dinner

Cocktails
Cranberry Mojitos
Sparkling Wine Garnished with Sugared Cranberries
Hors d'oeuvres
Cranberry Salsa served with an assortment of
crackers and tortilla chips
Crudités: Asparagus, Sliced Radishes, Cauliflower Florets,
Celery Sticks
Baked Brie with Roasted Cranberries
Salad
Spinach, Radicchio, Cranberry, and Pecan Salad
Cranberry-Pumpkin Rolls
Main Course

Thanksgiving Day Menu

Cranberry Stuffed Turkey Breast Roulade
Sweet Potatoes with Brown Butter and Parmesan Cheese
Roasted Brussels Sprouts with Bacon
Vegetarian: Stuffed Acorn Squash with Cranberries
Dessert
Cranberry Mojito Cupcakes
Cranberry Orange Cupcakes
Cranberry Cake with Lemon Glaze
White Chocolate Cranberry Cookies

Overnight Cranberry French Toast Casserole

SERVES 12

Ingredients
French Toast:

1 pound loaf, stale rustic white bread cubed into 1-inch pieces (gluten-free bread may be substituted)

2 cups milk (whole, 2%, or almond milk)

4 eggs

1/4 cup pure maple syrup

2 tablespoons brown sugar

1 teaspoon vanilla extract

1 teaspoon ground cinnamon

1-1/2 cups fresh (or frozen) cranberries, divided

Topping:

1/4 cup butter, cold and cut into small pieces

1/4 cup brown sugar

1/4 cup old fashioned rolled oats

1/4 teaspoon sea salt

1 teaspoon ground cinnamon

1 cup pecans, finely chopped

Instructions
French Toast:

Spritz a 9 x 13-inch casserole dish with cooking spray, then add the cubed bread to the dish. Set aside.

In a medium-sized bowl, whisk the milk, eggs, maple syrup, brown sugar, vanilla, and cinnamon together until thoroughly combined.

Pour the egg mixture over the cubed bread. Press the bread down into the liquid with the back of a spatula, until bread becomes partly saturated. Cover with plastic wrap and refrigerate overnight.

Topping:

In a medium-sized mixing bowl, combine the brown sugar, rolled oats, salt, cinnamon, and pecans. Using a pastry cutter or two forks, work the cold butter into the mixture until blended. Cover with plastic wrap and store in the refrigerator until needed.

Putting it together:

Preheat the oven to 350 degrees (F).

Remove the casserole from the refrigerator and stir the saturated bread to help soak up any egg mixture that may have puddled on the bottom of the dish. Top with 1 cup fresh (or frozen) cranberries and stir to combine. Sprinkle the remaining 1/2 cup cranberries over the top of the casserole.

Scatter the topping over the casserole.

Bake uncovered for 35 - 45 minutes, or until edges and topping are golden. Remove from oven and allow to cool for 10 minutes before serving with additional maple syrup.

Note:

If using frozen cranberries, do not defrost first.

Cranberry-Lemon Muffins
SERVES 12

Ingredients

1/4 cup butter, room temperature
1/2 cup granulated sugar
1/4 cup brown sugar
2 eggs
1/2 cup sour cream
1 teaspoon vanilla extract
1/2 teaspoon lemon extract
Zest from 1 lemon
1-3/4 cup all-purpose flour
1-1/2 teaspoons baking powder
1/2 teaspoon baking soda
1/2 teaspoon sea salt
3/4 cup whole berry cranberry sauce
Coarse sparkling sugar

Instructions

Preheat oven to 375 degrees (F) and line a 12-cup muffin tin with paper liners.

Using an electric or stand mixer, cream together the butter and sugars until light and fluffy, 2 to 3 minutes. Add the eggs one at a time, beating well after each addition. Mix in the sour cream, lemon extract, and lemon zest and beat until thoroughly incorporated.

In a medium-sized bowl, whisk together the flour, baking powder, baking soda, and salt. In 4 increments, add to the sugar mixture, mixing on low speed after each addition, just until combined. Don't overbeat, but batter should be smooth after the final addition of flour mixture.

Dollop the cranberry sauce over the surface of the muffin batter, then using a butter knife, swirl the cranberry sauce into the batter. You want to create a marbleized effect, so don't stir vigorously to make the sauce disappear completely into the batter.

Divide the batter evenly in the prepared muffin tin. Sprinkle the tops of the batter generously with coarse sparkling sugar, if desired.

Bake 20 to 23 minutes or until a wooden skewer inserted into the center of the muffins comes out mostly clean. A few moist crumbs clinging to the skewer is desired.

Cool muffins in the tin for 5 minutes then remove to a wire rack. Serve warm but cool completely before storing in an airtight container. Store in the refrigerator for up to 4 days.

Cranberry Mojito
SERVES 4

Ingredients
Cranberry Syrup
1/4 cup water
1/4 cup granulated sugar
1 cup fresh or frozen cranberries
Cranberry Mojito
16 sprigs fresh mint
4 tablespoons freshly squeezed lime juice
8 ounces light rum
16 ounces sparkling water
Extra mint sprigs, lime slices, and frozen cranberries for garnish
Instructions
Cranberry Syrup
Place the water, sugar, and cranberries in a small saucepan and stir together. Simmer over low heat for about 5 minutes or until the sauce thickens and the cranberries pop. Remove from heat and allow to cool then refrigerate until needed.
Cranberry Mojito
Divide the cranberry syrup evenly among four highball glasses.

Remove the mint leaves from the stems and place the leaves in a cocktail shaker. Add the lime juice and muddle together, pressing on the mint leaves 5 or 6 times.

Add the light rum to the cocktail shaker and shake several times. Add crushed ice to the highball glasses to about halfway full then divide the rum mixture among the glasses. Add sparkling water, about 4 ounces, to each glass and gently stir to combine ingredients.

Garnish each glass with a sprig of mint, a slice of lime, and frozen cranberries if desired.

Baked Brie with Roasted Cranberries

Ingredients
    1 (1 pound) brie cheese wheel
    2 cups fresh (or frozen) cranberries
    1/3 cup granulated sugar
    3 tablespoons white balsamic vinegar (or regular balsamic can be substituted)
    1/4 teaspoon sea salt
    1/3 cup toasted pecans
    Rosemary sprigs for garnishing (if desired)
    Crackers or toasted baguette slices for serving

Instructions
Preheat the oven to 400 degrees (F) and line two baking sheets with parchment paper.

In a medium-sized bowl, whisk together the sugar, balsamic vinegar, and salt. Add the cranberries (if using frozen, do not defrost), and gently stir to coat the berries. Spread the mixture on one of the prepared baking sheets.

Place the brie on the remaining baking sheet and place both the brie and cranberries in the oven.

Bake for ten minutes then remove the brie.

Roast the cranberries for an additional 5 minutes. If using

frozen cranberries, you may need to roast for an additional 10 to 15 minutes or until the berries are soft and have started to burst. Remove from oven.

Place the brie on a serving tray and top with the warm roasted cranberries. Sprinkle the toasted pecans over the cranberries and garnish with fresh rosemary sprigs if desired. Serve immediately.

Note:

Recipe can be halved if using an 8-ounce wheel of brie.

Cranberry-Pumpkin Rolls
MAKES 24 ROLLS

Ingredients
3/4 cup pure pumpkin puree
2 eggs
3/4 cup warm water (between 102 and 104 degrees F)
4 tablespoons unsalted butter, room temperature
4-3/4 cups all-purpose flour
1 teaspoon cinnamon
1/4 teaspoon ginger
1/4 teaspoon cloves
1/4 cup brown sugar, packed
1-1/2 teaspoons sea salt
1 tablespoon instant yeast
3/4 cup dried cranberries, coarsely chopped
1/3 cup crystallized ginger, finely chopped

Instructions
Add all the ingredients (from the pumpkin puree to the yeast, saving the cranberries and crystallized ginger to add in later) into the bowl of a bread machine in the order suggested by the manufacturer.

Select the bread dough cycle and press start. Once the mixture has kneaded for several minutes, check the consistency of the dough, since pumpkin can vary in moisture content. If too dry, add a little more water a couple of teaspoons at a time. If overly sticky, add in additional flour a tablespoon at a time. The dough should be soft and fairly smooth and forming a ball that pulls away from the sides of the bread machine bowl. When touched, the surface should be slightly tacky.

Add in the cranberries and crystallized ginger when kneading cycle is almost complete (my machine beeps to indicate when additions should be made).

Heavily grease two 8-inch round cake tins. Set aside.

Once the dough cycle is complete, and dough has risen and is puffy, form the dough into 24 equally sized balls and nestle them in the two prepared cake tins, 12 rolls per each cake tin. I place 9 rolls around the outer edge and 3 rolls in the center. Alternately, you can use greased cupcake tins to bake them in. Instead of 24 rolls, divide the dough into 16 pieces and nestle a single piece into each well of the cupcake tin.

Preheat the oven to 350 degrees (F).

Set the round cake tins (or cupcake tins) in a warm, draft-free area, and allow the dough to rise for an hour or until the rolls look puffy.

Bake the rolls for 25 to 30 minutes, until they're toasty brown, rotating once midway through baking. If you have an instant-read thermometer, the center should read 190 degrees (F). (The same baking time applies to rolls baked in both the cake tins and the cupcake tins.)

Remove the rolls from the oven and allow to rest for 5 minutes. Remove the rolls from the cake tins or cupcake tins. If desired, brush the tops of the hot rolls with butter. Allow to cool on a wire rack until ready to serve.

Store completely cooled rolls in an airtight container for 3 days.

Cranberry Stuffed Turkey Breast Roulade
SERVES 4 - 8

Ingredients
Turkey & Stuffing:
2 to 4 pounds boneless turkey breast, skin removed and reserved

1 teaspoon salt, divided

1/2 teaspoon freshly ground pepper

1 tablespoon olive oil

2 medium onions, divided

2 garlic cloves, minced

2-1/2 cups cubed stale bread (gluten-free bread can be substituted)

1/2 cup dried cranberries, soaked in hot water for 5 minutes then drained

1/3 cup chopped pecans

2 tablespoons fresh sage, chopped

2-1/2 cups low-sodium chicken broth, divided

1 bay leaf

Turkey Gravy:
2 cups of strained drippings from the turkey (use additional low sodium chicken broth if needed)

2 teaspoons fresh sage, chopped

1 tablespoon cornstarch
1 tablespoon low-sodium chicken broth
1 tablespoon cold unsalted butter
Salt and white pepper to taste

Instructions
Turkey & Stuffing:

Preheat the oven to 375 degrees (F).

Chop the 2 onions, reserving 1 of them. In a large Dutch oven over medium heat, brown the reserved turkey skin. Once golden, add one of the chopped onions and 1/2 teaspoon salt to the pot and cook until lightly browned, about 10 minutes, stirring frequently.

While the onion cooks, butterfly the turkey breast by slicing the meat horizontally, cutting almost to the other side. Open it like a book, and place it between two sheets of heavy-duty plastic wrap. Pound with a meat mallet to a thickness of almost 1/2 inch. Sprinkle the salt and pepper on both sides of the turkey. Set aside.

Discard the turkey skin from the chopped onions and reduce heat to low. Add in the garlic and cook 1 minute. Add the 1/2 cup chicken broth and stir to scrape up the brown bits on the bottom of the pot. Mix in the bread cubes, cranberries, pecans, and 2 tablespoons chopped sage. If stuffing seems dry, add a bit more chicken broth. The mixture should appear moist but not wet. Cook for 2 to 3 minutes, until mixture is heated through. Season with extra salt and pepper to taste.

Spread the stuffing over the pounded turkey breast, leaving 2 inches uncovered on all sides. Roll the turkey breast up and tightly secure with kitchen twine. If your turkey falls apart into 2 pieces, stuff and tie them individually.

Wipe stuffing residue from the Dutch oven then add 1 tablespoon olive oil to the pot. Heat over medium heat. Once the oil is hot, add the stuffed turkey breast and sear on all sides until lightly browned.

Pour in 1-1/2 cups chicken broth and stir the bottom of

the pot to scrape up the browned bits, being careful to not disturb the turkey breast. Add the bay leaf and sprinkle the remaining chopped onion around the turkey. Bring the broth just to a simmer then cover with a lid (or aluminum foil).

Roast in the oven for 30 to 50 minutes (depending on size of turkey breast. If turkey breast is in 2 pieces, it will cook more quickly). Begin checking temperature at 30 minutes with an instant-read thermometer. The thickest part of the turkey breast should register 160 degrees (F). (Carryover heat should raise the temperature to 165 degrees.)

Remove from the oven and transfer turkey breast to a cutting board. Immediately cover it tightly with aluminum foil and allow it to rest while you prepare the gravy.

Turkey Gravy:

Strain the juices from the Dutch oven. Press on the solids to extract as much liquid as possible then discard the solids. Return 2 cups of the liquid to the Dutch oven. If the juices from the turkey don't measure 2 cups, add enough chicken broth to make up the difference.

Add the fresh sage to the pot and bring to a simmer over medium-high heat. Once simmer is reached, reduce heat to low.

Mix the cornstarch with the 1 tablespoon of chicken broth. Slowly whisk the mixture into the simmering liquid. Bring the liquid back to a simmer and cook for another two minutes. Remove from heat.

Whisk the cold butter into the thickened gravy then season with salt and pepper to taste.

Remove the twine from the turkey breast and cut it into slices. Serve the gravy alongside.

Sweet Potatoes with Brown Butter and Parmesan Cheese
SERVES 8 - 10

A special thank you to my bonus daughter, Briana, for introducing me to this delicious sweet potato dish so many years ago and sharing her recipe! We've never been fans of sweet potato casserole with brown sugar and marshmallows, but this savory dish has become our go-to family recipe.

Ingredients

4 pounds sweet potatoes (tan-skinned are best), peeled and cut into 1-inch cubes

1/2 cup plus 2 tablespoons unsalted butter

1/4 cup fresh sage, finely chopped

1-1/4 cups grated Parmesan cheese

Salt and freshly ground pepper to taste

Fresh sage leaves for garnish

Instructions

Cover and steam the sweet potato cubes over boiling water for about 15 minutes, just until tender when pierced with a fork. Remove from the steamer and allow to cool.

Preheat oven to 400 degrees (F). Grease a 9 x 13-inch casserole dish. Add the cooled sweet potato cubes and set aside.

In a heavy pan, melt the butter over medium-low heat. As

the butter melts, swirl the pan frequently, and cook until the butter is golden brown, about 5 minutes.

Add the chopped fresh sage and 1/2 teaspoon of salt and 1/4 teaspoon of freshly ground pepper to the butter. Continue to cook until the butter is deep golden brown, about 2 minutes. Remove from heat and immediately pour over the sweet potatoes.

Sprinkle 3/4 cup grated Parmesan cheese over the sweet potatoes and stir to evenly coat. Add additional salt and pepper to taste.

Cover the casserole dish with aluminum foil and bake until sweet potatoes are heated through, 20 to 25 minutes.

Remove from oven and sprinkle the remaining Parmesan cheese over the top. If desired, garnish with fresh sage leaves right before serving.

Note

When browning the butter, it is best to use a stainless-steel pan instead of a dark, nonstick pan so you can easily monitor the changing color of the butter as it browns.

You can make this dish (and refrigerate) a day or two ahead of time then simply bake it while the turkey is resting.

Vegetarian Wild-Rice-Stuffed Acorn Squash
SERVES 4

Ingredients

2 medium acorn squash

2 tablespoons olive oil

1 onion, finely diced

2 cloves garlic, minced

8 ounces quartered baby button mushrooms

1 (15-ounce) can garbanzo beans (drained and rinsed)

3/4 cup dried cranberries

2 teaspoons cumin

2 cups cooked wild rice (or wild rice-brown rice mix)

1/2 orange, juiced and zested

1/2 cup grated Parmesan cheese, divided (or vegan Parmesan if desired)

2 cups (packed in measuring cup) baby spinach, coarsely chopped

1/2 cup slivered almonds, toasted

1 teaspoon sea salt or more to taste (divided)

Pepper to taste

Parsley for garnish

Instructions

Acorn Squash:

Preheat the oven to 375 degrees (F) and line a baking sheet with parchment paper.

Slice the top off about an inch below the stem and cut an inch off the bottom so the squash sits flat. Slice the squash in half, between the top and the bottom. Scoop out the seeds and fibers.

Brush the cut surfaces of the acorn squash with olive oil and sprinkle with salt and pepper.

Place the squash halves, cut side up, on the baking sheet. Bake for 25 to 30 minutes, or until a fork easily pierces squash. Remove from oven and cover with foil to keep warm.

Increase oven temperature to 425 degrees (F).

Filling:

Add 1 tablespoon of olive oil to a skillet and heat over medium heat. Add the diced onions, garlic, quartered mushrooms, 1/2 teaspoon sea salt, and several grinds of pepper. Stir to coat with oil. Cook for 8 to 10 minutes, stirring often, until liquid evaporates and the onions begin to slightly brown.

Add in the garbanzo beans, cranberries, and cumin. Stir to combine and cook for 3 to 4 minutes, until heated through.

Add the wild rice, orange juice, and zest to the skillet. Stirring often, heat until hot, about 3 to 4 minutes.

Stir in 1/3 cup Parmesan cheese, almonds, and spinach. Stirring constantly, cook just until the spinach is wilted. Season with additional salt and pepper if desired.

Putting it together:

Divide the filling among the four squash halves, mounding the filling as needed. Refrigerate any leftover filling.

Sprinkle each squash with the remaining Parmesan cheese.

Bake at 425 degrees (F) for 10 minutes, until the tops are golden brown.

Garnish with parsley, if desired, right before serving.

Cranberry Cake with Lemon Glaze

Ingredients

Cake:
1/3 cup packed brown sugar
3 cups fresh (or frozen) cranberries - divided
2-1/2 cups all-purpose flour plus 1 tablespoon - divided
2-1/2 teaspoons baking powder
1/2 teaspoon baking soda
1 teaspoon salt
1-1/2 cups granulated sugar
Zest from 1 lemon
1-1/2 cups (3 sticks) unsalted butter, room temperature
3 eggs, room temperature
1 teaspoon vanilla extract
3/4 cup buttermilk
2 tablespoons fresh lemon juice

Glaze:
1 cup confectioners' sugar
1 tablespoon + 2 teaspoons fresh lemon juice
Pinch of salt

Instructions

Cake:

Preheat oven to 350 degrees (F). Heavily grease and flour a Bundt cake pan.

Sprinkle brown sugar over the bottom of the pan then layer half the cranberries over the sugar. (*If using frozen cranberries, do not defrost first. Instead, add them right before pouring in the batter.)

In a medium bowl, whisk together 2-1/2 cups flour, baking powder, baking soda, and salt. Set aside.

Using an electric mixer, mix the granulated sugar with the lemon zest. Beat until the sugar becomes light yellow, about 2 minutes. Add the butter to the lemon sugar and beat on medium-high speed until light and fluffy. Add in the eggs one at a time, mixing well after each addition. Stir in the vanilla.

Stir together the buttermilk and 2 tablespoons lemon juice. With mixer on low speed, alternate adding the dry ingredients with the buttermilk in three increments. Mix until ingredients are incorporated.

Sprinkle the extra tablespoon of flour over the remaining cranberries (if using frozen cranberries, now is the time to remove them from the freezer) and stir to combine. Add the cranberries to the cake batter and fold in.

*If using frozen cranberries, now is the time to layer the first half of the cranberries on top of the brown sugar.

Spread the batter over the cranberries and brown sugar.

Bake 50 to 55 minutes, or until golden brown and a wooden skewer comes out mostly clean. A few moist crumbs clinging to the skewer is desired.

Transfer to a wire rack and allow to cool for 15 minutes. Invert the cake onto a serving platter or cake stand and remove the Bundt pan. If some of the cranberries and sugar stick to the cake pan, spoon it back onto the top of the cake. The glaze will hide any holes or cracks. Allow the cake to cool completely before drizzling the glaze.

Glaze:

Whisk the confectioners' sugar with the lemon juice until smooth. Drizzle over the cooled cake and allow to set before serving.

Cranberry Orange Cupcakes
WITH CRANBERRY CREAM CHEESE BUTTERCREAM

Makes 15

If you make the sugared cranberries for garnishing, you will need to plan ahead and start them one day prior to serving the cupcakes.

Ingredients

Sugared Cranberries:

1 cup granulated sugar

1 cup water

1 cup fresh (or frozen) cranberries*

1/2 cup superfine sugar**

Cupcakes:

1-1/2 cups all-purpose flour

2 teaspoons baking powder

1/2 teaspoon salt

1/2 cup unsalted butter, room temperature

1 cup granulated sugar

2 eggs, room temperature

Zest from 1 orange

3/4 cup buttermilk

1/2 teaspoon orange extract

1 teaspoon vanilla

1-1/2 cups fresh (or frozen) cranberries, roughly chopped

Cranberry Cream Cheese Buttercream:
1/2 cup fresh (or frozen) cranberries
1 tablespoon water
4 ounces cream cheese, room temperature
1/2 cup unsalted butter, room temperature
1/4 teaspoon orange extract
5 cups confectioners' sugar
1/4 teaspoon salt

Instructions

Sugared Cranberries:

Combine 1 cup sugar and water in a saucepan and cook over medium heat, stirring constantly, just until the sugar is dissolved. Don't allow the mixture to boil. Otherwise, the cranberries will burst. Remove from heat and allow the mixture to sit for 5 minutes. Place the cranberries in a bowl and add the simple syrup. Cover bowl and refrigerate overnight.

Drain the cranberries and roll them in the superfine sugar, making sure cranberries are thoroughly coated. Transfer to a baking sheet lined with parchment paper. Allow to dry for at least 2 hours.

Cupcakes:

Preheat oven to 350 degrees (F). Line cupcake tins with paper liners.

In a medium bowl, whisk together the flour, baking powder, and salt. Set aside.

Using an electric mixer, beat together the butter and sugar until light and fluffy. Add in the eggs 1 at a time, mixing until incorporated. Mix in the orange zest.

Combine the buttermilk with the orange extract and vanilla in a liquid measuring cup.

With mixer on low speed, alternate adding the dry ingredients with the buttermilk, in three increments. Mix until ingredients are incorporated.

Fold the cranberries into the batter.

Fill the cupcake liners 2/3 full.

Bake 15-18 minutes until a wooden skewer inserted into the center comes out mostly clean. A few moist crumbs clinging to the skewer is fine.

Remove the cupcake tins from the oven and cool for 5 minutes then remove the cupcakes and cool completely on a wire rack before frosting.

Cranberry Cream Cheese Buttercream:

In a small saucepan, add the cranberries and water. Cook over medium-low heat until they start to pop and the mixture turns into a jammy sauce. Stir frequently.

Remove from heat and using the back of a spoon, mash the cranberries to get a relatively smooth mixture. Refrigerate to cool completely and until ready to use. You can make this a day in advance.

In the bowl of a standing mixer, cream the butter and cream cheese until smooth. Add the orange extract and salt. On low speed, mix in half the confectioners' sugar a little at a time until incorporated into the butter and cream cheese mixture.

Add in 1 tablespoon of the cranberry mixture and beat to combine. Add in the remaining confectioners' sugar. Beat until blended then add in an additional 1 tablespoon of the cranberry mixture. Increase the mixer speed to medium high and beat until light and fluffy, about 5 minutes.

Using a large star tip, generously pipe the frosting in swooping swirls over the tops of the cupcakes. Garnish with sugared cranberries, if using.

If not serving immediately, refrigerate. Allow to come to room temperature an hour before serving.

Notes:

*If using frozen cranberries, don't defrost first. Keep them frozen until ready to add to the recipes.

**If you don't have superfine sugar, whirl regular granulated sugar in a food processor for 20 pulses.

Cranberry Mojito Cupcakes
MAKES 16 - 18 CUPCAKES

Ingredients
Cupcakes:
1/2 cup loosely measured fresh mint leaves, then roughly chopped

1 cup light rum

1/2 cup freshly squeezed lime juice (about 4 limes)

1 box white cake mix (I used Pillsbury Moist Supreme)

3 eggs

1/2 cup vegetable oil

Optional: 1/2 teaspoon peppermint extract if you prefer more than a subtle mint flavor

Zest from 1 lime

1-1/2 cups fresh (or frozen) cranberries, roughly chopped

Cranberry Mojito Buttercream:
1/3 cup fresh (or frozen) cranberries

1 tablespoon water

1-1/2 cups (3 sticks) unsalted butter, room temperature

6 cups confectioners' sugar

1/2 teaspoon sea salt

3 tablespoons of the rum mixture, reserved from cupcake recipe

Instructions
Cupcakes:

Place the fresh mint and rum in a saucepan. Heat over medium-low heat until it barely begins to simmer. Remove from stovetop and allow the mixture to steep for 15 minutes. Strain the solids from the liquid, pressing with the back of a spoon to extract as much liquid as possible. Discard the solids. Add the lime juice to the rum mixture and allow the liquid to cool to room temperature.

Measure out 1 cup of the liquid for the cupcakes and set aside the remaining liquid for the buttercream frosting.

Preheat oven to 350 degrees (F). Line cupcake tins with paper liners.

In a large bowl, combine the cake mix, eggs, vegetable oil, peppermint extract (if using), and 1 cup of the steeped rum mixture (make sure it's completely cooled). Beat on medium-high speed for 2 minutes, until batter is smooth.

Fold the chopped cranberries into the batter.

Fill the cupcake liners 3/4 full.

Bake 22-24 minutes, rotating once during baking, until a wooden skewer inserted into the center comes out mostly clean. A few moist crumbs clinging to the skewer is fine.

Remove the cupcake tins from the oven and cool for 5 minutes, then remove the cupcakes and cool completely on a wire rack before frosting.

Cranberry Mojito Buttercream:

In a small saucepan, add the cranberries and water. Cook over medium-low heat until they start to pop and the mixture turns into a thick sauce. Stir frequently.

Remove from heat and, using a fork, mash the cranberries to get a relatively smooth mixture. Refrigerate to cool completely and until ready to use. You can make this a day in advance.

In the bowl of a standing mixer, cream the butter until

light and fluffy. Add the salt and half the confectioners' sugar a little at a time until incorporated into the butter.

Add in the cranberry mixture and 2 tablespoons of the rum mixture and beat to combine. Add in the remaining confectioners' sugar. Mix on low until blended then increase the mixer speed to medium high and beat until light and fluffy, about 5 minutes. If the buttercream frosting is too stiff, add additional rum liquid mixture 1 teaspoon at a time, until desired consistency is reached.

Using a large star tip, generously pipe the frosting in swooping swirls over the tops of the cupcakes. Garnish with fresh mint leaves and lime wedges if desired, right before serving.

If not serving immediately, refrigerate. Allow to come to room temperature an hour before serving.

Notes:

If using frozen cranberries, don't defrost first. Keep them frozen until ready to add to the recipes.

White Chocolate Cranberry Cookies
MAKES 35 - 40 COOKIES, DEPENDING ON SIZE

Ingredients

1-1/2 cups all-purpose flour
1 teaspoon baking soda
1/2 teaspoon salt
1/2 cup (1 stick) unsalted butter, room temperature
1/2 cup packed brown sugar
1/4 cup granulated sugar
1 egg, room temperature
1 teaspoon vanilla extract
3/4 cup white chocolate chips
3/4 cup dried sweetened cranberries

Instructions

Line a baking sheet with parchment paper.

In a medium-sized bowl, whisk together the flour, baking soda, and salt. Set aside.

In the bowl of a stand mixer, cream the butter, brown sugar, and granulated sugar together until fluffy. Add the egg and vanilla extract. Beat until thoroughly combined.

On low speed, add the flour mixture and mix just until

combined. Add in the white chocolate chips and sweetened cranberries. Mix until incorporated.

Cover with plastic wrap and refrigerate for 45 minutes.

Preheat oven to 350 degrees (F).

Scoop the cookie dough into tablespoon-sized balls and place on the prepared baking sheet. Keep the dough balls at least 2 inches apart, since dough will spread while baking.

Bake 9 to 11 minutes, until the edges are beginning to turn golden brown. The center of the cookies should still appear slightly undercooked.

Remove cookies from the oven and allow to cool 5 minutes before removing them to a wire rack to cool completely. Repeat with remaining dough, making sure baking sheet is cooled before adding cookie dough.

Store cooled cookies in an airtight container at room temperature for up to 4 days.

Or roll cookie dough balls in granulated sugar and freeze on a baking sheet. Once solid, place in a freezer-safe ziplock bag and store in freezer. When ready to bake, remove the amount you wish to bake and place on a parchment-lined baking sheet. Allow to slightly defrost while the oven preheats. You may need to add a minute or two to the baking time.

Dedication

For Linda and Karen
I'm so happy you found each other!

Acknowledgments

It's true that it takes a village to create a book. I'd like to thank my husband, Dan, for reading and editing my manuscript several times. His engineering mind is invaluable in helping to keep my books (mostly logical).

A huge thank you to Mary Karnes, owner of Mother of the Bride wedding planner for helping me with the timeline of what needs to be accomplished leading up to a wedding. She happily gave me so much valuable information that I felt a bit guilty I couldn't use all of it in the story. Perhaps another wedding will take place in a future book and I'll get to share more of Mary's expertise!

Thank you to the lovely ladies of the Las Alegres group, who so willingly taste tested several of the recipes included in this book. I appreciate their enthusiasm as they shared an afternoon with me and allowed me to talk about my author journey with them.

Thank you to Janet Clause for being an early reader of my (very) rough draft. Your comments and suggestions always help in making my book so much better.

I greatly appreciate the talents of cover designer Karen Phillips. She captured the vision of my book and made it all the more special by managing to fit in the two special doggies in my life.

It was a delight getting to add Tracey My into the story after winning a character naming auction to benefit Make-A-Wish. Thank you for donating to such a worthy charity that is so close to my heart!

To all the bloggers who help me spread the word about my new releases and put up with my last-minute requests to review, I owe you a debt of gratitude! Readers and authors alike are fortunate to have you in our community. And to all the readers who take the time to read and review my books—you are appreciated! You're what makes me get up extra early to put my stories on the page. A special thanks to all the lovely people who follow my blog, Cinnamon, Sugar, and a Little Bit of Murder, and share in my love for delicious food and mysteries! You inspire me to create recipes to share with family and friends.

About the Author

Kim Davis lives in Southern California with her husband and puppy, Missy. When she's not spending time with her grand-daughters or chasing her energetic pup, she can be found either writing stories or working on her blog, Cinnamon, Sugar, and a Little Bit of Murder or in the kitchen baking up yummy treats. She has published the suspense novel, A GAME OF DECEIT, the award-winning Cupcake Catering cozy mystery series, and the Aromatherapy Apothecary Mystery series. She also has had several children's articles published in several magazines. Kim Davis is a member of Mystery Writers of America and Sisters in Crime.

MUDDLED MATRIMONIAL MURDER

Cupcake Catering Mystery Series Book 6

Cinnamon & Sugar Press

All characters and events in this book are a work of fiction. Any similarities to anyone living or dead are purely coincidental. Kim Davis is identified as the sole author of this book.

All rights are reserved. No part of this publication may be reproduced, stored in a retrieval system, or transmitted in any form or by any means, except for brief quotations in printed reviews, without the prior written permission of the author. Thank you for respecting the hard work of this author.

Copyright © 2023 Kim Davis

ISBN 979-8-9853601-3-4

ISBN 979-8-9853601-2-7

ISBN 979-8-2234976-1-5

Cover Design by Karen Phillips

Edited by Red Adept Editing

 Created with Vellum

Also by Kim Davis

The Cupcake Catering Mystery Series

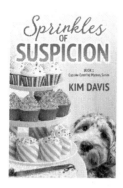

SPRINKLES OF SUSPICION

One glass of cheap California chardonnay cost Emory Gosser Martinez her husband, her job, and her best friend. Unfortunately, that was only the beginning of her troubles.

Distraught after discovering the betrayal by her husband and best friend, Tori, cupcake caterer Emory Martinez allows her temper to flare. Several people witness her very public altercation with her ex-friend. To make matters worse, Tori exacts her revenge by posting a fake photo of Emory in a compromising situation, which goes viral on social media. When Tori is found murdered, all signs point to Emory being the prime suspect.

With the police investigation focused on gathering evidence to convict her, Emory must prove her innocence while whipping up batches of cupcakes and buttercream. Delving into the past of her murdered ex-friend, she finds other people had reasons to want Tori dead, including Emory's own husband. Can she find the killer, or will the clues sprinkled around the investigation point the police back to her?

Praise for Sprinkles of Suspicion

"…there is enough action, including a few surprises—plus baking—to maintain a steady momentum. The breezy book concludes with a collection of unique recipes. An engaging cozy best enjoyed with a plate of cookies." – *Kirkus Reviews*

"The mystery, characters, and mouth-watering recipes will charm readers until the very end." – *InD'tale Magazine, Crowned Heart Review*

"You are going to love this delicious new cozy mystery! Kim Davis pens characters who come to life and a story you won't want to put down, not to mention recipes that will make your mouth water. Don't miss this scrumptious treat! – *Paige Shelton*, New York Times Bestselling author of the Farmers' Market, Country Cooking School, Dangerous Type, Scottish Bookshop mysteries, and Alaska Wild suspense series

"Sparkling prose, a deliciously twisty plot, and a colorful cast of characters make this debut cozy a surefire winner!" – *Linda Reilly*, author of the Cat Lady Mysteries, Deep Fried Mysteries, and the Grilled Cheese Mystery series.

"A delightful new cozy with a cool California setting and an imminently likable heroine." *Ellen Byron*, Best Humorous Lefty Awards winner and author of the Agatha Award winning and USA Today Bestselling Cajun Country Mysteries, The Catering Hall Mysteries, and the Vintage Cookbook Mystery series.

"This story moves along at a great pace and doesn't lag anywhere. There is always something happening, drama, twists, and yes, cupcakes. So well-plotted, I was totally taken in by the entire story and flabbergasted when the real killer was revealed." *Escape With Dollycas Into A Good Book*

CAKE POPPED OFF

Cupcake caterer Emory Martinez is hosting a Halloween bash alongside her octogenarian employer, Tillie. With guests dressed in elaborate costumes, the band is rocking, the cocktails are flowing, and tempers are flaring when the hired Bavarian Barmaid tries to hook a rich, hapless husband. Except one of her targets happens to be Emory's brother-in-law, which bodes ill for his pregnant wife. When Emory tracks down the distraught barmaid, instead of finding the young woman in tears, she finds her dead. Can she explain to the new detective on the scene why the Bavarian Barmaid was murdered in Emory's bathtub with Emory's Poison Apple Cake Pops stuffed into her mouth?

With an angry pregnant sister to contend with, she promises to clear her brother-in-law's name. As Emory starts asking questions and tracking down the identity of the costumed guests, she finds reasons to suspect her brother-in-law has been hiding a guilty secret. Her search leads her to a web of blackmail and betrayal amongst the posh setting of the local country club crowd. Can Emory sift through the lies she's being told and find the killer? She'll need to step up her investigation before another victim is sent to the great pumpkin patch in the sky.

FRAMED AND FROSTED

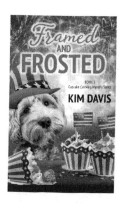

Framed and Frosted, the third book in the Cupcake Catering Mystery series, finds cupcake caterer, Emory Martinez, working at a Laguna Beach society Fourth of July soiree, with her sister and their new employee, Sal. With a host who seems intent on accosting both catering employees and guests alike, things go from bad to worse when he accuses Sal of murdering his long-dead son.

As the crescendo of exploding fireworks overhead becomes the backdrop for cupcakes and champagne, a deadly murder occurs. Can Sal and Emory explain why the cupcake the host ate, after shoving a trayful of buttercream-frosted cupcakes onto Sal, resulted in his death? Or will the detective and guests alike believe that Sal is a murderer? Emory and her octogenarian employer, Tillie, whip into action to find out who framed Sal after he was frosted by the victim.

FROSTED YULETIDE MURDER

Set against the holiday cheer of twinkling lights, costumed carolers, and a festive line of extravagantly decorated boats participating in the annual Christmas boat parade in Newport Beach, California,

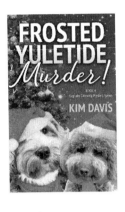

cupcake caterer Emory Martinez finds that the Grinch has crashed the party. Together with her sister Carrie, Emory is catering a delectable feast of holiday cupcakes and cookies aboard a luxury yacht for the new Mrs. Blair Villman and her guests.

Sparks fly when Carrie comes face-to-face with the hostess, who just happens to be Carrie's high school frenemy, and old grievances are dredged up. Adding fuel to the fire, Blair's stepson brings his mother, the former Mrs. Villman, to the party. Instead of celebrating holiday cheer, someone seems intent on channeling the Burgermeister Meisterburger and shutting down Blair's party permanently. When Emory finds a body aboard the yacht, she needs to discover who iced the victim before the Scrooge ruins not only her livelihood but her freedom as well.

BUTTERCREAM BETRAYAL

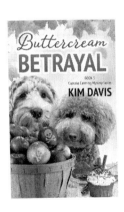

Intent on getting their two mischievous dogs under control, Emory Martinez and her half sister, Vannie, join a group dog training program led by Shawn Parker. With a graduation certificate just within grasp and a party to celebrate their hard-won achievements, what could go wrong? For starters, their two dogs have decided to wreak havoc during the party and tempers flare. It turns out not everyone is pleased with the dog trainer and his mother, the condo association president. Whispers of the mother and son's misbehavior, or worse, fly amongst the barks, whines, and growls of the canines.

When Emory finds the body of Mrs. Parker amidst an explosive situation, it becomes apparent there is more truth to the whispers instead of just gossip. Could one of the canine-loving participants be responsible? Or an outsider who hated her heavy-handed rule over the condo homeowners? Emory, Vannie, and octogenarian Tillie must sift through the clues to find out who has been betrayed and who has decided to take justice into their own hands.

Muddled Matrimonial Murder

With only two weeks left to finalize the arrangements for the nuptial ceremony and reception for Emory Martinez's best friend, Brad, and a Thanksgiving feast to plan, she has enough to keep her busy. But when Emory and Brad stumble across the body of his former stalker, with a wedding gift marble muddler lying next to the body, it soon becomes apparent someone is intent on framing the groom before vows can be exchanged.

How did the victim locate Brad, and how did she end up being murdered at the scene of the impending nuptials? Was someone so desperate to stop the wedding that they'd resort to murder? Or was she killed for revenge? As the countdown to the wedding speeds by, it'll take Emory and her family and friends pulling together to pick through the muddled clues to clear the groom's name.

Includes recipes.